'TIS THE SEASON TO KILL

Bettina appeared in the doorway, her face tightened by fear and her eyes wide. "It's Penny," she said, holding out the phone. "She tried your phone but you didn't answer."

"It's at home," Pamela said—but at that moment the whereabouts of her phone was the last thing on her mind. Pamela reached for the phone and the words rushed out. "Penny? What is it? What's happened?"

"Mom?" Penny's voice sounded small and faraway. "I'm down here at the nature preserve." The nature preserve occupied the westernmost edge of Arborville, beyond busy County Road at the bottom of Orchard Street where Pamela and the Frasers lived. Penny went on, "I found a body, Mom. Someone is dead." Penny stopped and it sounded like she was fighting back a sob. "I called the police."

"We'll be there," Pamela said, feeling breathless. "We're coming, right now." She handed the phone back to Bettina. "Someone is dead. In the nature preserve . . ."

D0980535

Books by Peggy Ehrhart

MURDER, SHE KNIT

DIED IN THE WOOL

KNIT ONE, DIE TWO

SILENT KNIT, DEADLY KNIT

Published by Kensington Publishing Corporation

SILENT KNIT, DEADLY KNIT

PEGGY EHRHART

KENSINGTON BOOKS
KENSINGTON PUBLISHING CORP.
www.kensingtonbooks.com

KENSINGTON BOOKS are published by

Kensington Publishing Corp.
119 West 40th Street
New York, NY 10018

Copyright © 2019 by Peggy Ehrhart

All rights reserved. No part of this book may be reproduced in any form or by any means without the prior written consent of the Publisher, excepting brief quotes used in reviews.

To the extent that the image or images on the cover of this book depict a person or persons, such person or persons are merely models, and are not intended to portray any character or characters featured in the book.

If you purchased this book without a cover you should be aware that this book is stolen property. It was reported as "unsold and destroyed" to the Publisher and neither the Author nor the Publisher has received any payment for this "stripped book."

All Kensington titles, imprints, and distributed lines are available at special quantity discounts for bulk purchases for sales promotion, premiums, fund-raising, educational, or institutional use.

Special book excerpts or customized printings can also be created to fit specific needs. For details, write or phone the office of the Kensington Sales Manager: Attn.: Sales Department. Kensington Publishing Corp., 119 West 40th Street, New York, NY 10018. Phone: 1-800-221-2647.

Kensington and the K logo Reg. U.S. Pat. & TM Off.

First Printing: November 2019
ISBN-13: 978-1-4967-2363-5
ISBN-10: 1-4967-2363-5

ISBN-13: 978-1-4967-2366-6 (eBook)
ISBN-10: 1-4967-2366-X (eBook)

10 9 8 7 6 5 4 3 2 1

Printed in the United States of America

For my sweet husband,
Norm Smith

ACKNOWLEDGMENTS

Abundant thanks, again, to my agent Evan Marshall, and to my editor at Kensington Books, John Scognamiglio.

Chapter One

"I'm not sure it was a fair trade." Bettina Fraser rested a hand on the graceful pottery vase, a rich shade of blue tinged with violet. "All I gave her in exchange was a scarf."

"It was a beautiful scarf, dear wife." Wilfred Fraser glanced up from the cookie he was decorating. "Beautiful, and warm. And just right for the season."

"Red with green stripes," Pamela Paterson added. "What could be more perfect for Christmas?" Pamela was the founder and mainstay of the Arborville, New Jersey, knitting club, nicknamed Knit and Nibble, and she had watched the scarf take shape over the past several meetings of the group. The cookies that the three friends were decorating were intended to provide the "nibble" portion of the next meeting.

"Still—to offer me this gorgeous vase in exchange . . . Of course, the craft shop is more of a hobby than anything else for Millicent. She certainly doesn't need money." Bettina gave the vase a final caress and picked up a cookie shaped like a wreath. "We're running out of green icing," she said, "so I might just as well eat this." She bit the cookie in half, sighed with pleasure, and added, "Your butter cookie recipe is heavenly,

Pamela. With your baking skills, I don't understand how you can be so thin." Bettina was not thin. Pamela was both thin and tall, and her lack of interest in dressing to play up her natural advantages was a source of great puzzlement to her friend.

"Well, I don't bake every day," Pamela said with a smile. "But at Christmas, and with Penny home from college for the break, it's fun to make special goodies—and of course we need nibbles for the group tomorrow night." She spread yellow icing on a star-shaped cookie and added a sprinkle of yellow sugar. The cookie decorating was taking place at the well-scrubbed pine table in Bettina's spacious kitchen. Woofus the shelter dog napped in the corner.

"Nell won't approve," Bettina said. "You know how she feels about sweets."

"But surely, at Christmastime . . ." Across the table Wilfred had dabbed the last bit of green icing on a cookie shaped like a Christmas tree and was arranging tiny silver balls to create the effect of a garland. He had tied an apron over the uniform of plaid shirt and bib overalls he adopted when he retired.

But Bettina didn't respond. Half to herself, she murmured, "I should really call Millicent to ask how she's doing."

"You just saw her this morning at her shop," Pamela said.

"Yes," Bettina replied. "I did, but something had happened to upset her and she didn't have time to tell me much. Her partner had just come in and she had to go over some shop business with her. But then she was going to run out on an errand. She'd already wrapped my scarf around her neck."

"See," Wilfred cut in. "That shows you how much she liked it."

"Was she upset about something that happened at the shop?" Pamela asked.

Bettina nodded. "Someone—a man, I think—wanted the shop to carry his work. Millicent turned him down and apparently he became quite angry." She reached for another undecorated wreath and bit into it.

"It's okay," Pamela said. "We have plenty for tomorrow night."

Two large platters held cookie stars, reindeer, Santas, wreaths, and Christmas trees, carefully spread with icing in bright shades and garnished with silver balls, sprinkles, and colored sugar.

"I'll call her right now, while I'm thinking of it." Bettina dusted cookie crumbs from her fingers. "My phone's in the living room," she added, and rose from her chair.

Bettina had barely reached the kitchen doorway when from the living room came the jinglejangle of her phone. Woofus jumped up in alarm.

"It's okay," Wilfred said soothingly, turning toward the huge, shaggy beast, who was cringing against the wall. "It's just the phone."

Then they heard a voice. It resembled Bettina's voice, but it quavered and then modulated into an urgent squeak. "Yes, yes!" the voice said. "She's right here. We're all right here."

Bettina appeared in the doorway, her face tightened by fear and her eyes wide. "It's Penny," she said, holding out the phone. "She tried your phone but you didn't answer."

"It's at home," Pamela said—but at that moment

the whereabouts of her phone was the last thing on her mind. Pamela reached for the phone and the words rushed out. "Penny? What is it? What's happened?"

Wilfred rose from his chair, bounded across the kitchen, and pulled Bettina into a comforting embrace. Her head nestled against his chest, her scarlet hair vivid against the faded denim of his coveralls. Looking around nervously, Woofus loped toward the dining room.

"Mom?" Penny's voice sounded small and faraway. "I'm down here at the nature preserve." The nature preserve occupied the westernmost edge of Arborville, beyond busy County Road at the bottom of Orchard Street where Pamela and the Frasers lived. Penny went on, "I found a body, Mom. Someone is dead." Penny stopped and it sounded like she was fighting back a sob. "I called the police."

"We'll be there," Pamela said, feeling breathless. "We're coming, right now." She handed the phone back to Bettina. "Someone is dead. In the nature preserve."

Bettina lifted her head from Wilfred's chest to nod. "She told me."

Of course. Otherwise why would Bettina have looked so . . . *stricken*? Pamela took a deep breath and added, "Penny called the police."

A siren underscored her statement, beginning as a thin whine, rising to a peak, falling off, and rising again. In a whirl of activity, Pamela and Wilfred grabbed their jackets and Bettina her coat, and they all hurried for the door. Wilfred's Mercedes, ancient but lovingly cared for, waited in the driveway next to Bettina's solid Toyota Corolla.

"I'll drive, dear ladies," Wilfred said, and helped his passengers into his car.

The police had already reached the nature preserve when Wilfred steered the Mercedes into the small clearing that served as a parking lot. A black-and-white car marked with the Arborville police logo stood empty at the head of a trail. The trail twisted among the dark trunks of the bare trees, their branches sketching complicated patterns against the gray sky.

Pamela thrust the car door open before Wilfred had even turned off the engine. She launched herself down the trail, stumbling a bit on the thick layer of fallen leaves. Through the gaps between the trees she could see the crime scene up ahead. Penny's violet jacket, a recent thrift-store find, stood out against the wintry tones of the landscape and contrasted with the subdued uniforms of the two police officers.

Penny caught sight of Pamela when she was about fifty feet away and started to run toward her, but was stopped by one of the police officers. The officer turned and Pamela recognized the young, gentle-voiced man who she'd most recently seen directing traffic at Arborville's main intersection on a morning when the traffic light inexplicably stopped functioning. The other officer was kneeling next to a bundled form that Pamela realized with a shock was the body.

"Mom!" Penny called. From some distance behind Pamela on the trail Wilfred's voice replied, "We're here too."

In a minute Pamela was standing next to her daughter. Penny's eyes were bright and her cheeks were rosy, and under other circumstances the effect would have been of a pretty young woman whose face showed the effects of a brisk walk on a wintry day. But the brightness in her eyes was caused by tears, some of which had dripped onto her cheeks, and her lips quivered and then tightened as if she was struggling to contain her emotions.

Pamela reached out and gathered her into a hug, resting her chin on the woolly cap that topped off Penny's ensemble. The officer watched but didn't say anything. Pamela nonetheless felt bound to supply that she was Penny's mother.

"I was sketching, Mom," Penny said, her voice a bit muffled by the hug. "And I came down here and followed that path and—" She gulped and a sob erupted.

"I'm Officer Anders, ma'am," the officer said, "and I'll need your name." He was already holding a pen and a little notepad.

"Pamela Paterson," she answered, and gave her address for good measure. "My daughter is home from college for the Christmas holidays."

"And I'm Wilfred Fraser and this is my wife Bettina Fraser—F-R-A-S-E-R," added a new voice, and Pamela felt a gentle hand on her shoulder. She released Penny, who looked slightly less stricken now that reinforcements had arrived. Wilfred had hurried into his jacket without bothering to remove his apron, but the apron didn't detract from the comfort offered by his bulky presence.

Officer Anders bent to his notepad but then looked up without writing. Nearby a siren had been interrupted in mid-squeal, subsiding into a drawn-out moan. The police reinforcements had arrived.

Bettina meanwhile had ventured a few steps in the direction of the bundled form resting on the thick bed of brownish leaves that covered the ground. "Oh, no!" she exclaimed suddenly, whirling around. "Wilfred! It's Millicent Farthingale."

"Excuse me, ma'am?" Officer Anders had returned to his note taking but now looked up again. "Are you saying that you recognize the deceased?"

"It's my friend Millicent Farthingale!" Bettina made a striking figure with her vivid hair and her pumpkin-colored coat, her hazel eyes wide with alarm.

"Are you sure, ma'am?" Officer Anders managed to look both quizzical and sympathetic. "The body is . . ." He waved uncertainly toward the bundled form. "You can hardly see . . ."

"That's her coat and those are her boots and that's her hair—she's blond, though not naturally of course—and she's small like that, slim and not very tall." Officer Anders nodded and Bettina went on. "I just saw her this morning at her shop. She owns"—Bettina gulped—"owned . . . a craft shop in Timberley."

Officer Anders wrote furiously. Meanwhile the officer who was kneeling by the body when they arrived had stood up. She positioned herself—the officer was a woman—as if standing guard over the person who had now been identified as Millicent Farthingale.

The reinforcements whose arrival the siren had announced proved to be another uniformed officer and Arborville's lone police detective, Lucas Clayborn. He acknowledged Officer Anders with a curt greeting and directed a nod in the direction of Pamela, Penny, Bettina, and Wilfred.

"We have an ID on the body, sir," Officer Anders said. "Ms. Fraser recognized the woman as a friend of hers"—he stared at his notepad—"Millicent Far . . . thin . . . gale."

"Is that true?" Detective Clayborn frowned at Bettina. His lived-in face was as nondescript as the dun-colored three-quarter-length coat he wore. Pamela thought he could have been a little more cordial, given that as chief reporter for Arborville's weekly paper, the *Advocate*, Bettina interviewed Detective Clayborn every few weeks for some article or another.

"Yes, yes." Bettina nodded vigorously. "I was with her this morning. This is exactly what she had on . . . except"—Bettina's eyes widened, and she lifted a hand to her mouth—"she was also wearing a scarf, a knitted scarf, red with green stripes at the ends." Bettina's voice faltered and her brightly painted lips twisted.

Wilfred had taken a few steps toward Bettina. Now he pulled her toward him. "It was a beautiful scarf," he said.

"I made the scarf," Bettina explained, "and I had just given it to her, and she liked it so much she put it on right then and there—" A large sob completed the sentence.

Detective Clayborn's homely features rearranged themselves into a vaguely sympathetic expression. "Officer Anders will take your statement," he said, "when you feel ready." Officer Anders nodded. He was still holding his little notepad. "And now"—Detective Clayborn fixed his gaze on Penny—"I understand it was you who found the body."

"Yes," Penny replied in a tiny voice, and Pamela rested a hand on the shoulder of the violet jacket.

"Your mother wasn't with you?" The skin around his eyes tightened. Pamela recognized the look. Detective Clayborn could be more perceptive than his usual expression suggested. She knew why he'd asked the question. For such an idyllic little town, Arborville had

a curiously high murder rate, and for some reason
Pamela Paterson was often on the scene when a body
was found.

"No," Penny said. "I'm home from college for
Christmas. I'd gone out sketching." As if suddenly
remembering something, she looked around and gestured toward a spiral-bound pad open to a graceful
pencil sketch of bare trees with branches interlaced
against the sky. "We don't live far . . . just across County
Road and halfway up Orchard Street."

"I know where you live," Detective Clayborn said.
He pulled a notepad and pen from his coat pocket.
"Let's start at the beginning. Your full name, please."

Twenty minutes later, Pamela, Penny, Bettina, and
Wilfred were climbing into Wilfred's ancient Mercedes. As they pulled out of the clearing at the edge
of the nature preserve, the huge silver van from the
county sheriff's department arrived. "It will all be
in the *Register* tomorrow," Bettina said. "I'm glad
we're getting away before that overly energetic *Register*
reporter shows up—or the radio and TV people."

"They'll find us though." Pamela reached over to
take Penny's hand.

"I'll have to write something for the *Advocate*,"
Bettina said from the front seat, swiveling around to
face them. "I'll have to mention Penny."

Pamela nodded. "But you'll be talking to Detective
Clayborn soon, and he'll know things. That was the
crime-scene unit arriving."

Chapter Two

"I suppose the police have contacted Pierre by now," Bettina said. Instead of crossing the street to their own house when Wilfred steered the Mercedes into the Frasers' driveway, Pamela and Penny had accepted Bettina's invitation to join her and Wilfred for dinner. The sun had begun to set as Detective Clayborn and Officer Anders completed their interviews, and they'd been glad to escape the shadowy woods when Detective Clayborn told them they were free to go.

Now it was nearly six p.m. and they were enjoying the familiar comfort of Bettina's kitchen. Pamela, Penny, and Bettina were sitting around the pine table, which had been cleared of cookies and cookie-decorating supplies. Instead it held a half-empty bottle and three glasses of red wine in various stages of consumption. Wilfred was across the room at the stove, the apron he'd neglected to remove for the trip to the nature preserve now serving the purpose for which it was intended.

He was flourishing a long-handled wooden spoon over a gleaming stainless-steel skillet, and the soothing aroma of onions sautéing in olive oil filled the room. "Plenty of food for all of us," he assured them. "Braised chicken thighs with tomatoes, olives, and capers are just the thing on a dark and chilly night like this."

Bettina had been uncharacteristically silent. Her face looked drawn and she stared gloomily at her wineglass, but she cheered slightly at Wilfred's announcement.

"Chicken is usually Tuesday night," she said. "Rotisserie chicken from the Co-Op. But with Wilfred retired now, we're eating like gourmets." A willing but uninspired cook, Bettina had served her family the same seven meals in regular rotation for most of her married life.

"How do you think Pierre will take the news?" Pamela asked.

Bettina shrugged. "She was more in love than he was. Not that looks are everything . . ." Her gaze wandered toward the stove. Pamela agreed with the unspoken thought. Genial Wilfred, with his bear-like physique and ruddy cheeks was truly a prize.

"Pierre will inherit, I suppose." Pamela took a sip of her wine and glanced toward Penny's wineglass. Her daughter had taken scarcely a sip.

"No children. Millicent married late in life. I hope there's a will—she's leaving behind a considerable estate, including the Wentworth mansion. Millicent's mother grew up in that house, then moved back in when her parents died. Her mother wasn't well, and Millicent lived with her and took care of her. Then when Millicent married Pierre, he moved in too. Lots of goodies for people to tussle over, and if that happens the lawyers will get a good cut too." Bettina sighed. "It's just so sad . . . nursing her mother all those years and looking after that huge house and she was finally free and ready to downsize—not that she wanted her mother to die . . . but I think the house is already on the market."

"Do you think Pierre will go ahead with the plans to sell?" Pamela had only met Millicent a few times, so the disposition of her estate wasn't of compelling interest. But talking about Millicent's house was at least a slight distraction from talking about her death.

"Probably," Bettina said. "A big house like that requires a lot of upkeep—and even if there's plenty of money to pay for it, organizing the upkeep takes time. Not that Pierre has that many demands on his time."

Pamela raised her brows. "I think you said once that he's a professor. They work pretty hard, don't they?"

"Some do," Penny commented with a slight laugh. "Some don't."

"Not exactly a professor," Bettina said. "Part-time lecturer in French at Wendelstaff College. And not exactly French either. He's from Montreal."

The cheerful voice seemed out of place. Pamela had been struggling to complete a knitting project, a huge swath of fuzzy wool that was somehow to figure in a funeral service. But the voice was assuring her that traffic was moving smoothly at the Hudson River crossings, including the upper deck of the George Washington Bridge. She opened her eyes to darkness. In the summer, the light coming through the white eyelet curtains at her bedroom windows served as an alarm clock of sorts. In the winter, however, she had to rely on the clock radio.

She rolled onto her back, stretched out an arm, and switched on the lamp on the bedside table. A soft form stirred at her feet, migrated up the side of her leg, and inched its way delicately across her torso. It eased its head out from under the down comforter that Pamela used on chilly winter nights. Two amber eyes stared at her from a heart-shaped face covered with silky jet-black fur.

"Catrina," Pamela murmured. "Good morning! Where are your children?"

This pleasant daily ritual was interrupted by a forlorn voice coming from the hall. "Mo-om!" Penny moaned. "Someone's coming up on the porch and I think it's reporters." Catrina scrambled off the bed and hurried to the bedroom door. If someone was stirring, there would be breakfast soon.

But Pamela's thoughts were less cheerful. It was barely seven a.m. What nerve reporters had! She flung comforter and sheet aside, sat up, swung her feet to the floor, and thrust them into her waiting slippers. A moment later, she had grabbed her robe and was hurrying down the stairs. She had just reached the landing when the doorbell chimed. She grabbed the railing to steady herself and continued her descent.

The porch light revealed a perky young woman bundled in a neon-green down coat with a fur-trimmed hood. "Marcy Brewer, from the *County Register*," she announced, tilting her head to meet Pamela's eyes. Despite her high-heeled boots, she was scarcely five feet tall, but her lipsticky smile and confident voice signaled that she was accustomed to getting her story. "Is Penny Paterson in?"

"Of course she's in," Pamela said, not bothering to soften the frown that she knew had furrowed her forehead and drawn her brows together. "It's seven a.m. And she doesn't wish to speak to the press. She doesn't have to, you know."

Marcy Brewer's smile didn't waver. "I take it you're her mother. Perhaps she'd like to answer for herself."

Pamela willed herself to look fierce. "You're right. I am her mother, and I know what's best for her."

"Will she be having a follow-up interview with the police today?" The smile was still in place.

"I expect so." Pamela stepped away from the door and pushed it closed.

In the kitchen, Penny had already set out a bowl containing several scoops of cat food. A black kitten was finishing his meal and Catrina joined her son. Penny was sitting at the table, still in her nightclothes, a fleecy pink robe tugged on over flannel pajamas. Her dark curls were still tousled from bed. She held a cat on her lap, the ginger kitten Pamela had adopted from the litter of six Catrina had presented her with at the end of the previous summer.

"She's getting used to me," Penny said, running her fingers over the kitten's fur. "She slept with me last night." The kitten's father was an impressive ginger tom and his three daughters had inherited his looks. Pamela had accordingly named the kitten Ginger. But being an avid cook and with all three ginger kittens underfoot till recently, Pamela had decided the coats of supposedly ginger cats could be better described as pumpkin pie—or butterscotch.

"You wouldn't have wanted to talk to Marcy Brewer from the *County Register*, would you?" Pamela asked. After she closed the door, she had realized maybe Penny *was* old enough to make such decisions for herself. What if something like this happened while she was at college? (Pamela shuddered at the thought.) Her mother wouldn't be there to protect her.

"No," Penny said. "I'm glad you chased her away."

"Did you sleep all right?" Pamela lowered herself into the chair across the table from Penny and studied her daughter's face. Penny's blue eyes were bright, but purplish shadows beneath them suggested her slumber had been less than restorative.

"I kept waking up, and then I'd see—" She grimaced. "And I kept wondering how she died. It wasn't obvious. She was just lying there. And the policeman led me away while the policewoman sort of studied . . . the body. I guess they're not supposed to touch anything or move anything in case there are clues. That is, if they decide it's murder. But they must have, because then they called for more police—" The fingers stroking the kitten's back began to move more rapidly.

"And that van came from the sheriff's department," Pamela supplied. "Bettina will talk to Detective Clayborn," she added. "Then we'll find out more from her." She stood up. "But for now, how about some coffee and toast?"

"Did you see the *Register* out there when you opened the door?" Penny asked.

"I'll get it now," Pamela said. "At least if Marcy Brewer is gone."

There was no reason, really, for Pamela to care if Richard Larkin saw her in her robe and slippers. The long fleece robe that reached nearly to the ground concealed more than a coat would. True, a fleece robe and furry slippers didn't constitute the most flattering of looks. But despite Bettina's urging to the contrary, Pamela refused to dwell on Richard Larkin's romantic potential. He *was* unattached, and a suitable age, and certainly attractive. But she preferred to consider him a neighbor with whom she had a cordial but detached relationship.

Now he stepped away from the back of his olive-green Jeep Cherokee—he'd apparently just been loading something into the vehicle—and caught sight of Pamela. He raised an arm in greeting and took several loping strides in her direction. He was wearing slim dark pants and a bulky jacket, also dark. Despite the chilly morning, his shaggy blond head was uncovered. Pamela had just stooped to retrieve the newspaper and it was dangling from her hand in its flimsy plastic bag.

"Are you and Penny okay?" Richard gestured toward the newspaper. "It's been on the radio, and TV too, of course." His face could look so stern, with its strong features and deep eyes. But probably he didn't mean to look stern now. He was just concerned.

"We're fine," Pamela said, tilting her head back. Richard Larkin was very tall, and being tall herself Pamela wasn't used to looking up at people.

"If there's anything I can do . . ." He hovered there uncertainly, his eyes fixed on her face. Then he spoke in a sudden rush of words. "I wish Laine and Sybil were here," he said, and his face relaxed as if he was relieved to have found a conversational topic. "It might help Penny, to have her friends next door. But they're spending the Christmas break in San Francisco with their mother."

"I wish they were here too," Pamela said. "This is going to be hard."

"Well, if there's anything . . ." He started to turn away.

"Thank you," Pamela said. She watched him lope

back to his car. But she was not to return to her warm house quite yet. Bettina was waving from the end of her driveway. She waited while Richard Larkin backed out and headed up the street and then she started across.

"I'm seeing Clayborn in an hour," she called before she reached the other side. "The first item on his agenda." She joined Pamela at the end of Pamela's front walk. "He's as anxious as I am to get the story into this week's *Advocate*. Even though Millicent lived in Timberley, it's Arborville's case because Arborville is where the body was found."

Pamela tucked the *Register* under her arm and hugged herself, rubbing her hands up and down the sleeves of her fleece robe. She was shivering. Her morning routine of fetching the *Register* in robe and slippers usually just involved a quick dash out and back. Bettina was already dressed for the day, her pumpkin-colored down coat topping off burgundy slacks complemented by sleek burgundy booties. She'd pulled a burgundy wool beret over her bright coiffure.

She intercepted one of Pamela's hands to give it a squeeze. "Are you and Penny okay this morning?" she asked, tipping her head to examine Pamela's face.

"Really weird dreams." Pamela smiled a sad half smile as she recalled the hand-knit funeral shroud she'd been tasked with by her dreaming mind. "And Penny looks tired. But we'll be fine once we've had some coffee. Do you want to come in? I'm just going to make some."

"I can't linger." Bettina released Pamela's hand. "I've got to stop by the *Advocate*'s office before I go to the police station." She turned toward the street but then swung back. "That was nice of Richard to take the time for a little chat. Even from my yard I could see he was concerned."

"Any neighbor would be," Pamela said in a tone designed to discourage further development of that theme.

Bettina got the message. "Well then," she said, "I'll be on my way. But I'll be back with a report just as soon as I finish with Clayborn." She paused. "And don't forget Wilfred Jr. is dropping by this morning to pick up the black kitten for his sons." She turned back toward the street, but she didn't move, and neither did Pamela, at least for a minute.

Heading toward them from the corner was a truck bearing the logo of the local TV station. "Oh, no," Pamela moaned. "I already chased away that Marcy Brewer from the *Register* this morning. Now . . . *them.*"

"I'll take care of it!" Bettina tightened her lips into a stern line. A slight wrinkle appeared between her carefully shaped brows. "You get yourself into the house."

Back inside and still bearing the plastic-wrapped *Register*, Pamela watched through the lace that curtained the oval window in her front door as a young man and a young woman descended from the truck, to be met at the curb by Bettina. The expressions on their faces suggested that they were very reluctant to abandon their assignment. But Bettina stood firm and eventually they climbed back into their truck and went on their way.

Penny had joined Pamela as she watched, now cuddling the black kitten against the pink fleece of her robe.

"Wilfred Jr. is coming for that kitten this morning,"

Pamela said as they turned away from the window. She reached an arm around Penny's slim shoulders and gave her a squeeze.

Back in the kitchen, Pamela deposited the *Register* on the kitchen table. Its account of the body found in the Arborville nature preserve could wait until they had been fortified with coffee and whole-grain toast.

Accordingly, Pamela's next action was to measure water into the kettle and set it to boiling on the stove. Then she slipped a paper filter into the plastic cone balanced over the mouth of the carafe and scooped coffee beans into the chamber of her coffee grinder. The coffee-making ritual was detailed and time-consuming, but it was a ritual. And predictable rituals were soothing when events like that of the previous day reminded one how unpredictable life could be.

With a clatter and a whir the beans were ground, and the aroma of coffee began to infuse the kitchen. Pamela spooned the fragrant ground beans into the paper filter just as the kettle began to hoot, and soon the coffee aroma grew more intense as the boiling water dripped through the ground beans into the carafe beneath.

Penny meanwhile had set down the black kitten, who had begun tussling in a half-hearted way with his bold sister, as if acknowledging that he was over-matched right from the start. Penny had taken cups and saucers from the cupboard, a pretty pattern featuring rose garlands. The cups and saucers were from Pamela's wedding china. She had resolved long ago to use her china every day because what was the point of having nice things if they just sat in a cupboard except for a few days out of the year?

As the coffee dripped, Pamela slid two slices of whole-grain bread into the toaster.

By the time the toast had popped up and was buttered, cut into neat quarters, and set on the kitchen table, Penny had extracted the *Register* from its plastic sleeve and unfolded it. Right there on the front page was the succinct headline: "Timberley Woman Found Dead in Arborville Nature Preserve." The thought of toast was suddenly not appealing, but Pamela fetched the carafe from the counter and filled each of the wedding-china cups.

"The article talks about me," Penny said, looking up with a woeful expression on her pretty face. "'Police told reporters that the body was found by Penny Paterson of Arborville, who stated she was home from college for Christmas and had gone to the nature preserve on a sketching expedition.'"

Pamela slipped around to Penny's side of the table and leaned over her shoulder to skim the article, waiting while Penny turned to an inner page for the continuation. A few sentences into the first paragraph on that page, Pamela heard herself gasp, and the sharp intake of breath was quickly echoed by Penny.

"Someone shot her," Penny whispered.

Pamela nodded. She quoted from the article. "'Police stated that the victim died from a gunshot wound to the chest. The medical examiner's report is expected to provide further information about the specific type of weapon used.'"

"I couldn't tell she'd been shot," Penny murmured, near tears. "She was lying on her side and her coat was kind of bunched up in front. Besides, I didn't really want to look." She sniffed a huge sniff and Pamela rested a hand on her back. "I have to talk to the police again. Eleven o'clock, they said. But I don't know what else I can tell them."

"They'll want to know if you saw anyone, I suppose. Or any clue, like a car down by where that path leads in." Pamela had returned to the other side of the table. She reached over the newspaper to take Penny's hands. "I'll come with you," she said. "Of course."

Penny sniffed again, but sat up straighter, suddenly resolute. "It's okay, Mom," she said. "I can go by myself. I know where the police station is."

"But . . ." Pamela felt her face pucker. "I'm your mother, and you're only—"

"I'm nineteen," Penny said, sitting up even straighter, "and I'm in college . . . on my own . . . all the way up in Massachusetts."

Pamela nodded. It was true. She'd been willing to let Penny go away for college—because her own parents had let her go away for college—even though that meant she'd be all alone in her big house. But Penny hadn't inherited Pamela's height, taking after her father's side of the family instead. Pamela was a full head taller than her daughter. That made it especially hard for Pamela to rein in her protective impulses, especially because Pamela and Penny had been their own small family since Michael Paterson's death six years earlier.

The two kittens had finished their tussle as Pamela and Penny talked, and had wandered from the room. Pamela suspected that they had joined their mother on the thrift-store Persian carpet in the entry and that all three were luxuriating in the patch of morning sun that made the carpet's colors glow.

The toast was cold but they frugally ate it anyway, and they sipped reheated coffee as they browsed through the rest of the *Register*. When the last drops of coffee had been drained from their cups, Penny stood. "You won't cancel Knit and Nibble tonight or anything, will you?" she asked, pausing near the tray of brightly decorated cookies, covered with plastic wrap, that waited on the counter.

"No," Pamela said, rising too. "We have to go on with our rituals."

Chapter Three

Upstairs, Pamela made her bed and arranged her collection of vintage lace pillows against the brass headboard. Then she dressed in her winter work-at-home uniform of jeans and a hand-knit sweater and stepped into the bathroom across the hall to run a comb through her dark straight hair. Penny had inherited her curls from her father's side of the family.

In her office Pamela poked the buttons that would awaken her computer and listened through the beeps and hums that signaled it was preparing to face the day. Five messages lurked in her inbox, three that could be dealt with later and two from her boss at *Fiber Craft* magazine. One of those was garnished with the stylized paper clip that indicated it brought with it attachments—i.e., work for Pamela. The other, at the top of the email queue, had been sent barely half an hour ago. With a click it was open.

Pamela, the message began. Pamela's boss eschewed the nearly universal custom of opening every email with the casual "Hi," no matter how serious the import. But in this case the formal greeting matched the seriousness of the message.

I've just heard the shocking news of Millicent Farthingale's death, the message went on. *This is a terrible blow to the* Fiber Craft *community. Millicent's shop was an important outlet for the work of tri-state textile artists and I am not sure that her partner Nadine will be able to keep it going—in fact I am quite sure that she will not.*

I know you are right there in Arborville and so know more about the skill of local law enforcement, but I do not have high hopes that a suburban police force will be able to bring Millicent's killer to justice.

Pamela took a moment to respond, keying in, *I'm sure they will do their best.*

The second email from her boss was more matter-of-fact. *Attached are five recent submissions to the magazine. Please read them and advise as to which you recommend for publication.*

The soothing rhythms of knitting were Pamela's first choice as an antidote for stress. But immersing herself in the worlds explored by the authors who submitted to *Fiber Craft* came in as a close second. Now she clicked on the first attachment and prepared to evaluate "Re-creating Traditional Turkish Weaving Techniques."

The second article was about jewelry made from the hair of dead people. Pamela fingered her chin as she skimmed the first paragraph. It is true that hair is a fiber, and making jewelry is a craft, but did the topic really fit the mission of *Fiber Craft*? It seemed so . . . macabre, particularly in light of Penny's grim discovery the previous day. But Pamela's boss must have seen the title, "Memorializing the Departed: The (Hair) Art of Victorian Mourning Brooches," and skimmed the article before sending it on to Pamela for a more in-depth reading. She shrugged and began reading more closely.

She'd barely read past the first paragraph when the doorbell chimed. Even from the landing Pamela knew that her caller was Bettina. Though veiled by the lace that covered the oval window in the front door, Bettina's pumpkin-colored coat stood out against the somber colors of the wintery landscape. Pamela hurried the rest of the way down the stairs and opened the door to greet her friend, who stepped inside murmuring about the cold wind. Once she was inside, she pulled off her beret and raised a hand to pat the tendrils of her vivid coif into place.

Catrina looked up briefly from the sunny spot on the rug where she was still dozing. The kittens had long since wandered off. A few balls of leftover yarn had found new lives as cat toys and the kittens often engaged in a morning game of capture the yarn ball. In fact, as Bettina slipped out of her coat, a ball of yarn rolled through the arch that separated the entry from the living room. Ginger followed in hot pursuit, trailed by her brother.

Bettina had come in looking both eager and intense, as if bearing news that she could hardly wait to impart. But her face softened as she watched the kittens.

"I hope Ginger won't miss her brother too much," she commented.

"Catrina still likes to play." Pamela reached out a foot to send the ball of yarn bouncing back toward the living room. Ginger watched it as fixedly as her undomesticated forebears must have watched mice or birds they hoped to capture for lunch, and then she pounced and rolled onto her back, clinging to it delightedly.

"I'd love some coffee," Bettina said, "and in return

I'll give you a full rundown on what Clayborn had to say. He knows more now than he knew when he talked to that *Register* reporter last evening. *Lots* more. I must say, the county medical examiner is very competent. But she's a woman, so . . . *of course.*" Now that her coat was off, Bettina's whole outfit was revealed: the burgundy slacks and sleek burgundy booties were topped off by a cozy burgundy sweater—"Not hand-knit," she said, fingering it—and a paisley scarf in rich tones of burgundy, rust, and green.

"I'm definitely ready for a coffee break myself." Pamela led the way to the kitchen and set to work boiling water and scooping more ground beans into a fresh paper filter.

But Bettina hesitated before reaching down cups and saucers from the cupboard, or splashing heavy cream into the cut-glass cream pitcher that matched Pamela's sugar bowl. She lingered by the tray of decorated cookies, their festive colors heightened by the shimmering plastic wrap that covered them.

"We probably don't need all of these for tonight, do we?" she said hopefully. "Nell is so suspicious of sugar, and Roland will say his doctor wouldn't approve, even though Roland is as skinny as a rail . . ."

Pamela turned and smiled fondly at her friend. "Yes," she said, "we can have cookies with our coffee." She opened a cupboard and took out a small plate garlanded with roses. "Put some on this."

In a few minutes they were seated with steaming cups of coffee in front of them, the rich and spicy aroma promising a perfect complement to the Santas and reindeer waiting to be nibbled.

Bettina bit off a Santa head. She took a sip of the coffee that she had sugared liberally and diluted with cream till the color was more coffee ice cream than coffee. Then she began to speak. "Millicent had been dead about six hours when Penny found her," Bettina said, the Santa body still in her hand. "Clayborn said the ME is pretty sure of that—they have ways of knowing. So that means she was killed not very long after I saw her at her shop."

"She was getting ready to go out while you were there, but she was still in the shop when you left." Pamela reached for a cookie, choosing a reindeer. She set the reindeer by her saucer and raised her coffee to her lips.

"That's right," Bettina said. "Nadine had just come in—Millicent had been waiting for her, because she couldn't go out and leave nobody there to look after things. But she was all ready. The scarf looked so nice with her coat."

"The body wasn't wearing a red scarf with green stripes," Pamela said. Bettina shook her head mournfully. "I wonder where the scarf is now." Bettina continued to shake her head. "Anyway," Pamela said, "did Millicent say where she was going?"

Bettina shrugged. "Just errands. But since we were both heading out, I asked if I should wait a few minutes and we'd walk to our cars together. But she had to explain something to Nadine, something about preparing checks for the people who sell their work through the shop. Christmas and all, and people like extra money for holiday expenses." Bettina bit the Santa body in half. "Millicent had no head for money, but Nadine can be a little slow on the uptake, so Millicent said I should just go on and she'd talk to me later." Bettina polished off the Santa body and reached for another cookie. Pamela noticed that even her nails carried out the burgundy theme today.

"So," Pamela said. "Millicent was killed yesterday morning. I suppose the police are searching that clearing in the nature preserve for clues."

"They did already," Bettina said. "They didn't find much of anything—but they realized she wasn't actually killed there."

"She wasn't?" Pamela set her cup back down on her saucer with a clunk. "A secluded place like that? It seemed just right if somebody wanted to commit a murder and get away with it." She paused, blinked, frowned, and thought for a minute. Then she added, "Of course the killer would have had to lure her there with some kind of a story. And it's hard to imagine what that story might have been."

Bettina nodded. "Millicent wasn't really the outdoorsy type."

"So what do the police think happened?" Pamela picked up the reindeer cookie and bit it in half.

"She was killed somewhere else and then the killer dumped the body there." Bettina took a sip of coffee. "The police could see by the way the dead leaves were disturbed that the body had been dragged from that parking area. And they didn't find any evidence that a gun had been fired in the clearing. But"—Bettina took another sip of coffee—"the ME recovered a bullet from her body." She smiled, the first Pamela had seen her smile since she'd fielded the call from Penny the previous afternoon. "That's a big clue," Bettina said. "Sometimes bullets go right through, and the police never find them. But now they know something about what kind of gun it was—a rifle, Clayborn said, like an old hunting rifle. And the bullet was lead, solid lead. That means it could have been homemade."

"People make their own bullets?" Pamela shuddered. "How creepy."

"Hunters, Clayborn said. The rifle could belong to some kind of hunter. Or somebody who knows a hunter could have had access to it."

Pamela shuddered again. "Did you tell him about the man who'd upset her that morning?"

"I did." Bettina bit into her second cookie, another Santa. "He was interested—like the only lead they really have. He said he'd follow up with Nadine—even though I clearly told him that Nadine wasn't in the shop yet when the man came."

"Maybe that wasn't the first time the man had been there."

Bettina studied the half Santa in her hand. "I think this is one of Wilfred's," she said. "He was so careful getting the red suit just right, and then the white beard, and the little red ball for the nose and two black dots for the eyes. It's almost a shame to eat it."

Pamela was spared watching the demise of the Santa cookie because just as Bettina raised the rest of the Santa to her mouth, the doorbell chimed. She motioned Bettina to stay where she was, and in a moment she was welcoming the Frasers' son, Wilfred Jr. She closed the door against the wintry gust of wind that had ushered him in.

Wilfred Jr. had Wilfred's genial face and thick head of hair, but he was thinner and his hair was still sandy. He gave Pamela a quick hug and greeted his mother, who had appeared in the doorway between the entry and the kitchen. "I can't stay," he said as Pamela offered to take his coat. He was carrying a boxy zippered satchel with wide mesh panels in the sides. "I came prepared," he added, displaying the satchel. "The boys are beside themselves with excitement, so I hope Midnight doesn't mind coming home with me." He laughed. "They already gave him a name. Not too imaginative."

Pamela laughed too, as Catrina and her daughter strolled in from the living room, curious about the visitor. "Meet Catrina and Ginger," she said. "Sometimes the first name that comes to you is the best."

Midnight—Pamela already thought of him as that— strolled in a moment later. But he took one look at Wilfred Jr. and veered past the group of humans to head for the stairs. He began to climb, rising on his back legs and stretching to his utmost to reach the next step. Pamela didn't want to alarm him further by snatching him up, so they watched his laborious ascent.

"Is he too young to go?" Wilfred Jr. asked, his face assuming a tender expression just like one that Pamela had seen on Wilfred Sr.'s face countless times.

"It's just that he doesn't know you," Pamela said. "He's used to Bettina because she's been around ever since he was a newborn."

"He's plenty old enough to be adopted," Bettina chimed in. "The others are in their new homes and doing fine, including my little Punkin." Punkin was the name she and Wilfred had given the kitten they'd adopted from Catrina's litter of six.

Catrina and Ginger were sniffing curiously at the satchel with the mesh sides, which of course was a cat-carrier.

"We'll let him calm down for a minute, then I'll go up and get him," Pamela said. "We'll put some kitten treats in the cat-carrier and he'll be more than happy to go home with you."

Bettina stepped to the bottom of the stairs and glanced up. "No sign of him," she observed. "He's made it past the landing."

Pamela reached for the cat-carrier and beckoned Wilfred Jr. toward the kitchen. "Come on and have a Christmas cookie while I get out the kitten treats."

But before they reached the kitchen door, Penny appeared on the landing holding the black kitten in her arms. "Look who came up to visit me," she said, scratching the kitten between his ears. He twisted his neck to study her face. Penny continued down the stairs. She had changed out of her pajamas and robe, and into an outfit rather nicer than her usual winter at-home uniform of leggings and a much-loved and much-worn sweater. She was wearing a pair of jeans in a dark navy blue and a navy pullover with a V-neck that revealed the collar of a crisp white shirt.

"Job interview?" Bettina asked.

"No," Penny said. "I'm supposed to talk to the police this morning." Bettina raised her fingers to her lips to smother a quick intake of breath. "No big deal. I suppose they want to make sure they got all the details right. Everything that happened before they got there. Things were kind of . . ." She grimaced. "Kind of confusing yesterday."

Bettina held out her arms and the kitten allowed himself to be transferred. Penny opened the closet and pulled out her violet jacket and the violet mohair scarf that Pamela had offered to share when Penny acquired the violet jacket. She slipped on the jacket, twisted the scarf into a cozy knot under her chin, and reached for the doorknob.

Pamela couldn't hold back the words that popped out. "Let me come! Please!" She dropped the cat-carrier, dodged around Bettina and Wilfred Jr., and pulled her coat out of the closet.

"*Mo-om!*" Penny groaned, but the expression on her face was sympathetic, not angry. "I can go by myself. *Really*. And I'll be back in no time."

Pamela stood with her coat in her hand, watching as her daughter opened the door. "Marcy Brewer might be waiting for you outside the police station," Pamela said. "She's the reporter from the *Register*, and she knows you're talking to Detective Clayborn today."

"I'll be fine," Penny said, and she was off.

In the kitchen, Bettina offered Wilfred Jr. a cookie and helped herself to another as Pamela took the bag of kitten treats from the cupboard. The cat-carrier waited on the kitchen table. The treats were shaped like fish, tiny fish the size of guppies. And they smelled like fish, though not in a way that Pamela thought would entice a human looking forward to a fish dinner. Clearly the manufacturers of the treats knew their market, however. As soon as Pamela had tugged apart the plastic zipper at the mouth of the bag, the kitten, still in Bettina's arms, lost interest in chewing at her fingers. He began to stare at the now open treat bag with an intensity that was comical in a creature so small.

Pamela reached into the bag and seized a few of the treats. She transferred them to the palm of her other hand and extended that hand toward the kitten. The kitten hunched himself up on Bettina's arm as if about to make a gravity defying leap right into Pamela's open hand. "Here we go," Pamela murmured, edging toward the kitchen table.

Wilfred Jr. unzipped the panel that constituted the carrier's door. Pamela reached in and deposited the fish treats on the floor of the carrier, which was covered in a smooth nylon fabric with a bit of padding beneath. "Yummy fish treats," she cooed, extracting her hand as Bettina advanced across the floor bearing the excited kitten.

Bettina stooped toward the table, extending the arm that the kitten was clinging to. The kitten hopped lightly onto the table and through the open door of the cat-carrier. Wilfred Jr. closed it quickly and, with a sound rather like the purring of a cat, the zipper was zipped and the kitten was captured.

"You'll be sure to report back," Pamela said, as she gazed through the mesh to watch the kitten savor his treats.

"Of course." Wilfred Jr. picked up the cat-carrier. "I can't wait to see the looks on the boys' faces," he added, and headed for the entry.

"I've got to be going too," Bettina said. "I want to write up my interview with Clayborn while it's still fresh in my mind." In the entry she retrieved the pumpkin-colored coat and buttoned herself into it. She was about to follow Wilfred Jr. out the door when she paused. "I wonder if Charlotte will come tonight. I don't think she was that close to Millicent, even though she was Millicent's tenant. But she seems like kind of a sensitive soul, and hearing that Millicent was murdered must have been a shock. Besides, she might be afraid that the Knit and Nibblers won't want to talk about anything else."

Pamela laughed. "She doesn't know us very well then."

"No." Bettina joined in the laughter. "Nell hates

gossip and Roland is in his own world and Karen is a shy little mouse, afraid of her own shadow. But Charlotte only joined when . . . ? A month ago?"

"I think so," Pamela said. "The first meeting she came to was at your house. She learned about the group from Millicent."

"So I'll see you tonight then." Bettina gave Pamela a hug.

When she was alone once more, Pamela rinsed the coffee cups at the sink and poured the leftover cream back into the carton in the refrigerator. Then she set to work preparing the house for Knit and Nibble.

She fetched the vacuum cleaner from the closet in the laundry room and, with the canister trailing along, vacuumed her way through the entry, the living room, and the dining room. Pamela's carpets were all thrift-store finds, old-fashioned carpets in the Persian style, with sinuous stylized foliage rendered in deep, rich colors.

When the vacuuming was done, she tidied the pillows along the back of the sofa, making sure the needlepoint cat wasn't standing on its head. Dusting was next, first the coffee table—which had to be cleared of magazines to make room for refreshments that evening. Then Pamela tackled shelves, cabinets, and tables, dusting her thrift-store treasures and tag-sale finds with loving hands and settling each one back in place.

As Pamela was returning the vacuum to its closet and disposing of the dust cloths, now scented with lemon oil, her stomach reminded her that coffee and one cookie were not going to fuel her through much more of her day. Pamela had made bean soup a few nights earlier, and lots of pork tenderloin was left from the dinner she'd welcomed Penny home with. The soup would be quick to reheat for the two of them before Knit and Nibble arrived, and she'd slice more of the pork and eat it on whole-grain bread for lunch.

After lunch, Pamela gave the kitchen floor a hurried mopping and then climbed the stairs to her office. After removing Catrina from her computer keyboard, she resumed reading "Memorializing the Departed: The (Hair) Art of Victorian Mourning Brooches." She was so caught up in it that she didn't notice Penny standing in the doorway until Catrina leapt from the shelf where she had relocated and Penny scooped her up and murmured, "Hi, kitty."

"You're back!" Pamela swiveled her desk chair to face her daughter. She studied Penny's face, still rosy from the brisk December wind. Pamela felt her forehead crease. "Was it . . . okay?"

"Detective Clayborn was okay," Penny said. "He was nice. He just went over what I told him and the other policeman down at the nature preserve yesterday and asked me to confirm that that was what I said. But"— she hesitated and Pamela held her breath—"that reporter was there. In the parking lot. I couldn't get away from her. And she had a photographer with her. He took my picture."

"Oh, dear." Pamela sighed. "Well, it's a big story and you're part of it. I suppose you'll be in the *Register* tomorrow, and people in town will recognize you, and everywhere you go somebody will want to hear your personal version of finding the body." She sighed again. "At least you'll be able to escape when you go back up to school."

"If the police solve the murder soon, the story will go away, won't it?" The hopeful expression on Penny's face made her look so vulnerable that Pamela's throat tightened. "So I hope the police get busy," Penny added.

"I'm sure they will do their best," Pamela said.

Penny stooped to lower Catrina to the floor. She was still wearing her violet jacket and the violet mohair scarf. "Lorie and I are going to the mall," she said. "And we're going to hang out at her house tonight. So don't worry about me for dinner."

Pamela waited until she heard the door close downstairs and then turned back to her computer.

Chapter Four

"There will only be six of us tonight," Holly Perkins announced as soon as she stepped through the door.

Pamela nodded. "It's understandable that Charlotte wouldn't want to come out."

"Charlotte?" Holly's large eyes grew larger. "No, I'm talking about Karen." Holly and Karen were best friends, young marrieds and only recently settled in Arborville.

"Is she all right?" Pamela asked, alarmed. Bettina had appeared in the kitchen doorway and she echoed the words, sounding equally alarmed.

"The baby . . ." Holly patted her own stomach through her stylish black-and-white houndstooth coat. Pamela and Bettina gasped in unison. "It's okay . . . I mean it's not here yet . . . but it might be coming. She called me a little while ago and said she and Dave were timing contractions."

"A Christmas baby." Bettina sighed. "So exciting."

"Hello, hello," said a cheery voice from the porch. Pamela advanced to the threshold and glanced out to see Nell Bascomb climbing the porch steps. Illuminated by the porch light and tousled by the wind, Nell's hair floated like a white halo above her kindly face. "Roland is just coming," Nell said as Pamela moved aside to let her enter. Holly came farther into the entry and handed Bettina her coat.

Pamela watched as Roland DeCamp's Porsche nosed into a spot at the curb. Roland climbed out, retrieved the briefcase in which he carried his knitting supplies, and strode up the front walk in his well-cut wool coat.

"Good evening, Pamela," he said once he had gained the porch. "I believe I may be a bit late."

"Not at all, Roland. Not at all." Pamela ushered him inside, just in time to hear Nell's soft squeal of pleasure as she absorbed the news that Karen's baby might be on its way. Nell's ancient gray wool coat joined Bettina's and Holly's coats on the chair in the entry, and Roland arranged his carefully on top of the pile.

"Only *five* tonight, it looks like," Bettina observed, "and we have so many cookies . . ." She took a seat on Pamela's sofa, moving a few pillows aside, and Holly joined her.

Nell started toward the living room but paused and took Pamela aside. "You're all right, I hope . . . after yesterday?" Pamela nodded. "And dear little Penny?"

"She went to the mall with one of her Arborville friends today," Pamela answered.

"Shopping," Bettina volunteered from the sofa. "That's the cure for everything." And she and Holly went back to a lively conversation about the likelihood of Karen's baby being born that night.

Nell set out again, heading for the sofa. Before she could get there, Pamela intercepted her. "Please take the comfy chair," she said, gesturing toward the comfortable armchair at the side of the fireplace.

Roland hesitated in the arch between the entry and

the living room, briefcase at his side. Bettina patted a spot on the sofa next to her. "Plenty of room here," she called. "Come and join Holly and me."

"But where will Pamela sit?" he asked, scanning the room, perhaps put off more by a sense that he had little to contribute to a conversation about childbirth than by genuine concern about a shortage of seating.

"I'll be fine on this footstool," Pamela said, tugging the footstool away from the armchair and toward the center of the room. She'd collected her knitting bag from its customary spot at the end of the sofa and was about to sit down when the doorbell chimed.

People had begun pulling out yarn and needles and projects in various states of completion, but everyone paused and watched as Pamela headed for the door and grasped the knob to swing it open.

"I know I'm late," said a small, breathless voice. The owner of the voice peeked around the door then tip-toed into the entry. "And I'm sorry to disturb you." It was Charlotte Sprague, looking like a romantic hero-ine in a voluminous coat and a lacy knit shawl that covered her head and her narrow shoulders. Her pale, oval face and huge dark eyes completed the image.

"We're scarcely disturbed," Roland said with a frown. He'd settled to work as soon as the latecomer made her identity known, and the pink angora rectan-gle hanging from his needles had already grown by half a row. He continued knitting even as he spoke.

Nell freed herself from the embrace of the comfy armchair and leaned forward. "We didn't think you'd come, dear," she said in her kind voice. "It must have been a terrible shock to learn that Millicent had been killed."

"It was," Charlotte said. "It was a terrible shock. But

I thought it would be better to come out and see people rather than sit home alone. The carriage house can get spooky at night, so far back from the road and with all those trees around." She removed the shawl to reveal dark hair pulled into an elaborate bun at the nape of her neck. Stray tendrils softened her hairline. Pamela held out her arms as Charlotte slipped out of her coat.

Charlotte perched on the rummage-sale chair with the carved wooden back and needlepoint seat, facing the sofa with the coffee table in between. Bettina leaned toward her. "How's Pierre doing?" she asked.

"Sad, of course," Charlotte said. She pulled a skein of sky-blue yarn from her knitting bag, which was sewn from flowered chintz and hung from wooden handles. "But he's also quite distracted at the moment."

"His teaching, I imagine . . . though Wendelstaff must be on break now." The expression on Bettina's face made the statement a question.

"Oh—not that. I mean, Pierre is a dedicated teacher of course and yes, Wendelstaff is on break." Charlotte reached into the bag again and came up with a wide swath of sky-blue knitting. Above a few inches of ribbing, an elaborate interlocking pattern commenced, Celtic in feel, like a braid woven from many strands. She studied it, smoothing it out on her knee. "Didn't Millicent tell you?"

Pamela had taken her seat on the footstool and set to work completing the last piece of the ambitious project she had started at the beginning of summer— a glamorous ruby-red tunic with (what seemed to her daring) peekaboo shoulders. But now she let needles and knitting rest in her lap and leaned forward.

Pamela was not a nosy person. Quite the opposite.

But she doubted even the most detached of persons could ignore words as tantalizing as *Didn't Millicent tell you?* And in fact Nell had abandoned her knitting too and was staring at Charlotte.

"Tell me what?" Bettina had no scruples about making her curiosity known.

"Millicent had a sister," Charlotte said. "An older sister—except Millicent never knew her because Millicent's parents put the sister up for adoption."

"Oh, my!" Nell's faded blue eyes looked positively tragic. "Why would people do that?"

"That's what this woman says anyway. She came around last week. Millicent had never laid eyes on her." Charlotte shrugged.

"The house," Bettina said. "When Millicent's mother died, the house should have gone to the sister—if she's the oldest."

"Depends on the will," Roland observed without pausing the steady rhythm of his needles.

Holly leaned across Bettina to flash Roland one of the dimply smiles that revealed her perfect teeth. "You must know everything there is to know about wills," she exclaimed.

"Inheritance law is hardly my specialty," Roland said, suppressing a tiny pleased smile. "But the basics are pretty basic. If the will says somebody gets something, then that somebody gets it."

Bettina tightened her lips into a thoughtful line. "Millicent's mother must have had a will—that huge house on that huge piece of land . . . in *Timberley*. The estate is worth millions, I'm sure. And Millicent cared for her mother for so many years before she died. It would be shameful if her mother just left everything for whatever heirs to fight over, while the lawyers all took their cut."

Pamela glanced at Roland, but he seemed more interested in the process of shaping his pink angora yarn into what seemed to be a sleeve than in following the conversation. "Millicent must have known the house was hers," Pamela said, "because she was going to sell it."

"True." Bettina nodded. "So what claim could this person think she has?" This question was directed to Charlotte.

Charlotte shrugged again, a delicate one-shouldered shrug that made the tiny gold locket nestled between her collarbones shift slightly. "DNA evidence. Isn't that what people do now?" Her pretty mouth shaped an apologetic half smile. "I'm not really supposed to know about this. I stopped by the big house to pay my rent last week and heard them talking before they saw me. They'd just come back from somewhere and were walking up to the porch."

"What will you do now?" Holly exclaimed, as if the thought had just occurred to her. "You'll have to move . . . unless Millicent's husband decides to keep the house, or this DNA person decides to stay . . ." Her voice trailed off.

"I was going to move anyway," Charlotte said. "I love living in that old carriage house, but I don't like paying rent when I could be buying something of my own. Morton-Bidwell just offered me a five-year contract and I've been looking at townhouses." Morton-Bidwell was a fancy private school in Timberley with a reputation as a sure conduit to the Ivy League.

Pamela surveyed the room. Holly's project looked new, and interesting, a rectangle knit from thick, fuzzy yarn in a dramatic shade of orange. Next to Holly, Bettina was intent on what Pamela knew was her most ambitious project to date: a Nordic-style sweater for Wilfred, navy blue with red ribbing and bands of snowflakes in red and white. Roland was still at work on the pink angora sweater destined as a Christmas gift for his wife, Melanie.

As if Holly had been doing her own survey, she suddenly spoke up, addressing Nell. "How many have you done so far?" she asked.

Nell looked momentarily startled, then blinked and smiled, as if a bit embarrassed to have been caught in the trancelike state that Pamela knew knitting sometimes induced. "This is number twenty," she said, holding the project up so it could be seen by all.

It was a stocking, nearly finished, bright red, and of a size to fit a foot larger than that of any human.

"There will be plenty of room for goodies in that," Bettina said.

Nell nodded. "Not too much candy though."

"But it's Christmas," Bettina protested.

"Healthful things, like nuts. And some little toys, of course. Educational toys. Heaven knows, the children at the shelter have so little." Nell volunteered at the women's shelter in Haversack, and most products of her knitting industry were designed as gifts for people temporarily lodging there.

Having satisfied her curiosity about Nell's progress, Holly leaned past Bettina and fingered the nearly completed sleeve that hung from Roland's needles. "Melanie is going to love this color," she exclaimed with another dimply smile.

Pamela had her doubts. She'd never seen Roland's soigné wife in anything but chic neutrals and fabrics like fine wool, linen, or silk. But Melanie was delighted that Roland's knitting hobby was serving as the stress-reducer his doctor had prescribed.

"Will you be finished in time?" Holly went on. "Christmas is just a week away."

"Eight days," Roland said with a frown. "And of course I'll be finished." Still knitting, he nodded toward the briefcase in which he carried his knitting supplies, which was open at his feet. Within were three knitted lengths of pink angora, folded neatly and nestled side by side. "This is the last sleeve, and I'll have plenty of time to sew them together."

"What about your project, Holly?" Pamela asked quickly. Most people came to Knit and Nibble to knit and talk (and nibble of course)—but Roland didn't do small talk and always seemed puzzled by Holly's conversational overtures. Now his lean face was serious as his finger caught up a strand of yarn and he plied his needles to form a stitch. It was the last stitch in the row. He studied his handiwork for a moment, then shifted the piece of knitting from his right hand to his left, turned it over, and started a new row.

"I'm making an afghan." Holly displayed the fuzzy orange rectangle. "Color block. Some pieces will be squares and others rectangles. Different sizes too, but they'll all fit together. It will look very sixties. And I'm using all my favorite colors—some other pieces will be turquoise, and I'm not sure what else yet. Maybe some kind of green, or—"

She was cut off by Roland, who had set his knitting aside in mid-row and pushed back his flawlessly starched shirt cuff to consult his impressive watch. "It's just eight," he announced. "Time for our break."

"—another shade of blue," Holly finished. Pamela gave her a sympathetic smile.

"I love those bright colors too," Bettina said. In fact, Bettina's hair, which she herself described as a color not found in nature, was nearly the same hue as the yarn Holly was shaping into the beginnings of her afghan. "And so clever—you can easily carry the project around because you're making one little piece at a time, then you sew them together and you have a whole afghan."

Meanwhile, Pamela was on her way to the kitchen. Before people started arriving, she'd set out seven cups and saucers from her wedding china on the kitchen table, and seven little plates, and seven spoons, and seven white linen napkins trimmed with lace. The napkins had been rescued long ago from the tail end of a tag sale, just as their owner, eager to downsize, was bagging up the unsold leftovers for the Goodwill. The cut-glass sugar bowl and creamer stood ready, the bowl freshly filled and the creamer ready for cream. In the absence of Karen, Nell would be the only tea drinker, but several scoops of loose tea waited in the teapot, a cherished thrift-store find. On the counter sat the coffee grinder, its canister full of fresh-ground coffee, and the carafe with a paper filter fitted into its plastic cone.

Pamela filled the kettle at the sink, settled it on the stove, and was just adjusting the flame under it when Bettina entered.

"That Roland," she muttered. "He has absolutely no social graces."

Pamela laughed. "Well, he *does* keep us on schedule."

"Just an excuse to show off that fancy watch of his. I

don't know how Melanie puts up with him." Bettina
expelled her breath in a disdainful puff.

"Not everyone is fortunate enough to have a Wilfred," Pamela said. *Or a Michael*, she almost said, but
stopped herself. Michael Paterson had been an ideal
husband, and the holidays always reminded her afresh
how happy their life had been. But Bettina needed
little encouragement to bring up one of her favorite
topics: the eligibility of Richard Larkin.

"What can I carry?" came a cheery voice from the
doorway. It was Holly, eyes shining and dimply smile in
place. She caught sight of the tray of cookies on the
counter. "Ohhh!" She clapped and her brilliant red
nails glittered in the bright kitchen. "Did you *make*
these?" She stared at Pamela. "I know you're an awesome cook, but these are just *too* amazing."

"I can't take all the credit," Pamela said. "I baked
them, but Bettina and Wilfred helped with the decorating."

Bettina stripped the plastic wrap from the cookie
tray. "Wilfred did most of the Santas," she added.

Holly leaned close to inspect the colorful assortment that included Santas, wreaths, reindeer, stars,
and Christmas trees. "The Santa even has eyes," she exclaimed, "and a little red nose." She reached for the
tray. "I'll take them in." Bettina retrieved the carton
of cream from the refrigerator and filled the cut-glass
creamer, then followed Holly to the living room bearing cream and sugar.

The hooting kettle summoned Pamela to the stove,
and in a few seconds the aroma of brewing coffee filled
the kitchen as the steaming water dripped through the
fresh grounds and into the carafe below. Pamela refilled the kettle and set it to boiling again for the tea.

From the living room came a chorus of praise for the cookies, a chorus that even included Roland's measured tones.

"Tea for Nell, of course, and everyone else wants coffee." Bettina had returned. "I'll take out these plates for the cookies then come back and pour some coffee," she said before picking up the stack of small plates and heading through the kitchen door again. Once back from that errand, she removed the plastic cone from the top of the carafe and transferred the carafe to the table where the wedding-china cups waited. She filled the cups, pouring the dark liquid into the pale porcelain traced with delicate rose garlands.

"Only five coffees," Pamela reminded her. "I put out an extra cup before I knew Karen wouldn't be here."

"Karen would be tea anyway," Bettina said, continuing with her coffee-pouring task. "One last cup to fill, then I'll start carrying them out."

"Take the spoons too," Pamela said, "and an empty cup for Nell. I'll bring the teapot and she can let it steep till it's the way she likes it."

When the kettle began to hoot, Pamela added the boiling water to the teapot and carried it to the living room, depositing it on the hearth near the armchair where Nell sat. A lively conversation was in progress.

"I think it's a perfectly fine use of my tax dollars," Nell was saying.

Pamela resumed her seat on the footstool. She didn't have to wait long to learn what use of tax dollars was being discussed and who wasn't in favor of it. Nell had barely finished speaking when Roland leaned forward. The action was so precipitous that if Bettina, who was next to him on the sofa, hadn't reacted quickly the plate balanced on Roland's pinstripe-clad knee would have slid to the floor.

"I don't need to see tinsel, colored lights, and blinking stars festooning every light pole along Arborville Avenue," he said, his lean face intense, "not to mention that they start appearing the day after Halloween."

"They're not on every light pole along Arborville Avenue." Bettina handed him the plate she had rescued, half-eaten Santa undisturbed. "Only the few blocks where the shops are."

"Then let the merchants pay to put the decorations up." Roland accepted the plate and returned it to his knee.

"Everyone enjoys the decorations," Nell observed mildly. "Winter is such a sad, dark time. People have always used light to remind themselves it won't last forever."

"It's a frivolous expenditure," Roland grumbled, "and our property taxes go up every year, and meanwhile the broken curb in front of my house has gone unrepaired for months."

"Everything doesn't always have to be practical," Holly observed. "Take these awesome cookies. They'd taste just as good if they weren't shaped and decorated to look like Santas and reindeer. But aren't we all enjoying them all the more because of the way they look?"

"I certainly am." Charlotte flourished a half-eaten reindeer. She'd pulled the rummage-sale chair with the carved wooden back and needlepoint seat closer to the coffee table, where her coffee cup sat, and she'd unfolded the lace-trimmed napkin and laid it neatly across her lap.

"I am too," Nell said, "though a little bit of sugar goes a long way."

"You must take some home for Harold," Pamela said. "I'll put them in a bag before you leave."

"The decorations are up in downtown Timberley too," Charlotte said. "I think all the towns have them."

"Does Timberley have Santa come around in a fire truck scaring everyone half to death?" Roland asked.

"Oh, Roland!" Nell laughed. "When people hear sirens in the afternoon on the Sunday before Christmas, everybody knows it's Santa. It's an old Arborville tradition. My children used to love it. They'd run out to the corner and watch him come up the hill, and they'd wave and wave."

"And what if there was really a fire while everyone was out having a good time?" Roland frowned.

"I'm sure lots of the firefighters stay back at the firehouse." Bettina turned toward Roland with an answering frown. "And there's more than one fire truck."

"Too many for a town this size. Toys for overgrown boys, paid for by the taxpayers." Roland's frown deepened.

Nell chuckled from the depths of the armchair, the delicate rose-garland cup that contained her tea poised halfway to her mouth. "Oh, you men all love your toys. And people are certainly happy to see those fire engines if there's a fire."

"I do not love toys," Roland said stiffly. "I do not have toys."

"What about that fancy watch of yours?" Bettina chuckled, but not as gently as Nell had done.

Roland swiveled toward her and, jarred by the sudden movement, the plate balanced on his knee slipped to the floor. "My watch is not a toy," he announced, his voice stern. "It's a precision instrument."

But that clarification was lost in the sudden bustle, as Holly and Bettina dove for the fallen plate and

Charlotte sprang from her seat. "It's your beautiful china," Charlotte moaned, leaning over the coffee table. Roland continued to frown, but he folded his arms across his chest in a defensive gesture.

Pamela had felt a pang as she saw the plate tip and then slide. But she'd decided long ago that she'd rather an incomplete set of china remained behind when she was no longer around to enjoy it than twelve place settings in pristine condition because they'd never been used.

Bettina's muffled voice came from somewhere near the floor. "It's okay," she announced as she straightened up and eased her hand, bearing the intact plate, past the edge of the coffee table and through the space between her knees and Roland's. "Your rug cushioned the fall, Pamela," she observed.

"And here's the rest of the cookie." At her end of the sofa, Holly triumphantly waved a Santa half. "I love your rugs, Pamela, and they go so well with your beautiful old things."

Looking chastened, and somewhat relieved, Roland accepted plate and cookie, and raised the cookie to his lips.

"You don't have to eat it after it's been on the floor." Pamela jumped up, seized the tray of cookies, and held it toward Roland. "There are plenty! Everyone, please have more." She waited while the group clustered around the coffee table helped themselves, then turned and offered the tray to Nell.

"No thank you! Really!" Nell patted her flat stomach. She was every bit as old as her white hair and faded eyes suggested, but her aversion to driving when she could walk and her devotion to healthful eating had kept her slim and limber. "You must save enough for dear little Penny to have her share. I *will* take a few for Harold though, before I go." She waved a wrinkled hand. "Just a few. He does love your creations."

Pamela turned back to the rest of the group. "There's more coffee in the kitchen. Whose cup can I refill?"

"No . . . none for me . . . I'm fine" came a chorus, and soon needles had been picked up and knitting resumed.

Chapter Five

Bettina was the last to leave, and lingered in Pamela's kitchen, where they'd worked together washing china and spoons, putting the cream away, and transferring the remaining cookies to a vintage cookie tin.

"You'll give some cookies to Richard Larkin, I hope," Bettina said as she pressed the lid, decorated with a scene of Santa, sleigh, and eight vigorous reindeer, down onto the tin.

"I can't just march over there with cookies." Pamela gave Bettina a fond but slightly chiding smile. "He'll be embarrassed because he won't have anything for me."

"He might have something," Bettina said. "You don't know for sure."

"Why would he?" Pamela shook out the dishcloth she'd been holding and hung it up.

"It would be a neighborly thing. After all, you and he are neighbors." Bettina studied Pamela's face, which Pamela struggled to keep neutral. "You know you like him," she said at last. "And it's obvious he likes you."

"And if we *did* . . . get together, and it didn't work out? What then?" Catrina strolled in from the entry and Pamela watched her make her undulating way across the floor toward the hallway that led to her bed in the laundry room. "I'm living here. He's living there. Our children are friends. It would be more than awkward."

"I think it would work out," Bettina said. "I know him and I know you." She turned and headed in the direction Catrina had just come from.

As she was slipping into her pumpkin-colored coat in the entry, she added one last thought. "You'll wear something flattering to my Christmas party, I hope." She accompanied the suggestion with a meaningful expression.

"You didn't invite Richard Larkin, did you?" Pamela wailed.

"Of course," Bettina said matter-of-factly. "He's a neighbor."

Pamela slid the *Register* from its flimsy plastic sleeve. She unfolded the paper and smoothed it flat on the kitchen table. Holding her breath, she hurriedly scanned the front page. Thankfully there was no photo of Penny or even any reference to Millicent's murder. The big story for the day involved an upcoming vote in the state senate on raising tuition at the state colleges.

Pamela poured the steaming water from the kettle into the plastic cone balanced over the carafe and slipped a piece of whole-grain bread into the toaster. As the coffee dripped into the carafe, she paged through Part 1 of the newspaper. It wasn't until she set Part 1 aside to reveal the Local section that she came upon what she had feared. Millicent's murder was no longer a breaking story but was certainly of ongoing interest, and would be until the killer was identified. And here was Penny, in her violet jacket and her mother's violet scarf, standing in the parking lot shared by the police station and the library and gazing uncertainly at the camera. The headline read, "Crime Scene Described by Woman Who Found Body."

"I didn't really feel like smiling," said a voice, "and besides, it didn't seem right." Penny had appeared in the doorway, her eyes still sleepy, dressed in her fleecy pink robe and flannel pajamas.

"The coffee should be ready," Pamela said, "and you can have that piece of toast. I'll make another."

As Penny helped herself to coffee, Pamela skimmed the article that accompanied the photo. It identified Penny as "Penny Paterson," mentioned where she went to college, and explained that she was home for Christmas break. The article was short—most likely, Pamela thought, because energetic as Marcy Brewer was, she had been unable to wrest more details from Penny than those Penny had given the police. And those details had appeared in the original report on the body's discovery. So tracking Penny down for a photo and interview had served no purpose that Pamela could see except making sure that every reader of the *Register* (including perhaps the very person who killed Millicent) knew that Penny had stumbled upon the body and knew exactly what Penny looked like.

Pamela was a levelheaded person, not prone to wild surmises. But *what if*—a voice in her head suddenly asked—*what if* the killer had left behind a clue and just now realized it and feared Penny had seen it and would suddenly remember it *if she wasn't silenced*?

"*Mo-om!*" Penny was staring at her from the counter,

a knife smeared with butter in her hand. "What on earth is wrong? You look like you've seen a ghost."

Pamela blinked and tried to smile. "I'm fine," she said. "Just . . . just . . . planning my day. So much to do . . . for Christmas."

Penny smiled back. "I'll pour you some coffee. And should I put another piece of toast in?"

"I'm not really hungry," Pamela said. "But I'll take some coffee."

Penny served her mother coffee, slipping a rose-garlanded cup in front of her and sitting down on her own side of the table with her own coffee and her toast. "Let's see what that reporter said about me," she murmured, reaching for the Local section and spinning it to face her.

An hour later, Pamela had checked her email, slipped on jeans and a sweater, and was gathering a few canvas shopping bags in preparation for a walk to the Co-Op. Cat food was already on the shopping list, and as far as meals for the humans went, she was thinking of making oxtail stew.

She'd always cooked proper meals, even after only she and Penny were left, wanting Penny to feel that in most ways her life was the same as it had been when her father was alive. And when Penny went away to college, she still cooked proper meals, though a meatloaf or roast chicken lasted a whole week. With Penny home for the Christmas holidays, though, she had an audience for more elaborate creations. A comforting pot of oxtail stew simmering on the stove would make the house fragrant with thyme and bay leaf.

Bundled in her warmest jacket and with a fuzzy hat

pulled down to her eyebrows and a fuzzy scarf knotted up to her chin, Pamela set out up the street, canvas bags in hand. The day was bright and still, though very cold. Evergreens and ivy offered the only flash of color in the wintry yards, aside from an occasional cluster of red berries.

At the corner she detoured through the parking lot behind the stately brick apartment building that faced Arborville Avenue and peeked behind the discreet fence that hid the building's trash from view. Pamela had rescued the occasional treasure there—people in the process of moving often discarded perfectly nice things that they didn't have time to donate to a thrift shop. The oxtail stew planned for that evening would simmer in a magnificent Le Creuset casserole she'd found there the previous summer, and she'd rescued a perfectly fine crystal vase. But nothing tempted her today.

The Co-Op anchored one end of Arborville's small commercial district. With its narrow aisles and wooden floors it was the antithesis of a modern supermarket, but it was cherished by the inhabitants of Arborville for its cheese counter, its bakery counter, and a meat department that offered meat from small, local farms. It was also cherished for the bulletin board mounted near the entry. Before the Internet, the bulletin board had kept Arborville informed of town doings and offered a venue where people could post notes about things they wanted to sell (or give away, like kittens). And many people still relied on it, rather than their computer screen, to keep them up-to-date.

The Co-Op indeed was Pamela's destination today, but instead of stopping when she reached it, she crossed Arborville Avenue. She continued on her way

their own or their friends' children—was unlikely to be impressed.

So she didn't hurry back the way she'd come and slip through the narrow passage between Hyler's and the hair salon to reach the police station and report her discovery to Detective Clayborn. Instead, she crossed Arborville Avenue and made her way to the Co-Op. There she plucked a basket from the nest of baskets near the door and made a round of the market, adding to it parsnips and a huge waxed turnip, three pounds of oxtails, and two cans of cat food.

She emerged from the Co-Op fifteen minutes later with a canvas shopping bag in each hand, eager to put the oxtails in the refrigerator and run across the street to tell Bettina about the scarf sighting. But as she stood at the corner waiting for the light to change, it suddenly appeared there might be more to report.

She was admiring the way Borough Hall, the small brick building that served as Arborville's administrative center, had been decorated for Christmas. The railings that flanked the half flight of steps leading to its entrance bore swags of greenery bound with wide red ribbons. Matching swags were draped around the door itself, which also sported a huge holly wreath trimmed with a red bow. Miniature Christmas trees twinkling with white lights flanked the door.

A young man had climbed the steps. He paused and stood aside as the door began to open, then waited while an elderly couple stepped out. They moved slowly and he turned to gaze toward the street, unable for a moment to enter. And as he did, he added a touch of seasonal color to the holiday tableau—a bright red scarf with green stripes at the ends.

Pamela stared, long enough to lose her chance to

cross the street. She stepped off the curb but the "Don't Cross" warning blinked in admonishment. She resigned herself to another wait, watching helplessly as, with a courtly nod to the elderly couple, her quarry disappeared through the wreath-bedecked door. He'd be somewhere in the building though. She resolved to track him down. As she waited for the light to change once again, she prepared mentally for the encounter.

Penny had been a cooperative and obedient child, especially in the past six years, as if she realized that with Michael Paterson gone, she and her mother had only each other. But Pamela still had a mother's instinct for the subtle signs of discomfort when an unexpected question required a quickly fabricated answer. When she located the young man, she would say, "Nice scarf! Do you mind if I ask where you got it?" And she'd watch his face carefully as he answered.

When the "Don't Cross" warning was replaced by the little striding figure that invited people to proceed on their way, Pamela stepped off the curb. She hurried to the other side of Arborville Avenue and thence up the steps and between the twinkling Christmas trees. Then she pushed open the door and entered Borough Hall.

A long hallway, carpeted in nondescript gray, stretched to the back of the building. To the left of the hallway, a steep staircase led to a second floor. The hallway ran past counters where people could pay their tax bills or parking tickets, apply for permits for home-improvement projects or garage sales, or request "Resident Parking" decals for their cars. Postings on a large bulletin board announced upcoming deadlines and advised that Borough Hall would no longer be able to process passport renewals. Beyond the counters, doors opened off either side of the hallway.

Pamela stopped at the first counter she came to. A chubby woman wearing dangling candy-cane earrings was sitting in front of a computer screen. Pamela asked her whether she'd noticed a young man in a red scarf.

"Can't say I did," the woman said, looking at Pamela over the half-glasses perched on her nose.

Pamela asked the same question at the other counters and got the same answer. Proceeding along the hallway, she peeked in each office but saw no sign of her quarry. She climbed the creaky stairs—Borough Hall was very old—but had no better luck on the second floor. All the while she was rehearsing in her mind *Nice scarf! Do you mind if I ask where you got it?* and various scenarios were playing themselves out.

In one, the one that made her heart come noisily alive in her chest, the young man in the red scarf replied, *I know why you're asking and I know who you are. You're the mother of Penny Paterson, the Miss Nosy who was nosing around in the nature preserve last Monday afternoon. And if you both know what's good for you, you'll mind your own business.*

She retraced her steps along the second-floor hallway till she was back at the top of the steep staircase, grasped the bannister, and made her way down. The grocery bags were getting rather heavy. At the bottom of the stairs, she took a deep breath to gather her nerve. There was no back door to Borough Hall, though more modern construction would have demanded a fire exit. The young man in the red scarf had to leave sooner or later. She'd stand by the entrance. It was only a matter of time.

And there was no reason to be afraid, she told herself. He didn't look like a killer, and he probably came by the scarf in some totally innocent way. But tracing the scarf's adventures between the time that Millicent wrapped it around her neck and the present could be useful—and revealing.

"Yoo-hoo, yoo-hoo!" The voice jolted her out of her reverie. The chubby woman with the candy-cane earrings was standing behind her counter, earrings bobbing as she waved at Pamela. Pamela looked up.

"You were lost in thought there," the woman said.

Pamela blinked and laughed. "Yes," she said. "I guess I was."

"He's gone," the woman said. "The red scarf. Headed down the stairs and out the door while you were back in the back there." She nodded toward the offices farther down the hallway and set the earrings bobbing again.

Pamela hurried back up the stairs, the grocery bags dangling from her hands. But nobody she encountered could—or would—tell her what the young man's business might have been.

Chapter Six

"It's the scarf I made for Millicent," Bettina exclaimed. "It has to be. Red, with three green stripes at each end."

"That was it." Pamela nodded. "Exactly. And one stripe was a different shade of green, where you ran out and had to use that leftover bit I had in my yarn basket."

"But if he's the killer—" Bettina interrupted herself to shoo away Woofus, who was avidly sniffing at one of Pamela's grocery bags. The shaggy creature looked up in alarm and slunk off toward the kitchen.

"Oxtails," Pamela observed, lifting the relevant bag. She had been so eager to tell her news, especially after the second sighting at Borough Hall, that she'd stopped off at Bettina's without going home to put her groceries away, and she had begun to speak the minute Bettina opened her door. Now she was standing in Bettina's living room.

"If he's the killer," Bettina continued, "how could he be so brazen as to wear a scarf he snatched from his victim? It *is* a nice scarf, but still . . ."

"I don't know." Pamela shook her head. "It's all very puzzling."

"Come on back here." Bettina took her friend's arm

and pulled her toward the arch that separated her
living room from her dining room.

When they reached the kitchen, Bettina stowed
Pamela's grocery bags on the counter, well out of the
reach of Woofus. "I almost forgot," she said suddenly.
"I was so distracted talking about the scarf." She paused
dramatically. "Karen's baby came—at three a.m.! I
talked to Dave this morning. They knew they were
having a little girl, and they had a name all picked out.
Lily—so sweet!"

"What happy news!" Pamela exclaimed. "And everyone's well?" Bettina nodded. Pamela went on. "I was
wondering, of course, after what Holly mentioned last
night. But I didn't want to disturb them too soon."

"Dave is on top of the world." Bettina laughed. "He
couldn't stop talking."

"I'll give them a call too," Pamela said.

"How about some lunch?" Bettina gestured toward
the stove. "I'll bet you haven't eaten anything but a
piece of toast all day. Wilfred made some of his five-
alarm chili last night and I was just heating it up."

Pamela had noticed the tempting smell of beef infused with onions, cumin, and dried peppers the
minute she stepped in the door, and she realized that
she was indeed very hungry. And she had noticed
that Bettina was wearing a protective apron over her
ensemble, a soft wool shirtdress in a red-and-green
plaid, complemented by festive red sneakers.

Already waiting on the counter was a wooden cutting board holding a wedge of Swiss cheese, pale
yellow and tunneled with holes, and a round loaf of
crusty bread sprinkled with seeds.

As Bettina stood at the stove tending the chili with

a long-handled wooden spoon, Pamela transferred two of Bettina's sage-green bowls from the cupboard to the counter and opened the silverware drawer.

"Oh, dear," Bettina moaned. "I'd forgotten about Millicent for a minute, but now looking at those bowls . . ." She sighed and the hand wielding the spoon was momentarily still. "They're from her shop." She watched as Pamela lifted two spoons from the drawer. "Napkins are in the drawer below," she said. Then she sighed again as Pamela retrieved two linen napkins with bright embroidery at the edges. "And those are from her shop too."

"My boss at *Fiber Craft* sent an email about Millicent's death," Pamela said as she patted Bettina's shoulder. "Losing her really is a blow to the craftspeople who sold their work there. My boss doesn't have much hope that Nadine will be able to keep the shop going—and she doesn't have much confidence in the abilities of the Arborville police."

"Well, I'm going to tell Clayborn that someone wearing Millicent's scarf is wandering around Arborville." Bettina gave the chili an energetic stir as if to emphasize the point. "If that isn't a clue, I don't know what is."

"I wasn't sure if we should," Pamela said hesitantly. "He might just say lots of people have red scarves with green stripes at the ends."

"Not with stripes that aren't all the same color of green." Bettina tapped the spoon on the side of the pot to knock off a few clinging beans and picked up a silvery ladle. Soon they were seated at her well-scrubbed pine table with bowls of steaming chili in front of them. Bettina carved thick slices from the crusty loaf of bread and gestured to Pamela to take one. "And have some of this cheese," she urged, turning her attentions to the imposing wedge of Swiss.

Woofus had retired to his habitual spot in the corner and was napping, flopped on his side with his legs stretched out at right angles to his body and his tail a shaggy extension of his backbone. Pamela buttered her bread and added a slice of cheese. Bettina did likewise and they were enjoying their first spoonfuls of the tempting chili when a small commotion drew their attention to the corner where Woofus reposed. With a startled whimper, he lifted his head and retracted his legs and tail, no more the image of blissful slumber.

The source of his distress was a lively ginger-colored kitten. She hadn't abandoned her interest in his tail even though it was now protectively lodged between his back legs. She was nudging it with a tiny paw as Woofus inched away from her, regarding her with alarm.

"It's going to take him a while to realize Punkin can't hurt him," Bettina said with a laugh: "She, on the other hand, has taken to us—especially Wilfred—as if she's known us all her life."

"She sort of has." Pamela echoed the laugh. "How's Midnight doing with Wilfred Jr.'s boys?"

"Oh, dear." A slight wrinkle appeared between Bettina's brows. "I was going to mention it . . . The boys might be allergic!"

"I guess this is their first exposure to a kitten." Pamela's lips twisted in sympathy.

"They're getting rashes. Itching." As if to comfort herself, Bettina cut another slice of bread and buttered it liberally.

"I'd understand if they have to return Midnight," Pamela said. "Allergies can be very unpleasant."

"Oh—we'd take him." Bettina smiled suddenly. "The more the merrier. We always had dogs when the boys were growing up, but never a kitten. I don't know why—Punkin is just a doll. And she'd have her brother to keep her company."

They turned back to their chili.

Packages waited on the porch when Pamela crossed the street to her own house half an hour later. She took the canvas bags containing the groceries to the kitchen and stowed the oxtails in the refrigerator. Catrina and Ginger prowled around her feet as if they knew the trip to the Co-Op had involved fetching cat food, and she promised them lunch would be forthcoming in a moment.

Ginger was eating regular cat food now, but more often than Catrina's morning and evening schedule. Keeping Catrina from sneaking bites of her daughter's meals was hopeless, so Pamela had settled on serving three small meals and letting the cats share.

She returned to the porch to fetch the packages, a small cardboard box and a larger one, and as she carried them inside Penny came down the stairs.

"From Grandma and Grandpa Paterson," Pamela said, holding out the smaller box. "And"—she consulted the mailing label on the larger box—"from my parents."

Pamela's parents lived in the Midwest, where Pamela grew up, and some years Christmas involved a trip to their house and a grand reunion with relatives of all sorts. But this year her parents had announced that they would be cruising in the Caribbean, a winter vacation that had been greeted by Pamela and her siblings as long overdue and well-deserved.

"The Christmas-tree lot will be open Friday night and all weekend," Pamela said. "And we'll just leave these boxes here"—she slid them under the mail table—"until we have it all up and decorated." Penny nodded. "And I'm making oxtail stew tonight. And Wilfred Jr.'s boys might be allergic to Midnight."

That wasn't quite all the news, but she didn't see that any good would come of telling Penny that she'd seen someone wearing Millicent's scarf.

Penny nodded again. "I'm going to Lorie's," she said. "But I'll be back for dinner." She opened the closet and took out the violet jacket. Pamela watched as she adjusted the violet scarf at her neck. Lorie Hopkins lived above Arborville Avenue, nowhere near the nature preserve, and nowhere near the commercial district where the young man wearing Millicent's scarf had been making his rounds.

"It gets dark at four thirty now," Pamela said. "Try to come back by then."

Upstairs, Pamela checked her email to find that a message from her boss at *Fiber Craft* had arrived while she was out. "Re-creating Traditional Turkish Weaving Techniques" and "Memorializing the Departed: The (Hair) Art of Victorian Mourning Brooches" were back, along with a third article, "The Mud Cloth Trade and Women's Textile Collectives in Mali." She was to edit them and return them by the next evening.

Pamela set to work without wasting a minute. The next day would be busy—she had a funeral to attend in Timberley, followed by a luncheon reception at the Carroll Inn.

* * *

"Pierre is handling his grief well," Pamela said as Wilfred piloted his ancient Mercedes into the parking lot of the Carroll Inn.

"I'd say so!" Bettina nodded. A hint of disapproval crept into her voice. "He didn't seem sad at all during the funeral. And when we were at the graveyard he was positively grinning." She leaned forward to address Wilfred—she and Pamela were riding in the back seat while Penny sat up front. "Don't park too far from the entrance. I'm not wearing my walking shoes."

"Your wish is my command, dear wife," Wilfred said cheerfully and turned into the closest open spot.

They climbed out of the car and started toward the main entrance of the Carroll Inn. Wilfred led the way in a smart woolen overcoat dating from his pre-retirement days. Bettina held his arm as she navigated the asphalt in slender-heeled pumps whose deep purple hue complemented her lavender coat. Both were bare-headed, Wilfred's white hair contrasting with Bettina's vivid scarlet coif. Suddenly Bettina whispered "Oops" and tugged Wilfred to a stop. Pamela and Penny halted too.

"I don't know if we should go in yet," she said, nodding toward a BMW in a far corner of the lot. "Maybe we're too early—that looks like Pierre."

"How can you tell from here?" Pamela asked. All that was visible through the driver's-side window was the back of a man's head.

"That's his car." She nodded again. "Didn't you notice him getting out of it at the graveyard?"

"Fancy car for a part-time lecturer," Pamela observed.

"Millicent bought it for him." Bettina continued

looking at the BMW. "She wasn't exactly a sugar mama, but he *was* quite a bit younger."

"Collecting his thoughts perhaps—before he faces the crowd again," Pamela said, taking a tentative step toward the entrance of the Carroll Inn. "Whether or not he's as sad as he should be, this has to be a stressful experience for him." Bettina seemed not to hear. She still gripped Wilfred's arm and now she seized Pamela's with her other hand.

The driver of the BMW leaned back in his seat, revealing himself to be, indeed, Pierre. The BMW's door opened and Pierre stepped out. "I think we can go now," Bettina said. "He's coming in."

They all turned away, but as they climbed the steps to the inn's double doors, painted a glossy white, Penny spoke up in a hesitant voice. "I think there was someone else in the car."

"Really?" Bettina whirled around, her eyes wide.

"I'm not sure," Penny said. "But I was still watching when you all started for the entrance. He leaned back in like he was talking to someone before he slammed the car door."

The Carroll Inn's lobby featured an enormous Christmas tree, decorated with garlands of popcorn and cranberries, and wooden ornaments that looked hand-carved. They were crossing the lobby at a leisurely pace when Pierre scurried past on the way to the Musket Room, which the directory next to the concierge's desk identified as the site of the Farthingale reception.

On the way to the Musket Room, they stopped off to leave their coats in a coatroom at the edge of the lobby. Pamela left her silky scarf knotted around her neck at the urging of Bettina, who advised that it added at least a bit of polish to her humdrum pants and jacket.

"Nice turnout," Bettina said as they entered the Musket Room. "Of course the funeral was well attended—Millicent's family has lived in Timberley forever, and then with the shop . . . artists, customers, the other tradespeople in town . . ." She scanned the room. "Quite a splendid venue." The décor was sedate, featuring paneled walls, chandeliers, and a grand fireplace with an ornate mantel. Guests had not been deterred by the initial absence of their host, but were prowling along the buffet table, where delicacies like crab puffs and smoked salmon on brown bread had been arranged on an expanse of starched white linen. Other guests were clustered in front of the bar, where a young woman in a crisp white shirt and a long blond ponytail was dispensing wine.

Pierre had hurriedly stationed himself near the entrance. Taking their cue, people—at least those who had not yet filled plates or collected wine—began to line up to greet him and offer condolences.

Pamela had never met Pierre and now she studied him. Bettina had said he was not really *French* French, but rather French Canadian. He was, however, tall and slim, with smooth dark hair and features that were sharp but symmetrical. To these natural gifts he had added careful grooming—his close-shaven skin fairly glowed—and a faultlessly tailored navy suit whose close-fitting cut suggested a Continental origin.

"Shall we pay our respects before we eat?" Pamela said, though Bettina's attention had wandered in the direction of the tempting buffet. Besides the crab puffs and smoked salmon, it offered delicate finger sandwiches, a cheese tray on which cheeses were identified with little placards, skewers with something interesting on them, a huge pile of jumbo shrimp with red dipping sauce, mini-meatballs, and a broad platter of raw vegetables arranged as gracefully as an artist's still life.

"Yes, of course!" Bettina turned back to Pamela, and the four of them joined the ragged line making its way toward Pierre. They listened as mourners described Millicent's encouragement in their artistic endeavors, involvement in community affairs, or self-sacrificing care as her mother faded. Pierre grasped hands, received hugs, and administered comforting pats to those who seemed especially stricken.

When their turn came, Bettina stepped forward first. "I'm so sorry, Pierre," she said. "Millicent was a dear friend and I'll miss her. What a shock for you!" She reached for both his hands and he arranged his features in an expression of grief that didn't detract from his good looks. When Bettina released his hands, Wilfred stepped up and offered a handshake and a sympathetic murmur.

Pierre acknowledged it with an answering murmur and then turned his glance toward Pamela and Penny. "And who are your friends?" he asked.

Bettina stepped aside to make way for Pamela and Penny and then said, "Pamela Paterson and her daughter Penny, my neighbors in Arborville. Pamela is the leader of our knitting group, and Penny is just back from college in Massachusetts for the holidays."

"Not Wendelstaff?" Pierre smiled a regretful smile and reached for Penny's hand. "Our loss," he said, bending over it then looking up to gaze into her eyes. He continued to hold her hand while he switched his gaze to Pamela. "Such a pleasure," he said. "And now

I must go on with my duties." He nodded toward the next person in line, an aged woman who might have been a contemporary of Millicent's mother. "Please enjoy yourselves," he added, finally relinquishing Penny's hand. "And perhaps"—he inserted an approximation of a Gallic shrug—"we will catch up later."

He would have winked, Pamela was sure, but she didn't believe French people—or people trying to act French—did things so lacking in subtlety.

Guests, most of them dressed in dark colors and talking in subdued tones, milled around. "Those meatballs look awfully tempting," Bettina said as they gazed toward the buffet table. A large crowd ebbed and flowed as people inched along the expanse of starched white linen, busily filling plates. Another crowd milled near the bar, where the young woman with the blond ponytail was serving wine—red here, white there—with admirable speed.

As Pamela watched, Charlotte stepped away from the bar bearing a glass of red wine that echoed the deep burgundy of her dress, a supple column of lace with an ankle-length hem, high neck, and long sleeves.

"Charlotte"—Bettina nodded—"nice of her to come, though she could hardly have stayed away."

Between the crowds at buffet and bar, a smaller crowd had formed, and it was hard at first to make out what its focus was. A tight knot of people had clustered around someone, but a someone considerably shorter than the people in the clustering group.

Bettina clutched Pamela's arm. "It's Nadine, Millicent's partner! Come on!" Meatballs forgotten, Bettina took a few steps, tugging Pamela with her.

Pamela resisted, murmuring, "Bettina . . . really . . . she's already attracted a crowd." Pamela was actually

glad to see that someone else was the focus of attention.
Since Penny was the one who found Millicent's body,
she'd been afraid that her daughter would be the most
in-demand conversation partner at the reception.

"We'll rescue her," Bettina said. "She's terribly shy.
She must be a bundle of nerves with all these people
she barely knows quizzing her. Then we'll see if she
can tell us anything useful. She'll relax with me."

They'd already gotten close enough to hear Nadine
say, in a mousy little voice, "I can't tell you any more
than I know. Millicent left the shop at about ten a.m.
and that was the last time I saw her."

Bettina let go of Pamela and strode purposefully
toward Nadine. "You poor thing," she declared.
"You haven't had a chance to eat anything at all yet,
have you, with so many curious people wanting to talk
to you." A man and a woman backed away, looking
sheepish, as Bettina put an arm around Nadine and
led her toward Pamela. Bettina wasn't tall, but Nadine
was tiny and sparrowlike, an impression enhanced by
her drab suit and no-color hair.

Wilfred and Penny, meanwhile, had joined the line
at the buffet, which had dwindled considerably. Wilfred was standing protectively near Penny and gazing
around as if warding off anyone who might recognize
Penny and want to hear firsthand what it was like to
come upon a dead body in the nature preserve. Most
of the attendees were now supplied with food and
drink, and conversational groupings were forming
and breaking up here and there.

The main part of the room was set up to suit the reception format—buffet table and bar, and lots of open
space for people to mingle, meet, and greet. But at the
end near the grand fireplace, where a pleasant fire

crackled, was a small seating area consisting of four wing chairs and a low table. Pamela followed as Bettina led Nadine there and settled her into one of the wing chairs, the one in the most shadowy corner.

"Now you just wait here," Bettina said, "and Pamela and I will bring some food and wine and we can all relax."

Pamela was happy to see that Wilfred and Penny had filled plates and were chatting with a man of Wilfred's age, who was paying little attention to Penny, a sign that he either didn't realize it was she who found Millicent's body or was too well mannered to think of quizzing a young woman about such a grisly topic.

She relaxed and focused on the platter of mini-sandwiches in front of her, choosing a mini–corned beef on rye and a mini–ham on a biscuit before moving on to the cheese and the vegetable tray. Bettina had filled a plate for Nadine and now she handed it to Pamela to deliver before starting through the line again.

Soon the three of them were comfortably set with food and drink, and for a few minutes they ate and drank in companionable silence.

"Have you been going to the shop every day?" Bettina asked after a bit.

"I'm not there now," Nadine said, blinking at Bettina and then at Pamela. Her tone suggested she herself had just realized that fact. "I was there yesterday—it was all so confusing though, with artists calling every minute." She paused as if to sort out details before speaking again, then she went on. "I was there Tuesday, but the police came and I had to close the shop while they were there."

"I was there Monday," Bettina said.

"I remember." Nadine nodded.

"You weren't there yet." Bettina had taken a glass of the deep burgundy wine and she sipped it now.

"I wasn't." Nadine nodded again. "But then I came in before you left."

"Millicent was upset about a man who had been there first thing that morning. He wanted the shop to carry his work but she turned him down and he became angry." Bettina set the wineglass back on the table and picked up a crab puff.

Nadine had barely eaten anything, but her wineglass was nearly empty. "A lot of people ask to sell their work through the shop," she said, reaching for the glass. "But Millicent wanted the shop to be a certain way. Special things, not just anything."

Pamela was watching and listening carefully. She was sure the police had been thorough when they talked to Nadine on Tuesday, but they had talked to Nadine before Bettina had her conversation with Detective Clayborn. Bettina had told Detective Clayborn about the angry man who'd been in the shop on the morning of the day Millicent was killed. But would Nadine have thought to volunteer that information? She seemed a little disconnected. And would the police have gone back to ask if Nadine knew who the angry man might have been after Bettina told Detective Clayborn about him?

Bettina had made short work of the crab puff and was nibbling on a giant shrimp, so Pamela took the opportunity to ask a question of her own. "Nadine?" she said, and waited until Nadine looked her way. Nadine's gaze was disconcerting, like the wondering gaze of a young child. "When the police came to the shop to talk to you, did you tell them about the angry man?"

"Oh, no," Nadine said. "I didn't know about him."

"You didn't know he'd been there that morning," Pamela said, "but maybe Millicent had talked about him in the past."

"She talked about a lot of people," Nadine said. "A lot of people wanted her to sell their work."

Pamela sighed to herself and studied the plate of food before her. The slice of brown bread garnished with smoked salmon and dill looked very tempting and she lifted it to her lips. But she was interrupted in mid-bite by a cheerful wave and a shout—somewhat out of place given the circumstances.

Chapter Seven

Pamela's chair was the only one oriented toward the room. Bettina and Nadine faced the fireplace and were sheltered from view by the enveloping backs of their chairs. So it was Pamela whom the woman singled out to greet. "Hello there!" she boomed, drawing closer. "I just wanted to introduce myself"—she leaned toward Pamela and extended a hand—"Millicent's sister, Catherine Calvin. But you can just call me Coot."

The woman looked to be in her sixties, and her skin reflected her age—especially since she'd apparently spent a great deal of time outdoors, ignoring the effects of wind and sun. But the time outdoors was perhaps also responsible for her athletic physique and easy movements. There was a twang to her voice that evoked an upbringing far to the west of Arborville, New Jersey.

She noticed Bettina and Nadine. "Millicent's sister, Coot," she repeated, and held out a hand toward Bettina. Bettina took the hand, frowning, and introduced herself. Nadine held out a meek hand and murmured her own name.

"And I'm Pamela Paterson," Pamela said, but she felt

herself twitch in alarm. This must be the supposedly long-lost older sister that Charlotte had mentioned at Knit and Nibble. What incredible nerve this person had!

The incredible nerve was confirmed when Coot claimed the fourth chair without asking. "You're all probably wondering what my story is," she said.

Well, they were—at least Pamela was, but . . .

"I could be bitter," Coot went on. "But I'm not, even though I was basically given away by my real parents."

Charlotte had said Millicent's parents put the older sister up for adoption. And she had been clear—not Millicent's *mother*, but Millicent's *parents*. And now Coot was confirming that aspect of the story. But Millicent's mother and her husband couldn't have been a destitute young couple with no resources to raise a child. The Wentworth mansion in Timberley had been in Millicent's family since it was built in the Victorian era. And the Farthingales, Millicent's father's family, were equally well established.

"My birth mom got knocked up, basically," Coot announced in the same cheery tone.

"But . . ." Pamela twisted her lips into a puzzled knot. "When people got married didn't they expect . . . ? At least back then . . . ?"

"They weren't married." Coot's voice boomed. "That's the thing. Prep school sweethearts."

In her mind Pamela was calculating. Millicent had been nearly sixty, so let's say her mother had been about eighty. The elder Ms. Farthingale, née Wentworth, would have been in high school in the fifties—not an era when keeping your baby and raising it yourself was done. Humans being humans, though, Pamela had no doubt there were many unintended pregnancies. And more than one possible solution.

As if reading her mind, Coot answered the unspoken question. "Yep, my birth mother was hustled off for a visit to an aunt—who happened to live in Texas, and when I was born I was put up for adoption. Then, as it turned out, the prep-school sweethearts stayed in love, and six years later they got married and had Millicent. And there you have it." She clapped briskly and beamed at her audience. "Until—just on a whim, really—I did one of those DNA tests, and that led me to a Texas cousin who knew the whole story."

Pamela and Bettina both spoke, their words overlapping. The result was, "So, you came out here. What are your plans?"

"Well, I didn't think Millicent would be dead almost as soon as I got here, for one thing," Coot said in a matter-of-fact voice. "Of course, I never actually knew her, but she *was* my sister, and blood is blood." She paused. "So now there's the house. I've only been out here a few days, but I can already tell you I hate New Jersey. The weather! How can anyone live here? So I don't want to live in the house, but it's worth a lot of money. I can sure see that."

"The house will go to Pierre," Bettina said. "Even if she didn't leave a will. They were married."

"Don't be so sure about that." Coot smiled a smug little smile and scrunched up her face till her eyes peered out from nests of wrinkles. "She was still Farthingale, you know. Not Mrs. Pierre Lapointe."

"Women keep their own names all the time now," Pamela observed. "That doesn't mean anything."

"Maybe it does though," Coot continued. "Maybe he was just her"—she snickered—"*fancy man.*"

"Oh, I don't think—" Bettina looked shocked.

"We'll see. I hired a lawyer before I flew out here." And with that, Coot stood up and strode toward the buffet table.

Nadine seemed to have fallen asleep. The room was a bit warm with all the people crowded into it, and then there was the fire in the fireplace as well, and she had drunk a large glass of red wine.

Pamela and Bettina looked at each other. Pamela was the first to speak. "She thinks she was entitled to a share of the inheritance when Millicent's mother died."

Bettina added, "So she came out here to claim it."

Pamela went on, "But now, with Millicent dead . . ."

Bettina took up the thought. "She thinks the whole thing should be hers."

"She looked awfully strong," Pamela said. "And people from Texas know how to handle guns."

"She did look strong," Bettina said, "but if she thought the DNA could prove her claim, why would she need to kill Millicent?"

"She didn't really look very much like Millicent," Pamela observed.

"No," Bettina said, "she didn't."

"It didn't sound like Millicent's DNA is in the database. I guess she was going to demand that Millicent get it tested."

"Can you do that?" Bettina asked.

"I don't know."

"I didn't get a chance to sample those mini-meatballs yet." Bettina rose from the wing chair, empty plate in hand. "When I got to them, someone else had grabbed the serving spoon and was really digging in. Shall we see what's left on the table?"

"I'd eat more of those vegetables," Pamela said. "I've never seen that many kinds of baby heirloom tomatoes all in the same place. I wonder where they come from this time of year."

Nadine was dozing peacefully, complete with soft snores, so without bidding her good-bye they set out across the floor. The buffet table was still well stocked with food, though the crowd had thinned considerably. There was no sign of Coot, who had apparently introduced herself to everyone she cared to meet and gone on her way.

Pamela noted that Wilfred was still looking after Penny, and whatever he was saying to her had provoked a small giggle. Pierre was standing near the door accepting thank-yous and condolences from departing guests.

Bettina cooed with delight when she discovered that the meatballs had recently been replenished. They nestled cozily in a rich and creamy gravy, but a supply of large toothpicks nearby made them suitable as finger food. Bettina served herself a generous portion as Pamela moved ahead toward the vegetable platter but paused to help herself to another giant shrimp and a scoop of spicy red sauce.

As they turned away from the table, Pamela's attention was drawn to a small commotion near the door. A woman on her way in—quite a ravishing woman— had nearly collided with a man on his way out. He apologized profusely and made his exit.

Either the apology hadn't been deemed sufficient or the near-collision had only added to a preexisting dissatisfaction. A vertical line between her perfect brows was all she allowed herself in the way of a frown, but the rigid line of her jaw and the sharp click of her stiletto heels as she strode farther into the room completed the message. She was dressed in black, but the little black dress that followed the elegant lines of her body was more cocktail party than funeral. She glanced toward Pierre, who was bending to receive a hug from a white-haired woman, then she lifted a graceful hand to consult a dainty watch and continued on until she reached the bar.

Wilfred and Penny strolled over as Pamela and Bettina nibbled on their food. Wilfred tapped his watch and Bettina nodded, her mouth full of meatball. "Yes," she said, after she swallowed. "It looks like things are winding down." And a server was hovering nearby with a tray ready to receive empty plates.

But before Pamela and Bettina could hand their plates over, their group was suddenly joined by Pierre, who had apparently been on his way to the bar but had suddenly veered in their direction.

"Thank you so much for coming," he said with a graceful tilt of his head. He seized Bettina's hands. "Millicent valued your friendship so much." As he uttered the words, his eyes roamed toward Penny. She looked all the younger and tinier surrounded by the four adults, each of whom was imposing by reason of height or bulk or—in the case of Wilfred—both. "And mademoiselle will go back to her college then?"

"After Christmas." Penny nodded shyly.

"Such a pity." The look he gave her daughter seemed so invasive that Pamela was delighted when Bettina spoke up.

"We met Coot," she said.

Pierre gave a start and focused his gaze on Bettina. "She has no claim," he said. "No claim at all." He tapped the side of his head and rolled his eyes comically. "*Fou*, as we say in French. *Complètement fou.*"

The server appeared at Pamela's elbow. Pamela slipped her plate onto the tray, then reached for Bettina's and added it as well. Wilfred shook Pierre's hand. Pierre reached for Penny's hand and for a horrified moment Pamela thought he was going to kiss it. But instead he whispered "*Adieu*" and relinquished it. More nods and murmurs all around and then they started for the door.

But they didn't get far before he was at their side again. "The house," he said. "It will be sold, of course, as Millicent planned. All the more reason now. So you must come to my grand estate sale. Millicent had already hired a company to manage it, and they are very much in demand, so I must go ahead now even though it is so soon. The carriage house and its attic are full of old, old things. The sale starts tomorrow." Another meaningful look at Penny. "You must *all* come. I'll tell them to let you take whatever you want for free. *Voilà!*" He kissed his fingertips. "*Bien sûr*, it is all mine now, isn't it?"

Pierre left the Musket Room when they did, explaining that he needed to pop into the catering office. They all headed down the hall together, but Pierre veered off before they reached the coatroom. In the coatroom, their coats were hanging right where they left them, among sedate wool, fashionable puffers, and a few furs, and in a few minutes they were bundled up and ready to brave the chilly outdoors. But as Pamela watched Penny adjust the violet mohair scarf,

she realized that her own neck was bare. She turned
back to the long rack of coats and located the hanger
from which she had claimed hers. No scarf had lingered behind on the hanger. She studied the floor,
then stooped to peer into the shadowy recesses under
the crowded racks.

Bettina and Penny had already stepped out into the
hall, but Wilfred had lingered. "Did you lose something?" he asked, looking concerned.

"I can't find my scarf." Pamela shrugged and held
up her empty hands.

Bettina leaned back into the doorway. "You left it
on," she said. "Remember?"

"Oh, yes!" Pamela touched her bare neck. "It's
probably in that chair by the fireplace. I'll just run
back and grab it." She slipped past Bettina and started
down the hall.

"We'll bring the car around," Bettina said.

"See you in a minute," Wilfred added.

But it was more than a minute. Because as eager
as Pamela was to reclaim her scarf, she couldn't resist
dallying as she passed the Forge Room, one of the other
rooms the Carroll Inn made available to people hosting
private events. The door was partly ajar, thus allowing
the sound of gleeful laughter to reach the hall.

It was a woman's laughter, and as Pamela halted
and peered through the four-inch gap between the
door and the doorframe, she soon realized exactly
which woman it was. First a slender leg came into view,
made more shapely by the ultra-high stiletto heel that
encased its foot. Then Pamela recognized the little
black dress that was more cocktail party than funeral.
The woman's face was turned away, giving Pamela a
good view of her lustrous blond hair. But judging by

the laughter still issuing from the woman's mouth, Pamela guessed that her mood had lightened considerably since she strode angrily into the reception.

She was not alone. Deeper laughter echoed the woman's, then a male voice observed, "So you are not angry anymore, *chérie*?"

"I was missing you, Poody," the woman said in a cooing tone that Pamela sometimes used with her cats. "Couldn't you get rid of all those people sooner so your little *chérie* didn't have to spend the whole afternoon alone? It's almost four o'clock."

"We have the whole *evening*." This was the male voice—which of course was Pierre's voice.

Now no one was visible through the gap between the door and the doorframe. Pamela could see only a large painting of a blacksmith shoeing a horse. A series of sighs and moans suggested that verbal communication had been deemed inadequately expressive. But before Pamela turned away to resume her quest for her errant scarf, Pierre spoke again. "We'll have the whole *rest of our lives* together," he assured the woman in the little black dress.

Nadine was still snoring quietly when Pamela retrieved her scarf. The servers were clearing off the buffet table and only a few guests lingered, moving slowly toward the door as they continued to chat. No sounds at all came from the Forge Room as Pamela retraced her steps down the hall, though the door was still ajar.

She entered the lobby, passed the splendid tree, and stepped out onto the Carroll Inn's porch. Wilfred's Mercedes waited on the circular drive below, and in a moment Bettina had pushed one of the car's back doors open and was beckoning to Pamela.

Pamela had been debating whether to reveal her fascinating discovery to the whole group on the way home or wait until she and Bettina were alone. But, after all, the mystery was as much Penny's business as anyone else's—and Wilfred had been a useful adviser in Bettina's and Pamela's earlier crime-solving exploits.

So as Wilfred steered the Mercedes through Timberley's charming commercial district, Pamela described the encounter between Pierre Lapointe and the glamorous stiletto-heeled woman she had heard—and partially seen.

"Oh, my goodness!" Bettina said, latching onto Pamela's forearm in her excitement. "Motive! That's for sure!"

"We'll have the whole *rest of our lives* together," Pamela murmured.

"With all the money we need," Wilfred chimed in from the front seat.

Penny turned around, her face troubled. "But . . . Mom, he was so . . ." She twisted her pretty mouth into a little knot. "That woman must know how he is. Could she really think . . . ?"

"Love can be quite blind," Bettina said. "I hope you'll always keep your eyes wide-open."

"He's on Christmas break," Pamela said. "So he could have been at home on Monday morning. Suppose Millicent stopped off at home on her way to do her errands. And that was his chance, and he took it."

Bettina was nodding enthusiastically, the scarlet tendrils of her hair vibrating and her earrings swinging wildly. But suddenly she stopped. "Clayborn interviewed him," she said. "Of course, right away. The spouse is often the first person the police suspect. He has an alibi."

"Ohhh!" Pamela, Penny, and Wilfred all groaned simultaneously.

Bettina went on. "He went to the campus about ten-thirty Monday to turn his grades in. Then he went to his office and did some paperwork, and he had an early lunch with a colleague."

"Clayborn had checked on all of that by the time you talked to him Tuesday morning?" Pamela asked. They were cruising south on County Road now and soon the nature preserve would come into sight.

"No," Bettina said, "but that's what Pierre told him, and I'm sure Clayborn has verified the story by now. I'm sure the police searched Pierre's car too. Pierre is still running around free, so I guess his colleague vouched for him and there weren't any bloodstains in his trunk."

They all fell silent as Wilfred drove past the nature preserve, already shadowy in the early winter dusk. He made the turn onto Orchard Street and soon they had climbed out of the car and were standing on Bettina's driveway.

"So," Penny said after they had exchanged good-byes, "what time shall we leave for the estate sale tomorrow?"

Pamela was sure the look on her own face mirrored Bettina's expression—eyes wide and lips parted in amazement. Both women stared at Penny.

Pamela spoke first. "You can't be serious! I mean, the way Millicent died—and you found her body. And then today Pierre was so . . . forward. Grabbing your hand like that! Who knows what he'd try to do if there weren't people around?"

"Oh, Mo—om!" Penny laughed. "He was totally creepy, but if we all go together—"

"Well, I for one am not going," Bettina cut in. "I would feel like a ghoul, pawing through my friend's things." She folded her arms across her chest.

"I'll go by myself then." Penny laughed again. "I wish Laine and Sybil weren't in California. I'll bet there are some great vintage clothes."

"You absolutely will not go alone," Pamela said. She reached an arm around Penny's waist and tugged her close.

"I'm nineteen years old, Mom." Penny tilted her head to meet her mother's eyes. "I'll go on the bus if you won't let me use your car."

Wilfred meanwhile was standing at a diplomatic remove from the conversation.

Pamela sighed. "You won't go on the bus," she said. "I'll take you." She certainly didn't want Penny to venture into the clutches of Pierre Lapointe on her own—and she had to admit that she herself was curious about the treasures the Farthingales and several generations of Wentworths had accumulated.

"But—" Bettina's brightly lipsticked mouth stretched wide with alarm. She grabbed Pamela's right arm and Penny's left. "If you're both going, I'm going too. And we'll all stick close together."

Chapter Eight

Many emails, work-related and other, lurked in Pamela's inbox. But before she opened them, she brought up the Google page and keyed *Wendelstaff College* into the search box. A few seconds later the Wendelstaff home page appeared on her computer screen. The home page showed a group of students chatting happily on the college's attractive quadrangle, with an ivy-covered building in the background.

But Pamela already knew the Wendelstaff campus was pretty. What she was curious about was the college's faculty—specifically, which faculty members Pierre Lapointe might count among his own particular colleagues. She clicked on the tab for "Departments" and from the list that came up selected "Foreign Languages." Three people taught French, two of them full-time professors and one of them Pierre Lapointe. One of the full-time professors was a woman named Ida Wilma Merten. Would someone named Ida Wilma Merten wear close-fitting sheath dresses and stiletto heels? Pamela asked herself that question as she waited for Professor Merten's profile to come up.

She might or might not, Pamela decided as she studied the photograph that accompanied the impressive list of Professor Merten's accomplishments. Professor Merten was young and attractive, but her hair was jet black and cut in a gamine style that made her resemble Audrey Hepburn in an old movie.

In addition to French, Wendelstaff College offered other foreign languages. Pamela browsed among them, bringing up the profile of every faculty member with a woman's name. Professor Svetlana Romanoff was blond, but not young, and Professor Angelica Castro was young but not blond. But after a few more disappointing tries, Pamela found herself whispering *Yes!* as she stared at the photograph of Jeannette Thornton, Lecturer in German.

The photo showed Jeannette Thornton only from the shoulders up. But Pamela recognized the perfect brows, minus the frown that had marred them at the reception, and the curve of jawline now relaxed into a smile. And of course the carefully careless sweep of blond hair.

Jeannette Thornton was the woman in the stiletto heels now looking forward to spending the rest of her life with Pierre Lapointe. Pamela couldn't be sure, but she strongly suspected that she was also the colleague who had given Pierre his alibi for the morning Millicent was killed. This discovery would have to be reported to Bettina.

But there were emails from her boss at *Fiber Craft* to be read and digested. In fact, a new one popped up the moment Pamela closed the Wendelstaff website. The stylized paperclip that accompanied it signaled the presence of attachments, and attachments meant work.

Pamela had labored until seven p.m., finally pushing her chair back from the computer and raising her arms in a welcome stretch when Penny tapped at her office door to ask plaintively whether there would be dinner. Had Penny not been home, Pamela would have been summoned much earlier by hungry cats, but Penny had taken over many feeding duties during her visit.

"I'll warm up the oxtail stew," Pamela said, "and we can have salad and there's plenty of whole-grain bread."

Later, they settled at opposite ends of the sofa, a British mystery unfolding on the screen before them. Pamela had finished all the pieces of the glamorous ruby-red tunic and was beginning to assemble it. The back and the front formed a cozy lap rug as she methodically stitched the long seam that would join one side from hem to armhole. Catrina had tunneled under the swath of knitting that draped onto the sofa and was snuggled against Pamela's thigh.

For her part, Penny was browsing through the latest issue of Pamela's favorite knitting magazine. One of her Christmas gifts from her mother was to be a sweater knit to a pattern of Penny's choosing from yarn that Penny would select from the fancy yarn shop in Timberley. Of course the sweater wouldn't be ready by Christmas morning, but the trip to the yarn shop would be scheduled for Christmas week.

Penny had a cat of her own to keep her company— or a kitten rather. Ginger had taken up residence in her lap and was signaling her contentment with a soothing purr.

"Snow today, for sure," Bettina said from the porch as Pamela opened her front door the next morning.

north, past shops, Hyler's Luncheonette, the Chinese takeout, and When in Rome Pizza. At the end of that block, she crossed another street. A small forest of evergreens loomed in front of her, their boughs rustling in the wind and their spicy fragrance infusing the air.

This was the town Christmas-tree lot, set up every year by the Aardvark Alliance (named for the Arborville High School football team) to benefit the school's sports programs. An evergreen wreath on Pamela's front door had welcomed visitors since the beginning of December, but with Penny home now to help, it was time to put up a tree.

She didn't plan to buy a tree at this moment—it would be impossible to carry home on foot—but she wanted to check the lot's hours. The lot was surrounded by a makeshift barrier consisting of stakes and chicken wire, with a gate along the stretch facing Arborville Avenue. From her position on the corner, she could see a sign on the gate, but she couldn't make out what it said. So she proceeded along the chicken-wire barrier, inhaling deeply of the rich piney scent. Just as she was absorbing the information that the lot would be open for business the following Friday night and both weekend days from 10:00 a.m. to 8:00 p.m., the sight of a young man climbing into a car parked at the curb distracted her.

He paused for a moment and leaned over the roof of his car toward the Christmas-tree lot, as if he too was wondering about its hours of business. Pamela turned to get a better look at him and they locked eyes for a moment. He flashed her a genial smile, even slightly flirtatious—though he was truly a *young* man, closer to Penny's age than her own. He was quite attractive in a

raffish way, but it wasn't his attractiveness that had
caught her attention. It was his ensemble—specifically
the knitted scarf wrapped around his neck in a casual
twist that let the wind tease it.

The scarf was bright red, with green stripes at the
ends. It was the scarf Bettina had traded Millicent
Farthingale for the blue and violet vase, the scarf
Bettina had seen Millicent wearing as Millicent prepared to go out on errands the morning that turned
out to be the morning of her death. Pamela was sure
this was the same scarf.

Pamela thought she must look the way people look
when captured in an unexpected photo—frozen in an
awkward attitude of surprise. For a moment she didn't
move, and nothing else seemed to move either. Then
the young man waved a cheerful wave, lowered himself into his car, slammed the door, and drove away.
By the time Pamela thought to run to the curb and
peer after him in quest of a license plate number, a
contractor's van had slipped in behind him and his car
was hidden from view.

There were clues, and then there were clues. Pamela
knew that. Lobbing clues willy-nilly at Detective Clayborn could result in no clues being taken seriously.
Pamela knew that too, and Bettina's reporter job for
the *Advocate* had provided both Pamela and Bettina
with insight into the police mind.

Though Pamela now knew that a young man was
wandering around Arborville wearing a scarf that
could only have come from Millicent Farthingale's
neck, that knowledge depended on a personal ac-
quaintance with the scarf in question. And Detective
Clayborn—unaware that knitters recognize their own
or their friends' creations as readily as they recognize

Indeed, the no-color clouds hung low, as if weighed down by snow crystals soon to be released. Bettina's pumpkin-colored coat was a welcome spot of color against the bleak landscape. She held out a slender newspaper wrapped in plastic. "It was under your car," she said.

"I wondered where the *Advocate* was." Pamela reached for the paper. "Not that I need to read it to know the latest on the Farthingale case."

"Well"—Bettina feigned insult with a comical pout—"when a paper only comes out once a week . . ."

"I've made a connection Detective Clayborn hasn't made." Pamela smiled mysteriously and raised her brows.

"What?" The pout turned into an excited smile. Bettina's lipstick was exactly the same shade as her coat. The effect was stunning with her scarlet hair. She sniffed the air. "Is there coffee? I think we can spare a few minutes before we drive over to Timberley."

"Penny's still getting dressed," Pamela said. "Come on back to the kitchen."

Ginger watched curiously as Bettina slipped off her coat and took a seat, and then the kitten crept forward to sample what exotic scents might have come in on the toe of Bettina's chic boot. Meanwhile Pamela poured a cup of coffee for Bettina, fetched the heavy cream from the refrigerator, and set sugar and cream before her friend.

She took a seat across from Bettina and waited as Bettina sugared her coffee and stirred in cream till the coffee reached the exact shade of pale mocha that she preferred. Then she began to speak.

"Detective Clayborn probably tracked down the colleague who gave Pierre his alibi," Pamela said.

"Probably." Bettina nodded. "He's very thorough. He'd have verified the alibi."

"So he knows that colleague is Jeannette Thornton, lecturer in German at Wendelstaff."

"How do *you* know who she is?" Bettina paused with her coffee cup raised to her lips and frowned at Pamela over the rim.

"Wendelstaff website," Pamela said with a triumphant grin.

"But there must be lots of people in the foreign language department at Wendelstaff," Bettina protested, coffee still untasted. "Any one of them could be described as his colleague."

"But only one of them is the same person who showed up at the reception in a black cocktail dress and stiletto heels and was later overheard—by me—in a compromising tête-à-tête with Pierre." Pamela continued to grin.

"Oh, my!" Bettina set her coffee down without drinking.

"You know what that means," Pamela said.

Bettina nodded, her eyes gleaming with delight. But before she could speak, an unexpected voice chimed in. "His alibi isn't really an alibi!"

"Penny!" Pamela and Bettina spoke in unison, heads swiveling toward the doorway.

"No secrets," Penny said, advancing farther into the kitchen. "It's my mystery too."

Bettina had already fastened onto the implications of Pamela's fascinating revelation. "Is he the kind of person who could make his own bullets?" she asked. She raised her cup back to her lips and took a long sip, as if a bit of caffeine would aid in formulating an answer.

Penny wrinkled her nose. "He seemed kind of like . . . like someone who wouldn't want to get his hands dirty."

Pamela nodded. "I can't picture him in . . . whatever people wear when they make their own bullets."

"Grubby clothes?" Penny suggested.

"On the other hand"—Bettina returned her cup to its saucer with a gentle clink—"Pierre *is* a Canadian. Wilfred and his cousin go up into Quebec to fish sometimes, and the woods are full of guys tramping around with guns looking for moose."

Pamela focused her gaze on Bettina. "You need to talk to Detective Clayborn," she said. "He needs to know that Pierre had a motive to want Millicent dead. With his wife out of the way, his affair with Jeannette Thornton wouldn't have to be kept secret anymore. I'm sure Jeannette Thornton is the colleague who gave Pierre his alibi, and I'm sure once Detective Clayborn knows they were more than just colleagues, he'll realize she had every reason to lie."

"I'll be checking in with Clayborn Monday," Bettina said, "to see if there's anything new on the case to report to readers of the *Advocate*." She frowned and tightened her lips into an unhappy grimace. "But if I tell him what we know, he'll ask if *I* actually witnessed the scene, and I'll have to say I didn't. And he'll wonder how I'm so sure that this woman is the same person who gave Pierre an alibi. And I'll have to say my friend looked her up on the Wendelstaff website. And he'll know my friend is you. Then he'll tell me you and I pay taxes so we don't have to personally solve Arborville's murders and that's what the police are for."

Sighing, Pamela nodded. "And Detective Clayborn

might know more than we know. Perhaps the police don't just take one person's word for it when they're confirming an alibi. He might have asked around at Wendelstaff to make sure other people saw Pierre that morning too."

"But he might not have," Bettina said firmly. She took another long swallow of coffee and when she spoke again it was to change the subject. "This coffee is really good," she said. "Is it still that Guatemalan kind?"

Pamela wasn't paying attention. She was staring straight ahead, but at nothing in particular, and fingering her chin. "I wonder if we should really go today," she said. "Pierre could be a very dangerous person."

"We'll all be together." Penny's young face looked so trusting that Pamela felt her throat tighten. "And it sounds like the best sale ever. And why would he want to hurt us?"

"He could be Millicent's murderer," Pamela said. "He could think we know things that might help the police finger him. Because we were her friends."

"We were her friends." Bettina drained her coffee cup and stood up. "That's why we should go. Who knows what secrets might turn up in all that old family stuff?"

Bettina insisted on driving. Wilfred, accompanied by Woofus, came out onto the porch as they all climbed into her faithful Toyota. "Be careful!" he called as Bettina backed out of the driveway. "Better safe than sorry!"

The Wentworth mansion was a fanciful woodframe structure, three stories tall, with bay windows, turrets, and multiple chimneys. It was painted a deep cranberry red with dark gray and cream accents, and its surface alternated between clapboard and curving shingles that overlapped like fish scales. It loomed through bare trees, set far back from a road that curved past other houses of similar age and splendidness.

"Lovely, isn't it?" Bettina commented as she slowed down so her passengers could appreciate the house from its most impressive angle. "But I can see why Millicent was eager to downsize. Can you imagine searching for a painting contractor who'd want to take on that job? Not to mention dealing with wiring or plumbing problems." She continued driving until she came to a street that cut off to the left, skirting the edge of the Wentworth property. Like the main road, this street had no curbs or sidewalks, and cars were crowded along both sides, parked half on the asphalt and half on the scrubby winter grass that fringed it.

Bettina passed a row of twenty cars before reaching an empty stretch and guiding the Toyota into a spot just in front of a tired-looking compact. "I wore my most comfortable boots," she announced as she twisted the key in the ignition and the Toyota's engine rumbled into silence. "Good thing, too."

They strolled back the way they'd come until they reached a gap in the string of cars where a graveled driveway led back into more of the woods that sheltered the mansion from the main road. A bright orange sign fastened to a stake featured an arrow pointing into the woods and the words ANOTHER GREAT SALE PRESENTED BY EVERGREEN. FRIDAY, SATURDAY, AND SUNDAY 10:00 TO 5:00.

Pamela, Penny, and Bettina crunched over the gravel, passing a few people who had apparently already exhausted the sale's delights. These people were heading the other way, bearing their treasures away in plastic bags on which Pamela recognized the logo of the upscale grocery store that had an outpost in Timberley.

They could see their destination up ahead. In a small clearing stood a building with four pairs of wide double doors across the front and a steep, peaked roof that suggested a capacious attic above. Like the main house, it was fashioned of wood, but the wood was weathered and worn, and the structure blended into the faded grays and browns of the bare trees that surrounded it.

"It's the old carriage house," Bettina said as they proceeded. "The groom's quarters, where Charlotte lives, are around the side. They're part of this, but they have a proper front door. She halted for a moment, and Pamela and Penny slowed down.

"Did you hear something?" Pamela and Penny turned to see Bettina tilting her head.

"Like what?" Pamela asked.

"Like that!" Bettina tilted her head further and closed her eyes in concentration.

"It's a sneeze," Penny exclaimed. "Someone is sneezing."

They all stared in the direction of the sneeze. A figure was moving among the trees, a figure dressed in periwinkle blue.

They continued on their way. The gravel became sparse as they drew nearer, giving way to rutted earth sprinkled with a few shriveled autumn leaves whose color now blended with the dirt. One pair of the structure's doors stood open, giving a glimpse into a shadowy interior. Near the open doors but at the edge of the clearing sat a round cast-iron table and two matching chairs, their white paint sadly chipped and streaked with rust.

On a balmy summer afternoon with trees in full foliage rustling overhead, the chairs could have invited dallying and the table could have accommodated a pitcher of lemonade or a bottle of wine. On a chilly winter day, however, with snow threatening, Pierre Lapointe looked incongruous perched on one of the chairs, bundled in a bulky but chic down jacket and sneezing. He was not, however, the sneezer they had glimpsed through the trees. His jacket was loden green, not periwinkle blue.

"Dust," he said, stifling another sneeze and rising to his feet. "It's very dusty in there." He gestured toward the open door. "*Bonjour* and welcome, ladies. I hope you are not as susceptible to the dust as I am." He stepped toward the door. "I will tell them you are not to be charged for anything. I know Millicent would have wanted her friends to help themselves."

They followed him into the shadowy interior, straining to see anything at all as their eyes adjusted to the darkness. The room that they had entered was quite spacious—it had obviously housed the carriage in earlier times. But now it was filled with piles and piles of . . . everything. Tables and chairs, an iron bedstead, a Victorian-style sofa with a carved wooden frame, and boxes and boxes and boxes, piled in teetering stacks on armchairs that were themselves balanced precariously on mountains of old magazines and ancient trunks. Here and there a lamp had been pressed into service, perhaps by Evergreen, and glaring pools of light punctuated the dimness. The only other illumination came feebly through high windows in the back wall, windows so grimy that the glass seemed smoked, or from people moving through the gloom with flashlights.

Just ahead, a rustic stairway—little more than a series of boards with handrails on either side—led to the attic. And to the left was a rough wooden door with heavy iron hardware. A recent-looking sign read CLOSE DOOR WHEN YOU GO IN OR OUT.

To the right a makeshift table had been created from a pair of sawhorses and a broad plank. An assortment of jewelry was displayed in a glass-topped case but otherwise the table held only a calculator and a stout cash box. Behind the table sat a sturdy older woman with jet-black hair.

"These are Millicent's friends—and mine," Pierre informed her. "They are to have *carte blanche.*" He stifled a sneeze. "Whatever they want to take."

He pulled Penny aside as Bettina started down one of the makeshift aisles that separated the piles of castoffs. "*Bonne chance, mademoiselle,*" Pamela heard him whisper. "I hope you find many treasures—and that you will stop and say good-bye before you leave." Pamela lingered near her daughter.

Chapter Nine

As Pierre turned and headed back outside, the door to the left opened and a young couple stepped out carrying a pile of old books and a lamp. In the brief moment that the door was open, Pamela could see that the room behind it was much brighter than the dim space they now stood in.

"Let's look around in there first," Penny suggested. "It's hard to see anything out here." She grabbed the heavy iron door pull and tugged the door open as Pamela retrieved Bettina.

They stepped into a huge space that had obviously been the stable. Four horse stalls still remained along the wall to the right—at least the partitions that had formed the sides of horse stalls. Or perhaps the horses had remained happily in their stalls with no gates to confine them. As in the other room, walls, ceiling, and floor had been constructed of roughly finished lumber and never painted. They now had the rich patina of very old wood.

This room had the same small, grimy windows as the other room, but at some point large hanging light fixtures had been installed, three of them, and the castoffs of many generations, ranged around the room, were clearly illuminated. Ten or so other people poked among them. One of the horse stalls had been fitted up as a kitchen, but long ago. The stove, white enamel now yellowed and stained, stood on legs, and the counter that surrounded a similarly yellowed and stained sink was stacked with battered kitchen ware. Another horse stall contained a narrow cot, still made up with sheets, a pillow, and a faded wool blanket. A small dresser held a dusty collection of mason jars. A drawer had been explored and left half-open, disclosing a tangled garment that might have been long underwear.

The other horse stalls were piled with boxes—old wooden boxes, dusty and discolored, and cardboard boxes, some looking as if animals had nibbled on them. Some boxes had been opened and abandoned, evidently by bargain hunters unimpressed with their contents: random dinnerware, mysterious newspaper-wrapped shapes, small parcels of fabric in antiquated prints, reels of lace and faded ribbon. An old dress form stood in the corner of one stall, a headless and armless torso on a metal post. The same stall held a treadle sewing machine, its glossy black paint dimmed by dust but its oak cabinet and the cast-iron filigree of its stand still impressive. In the middle of that stall's floor stood a large cardboard box with its flaps folded back to reveal balls of yarn in various sizes and colors.

A haphazard arrangement of tables and shelves occupied the long wall that faced the horse stalls. Some tables were covered with books, old books with cloth covers, arranged in rows with their spines facing up. Shelves held more books. A young man sitting on the floor was picking out one book at a time from a lower shelf, examining it, and then consulting his mobile device. "Found any first editions yet?" an older man inquired in a joking tone.

Other tables and shelves held dusty glassware, framed pictures and empty picture frames, vases, lamps, knickknacks of all sorts, and stacks of ancient magazines with faded covers.

"Ohh! I know what I'm going to look at," Penny exclaimed. A huge trunk stood at the far end of the room with its heavy lid thrown back. A few young women had been examining the contents but moved away to reveal tantalizing folds of silk and velvet draped over the trunk's rim, as well as a length of lustrous fur that sported a tail and a pair of legs. Penny darted across the creaking wooden floor and was soon dipping into the trunk's recesses.

"I'm going to rummage in that box with the old yarn," Pamela said.

"Maybe I can find Wilfred something interesting for his den walls." Bettina pointed at a table with a particularly large stack of framed pictures. "You know how he likes anything historical." She set out toward the far corner of the room.

Pamela turned and walked a few steps back to the stall that held the treadle sewing machine, the dress form, and the box of yarn. She squatted and began to pull out the balls of yarn and pile them on the floor. Beneath the yarn she came upon a knitting pattern book, dating from the 1940s to judge by the ensemble modeled on the cover—a young women in saddle shoes and bobby socks, complementing her pleated plaid skirt with a hand-knit twinset. Assuming each ball of yarn represented the leftovers of a project, the owner of this trove had been a busy knitter. And given the likely age of the trove, it was a wonder these remnants—which all seemed to be wool and not acrylic—hadn't succumbed to moths.

At the very bottom of the box, Pamela came upon a charming knitting bag, needlepoint in a flowered pattern, with Bakelite handles. Inside the bag was an assortment of knitting needles and some bobbins. Pamela returned the equipment to the bag, and the bag and pattern book to the box, as well as the random balls of yarn. Even if she found nothing else at the sale, this find would make the trip worthwhile.

"Hey, Mom!" said a voice behind her. Pamela stood up and turned to see Penny's face beaming at her above the fur piece from the trunk, which was wrapped around her neck. The mouth of the creature (which seemed to be a fox) was snapped securely onto its own tail. "Did people really wear these things?" Penny asked, her blue eyes wide with amazement.

"*I* didn't wear them," Pamela said, laughing. "But I think my grandmother did. In movies and photographs from the thirties and forties, it seems a woman had to have one if she was to be stylish. Sometimes they even wore ones made out of several animals all fastened together. Dangling feet and tails all over the place."

Penny stroked the fur, which was still in very good shape. "It's quite cozy," she said. "But I can't take it back to school. Some of my friends are in PETA and they'd never speak to me again." She unclipped it and draped it over her arm. "What's that weird thing?" she asked suddenly, having just caught sight of the dress form.

"It's for sewing," Pamela explained. "Dressmakers used them to size clothing they were making for clients—and home sewers used them too. They're adjustable—see those gaps down the sides and in the front. They can be pushed together or pulled farther apart to make it bigger or smaller. My mother had one, but I never wanted to sew—just knit."

"Can we take it?" Penny said.

"Sure." Pamela laughed. "What will we do with it?"

"Laine and Sybil might like it. Sometimes they have to fix the thrift-store clothes they find."

Pamela shrugged and smiled. "I doubt if anybody else is going to grab it in the next few minutes, so when we finish in here we'll take it out to the table by the door and ask that woman to look after it while we browse upstairs."

"I found some other really good things in the trunk," Penny said. "Do you want to see?"

"I do." Pamela folded the flaps closed on her box of knitting treasures, stooped to pick it up, and followed Penny across the floor to where the trunk stood open. Penny had arranged her finds in a pile on the floor. She returned the fur to the rim of the trunk and Pamela set her box down. Bettina was standing at a nearby table, engrossed in sorting through a pile of unframed engravings.

Penny held up a black-and-white checked wool jacket, tailored with a nipped-in waist. The collar and cuffs were black velvet edged with giant black rickrack. "It fits," Penny said. "I tried it on. And there's a skirt." She laid the jacket over the rim of the trunk and picked up a skirt in the same black-and-white wool check. "I didn't try this on, and it has something like a coffee stain on the front. But if it doesn't fit, even just the jacket will be great."

Bettina had noticed them and turned away from her rummaging, bearing a few engravings on heavy paper. "These look really old, don't they?" she said, displaying the top one, which showed a landscape as if seen from the top of a hill, with a caption in flowing script across the top. "The men in red coats could be the British, and here's a burning house with a plume of smoke going up into the sky, and there are other soldiers behind these trees . . . I guess they're soldiers because they have long guns . . ."

Pamela leaned closer and studied the writing. "It says 'Battle of . . .'"—she leaned still closer—"'Lex . . . ing . . . ton.'"

"It could be a real find," Penny exclaimed. "We did the American Revolution in history this term."

"Perfect then." Bettina looked delighted. "I'll have it framed for Wilfred's den—maybe I can even get it done in time for Christmas." She gestured toward the clothes Penny had picked out of the trunk. "What goodies do you have?"

Penny displayed the black-and-white checked suit, and then a minidress made from purple jersey printed with orange peace symbols. "Sybil will love this," she said, "and I found these for Laine." She held out a pair of navy wool bell-bottoms with a button-up fly. "And a minidress for me, or it could be a long top with jeans." The garment was chartreuse velour with long loose sleeves and a V-neck. "Then, finally"—she dipped to the floor to retrieve what looked like a shapeless mass of dark, velvety fabric—"a *cape*!"

Penny shook the garment out then swirled it around, passing one arm over her head, until it came to rest on her shoulders. It was so long, the excess fabric pooled on the floor around her. "It even has a *hood*!" She reached back and tugged at the hood until the front edge flopped down over her eyes.

"Are they wearing capes in college these days?" Pamela asked with a fond laugh.

"*Mo—om*!" Penny laughed in return. "It's for Halloween. It will be perfect."

"We can use the dress form to hem it up," Pamela said. "I can manage that much sewing and I don't want you tripping when you go out in it."

"Dress form?" Bettina raised her brows.

"Over there." Penny pointed toward the stall at the end of the row. Though headless, the dress form stood like a pale monitor, watching the proceedings from its corner. "We're taking it home."

"Will it fit in my car?" Bettina said dubiously.

"It's adjustable," Penny responded, as matter-of-factly as if her knowledge of dress forms hadn't been acquired only a few minutes earlier.

"Are we finished in here then?" Bettina asked. "There's a whole upstairs with tons more stuff."

Pamela and Penny nodded. Penny folded the cape and her other finds and stacked them on top of the cardboard box full of knitting supplies. "I'll take this stuff out and leave it with that woman at the entrance," she said. "Can you get the dress form?"

Pamela nodded again and Penny headed toward the door that separated the stable from the room that had housed the carriage.

Meanwhile Pamela, followed by Bettina, made her way through the small crowd of roaming browsers toward the stall that held the dress form. Once there, she edged among the stacks of boxes and grabbed the dress form with one hand on each side of its solid waist. The metal post that supported it was anchored to a heavy metal base. She was struggling to free the base from the crush of boxes when a pleasant male voice behind her said, "Let me give you a hand with that."

Pamela let go of the dress form. It teetered briefly and then steadied. She turned to see a friendly looking man with salt-and-pepper hair reaching out an arm toward the dress form. "It's okay," Pamela said. "Really. I can do it."

"A couple of these boxes are probably holding the base down," he said. Before she could protest again, he began lifting boxes and re-piling them near where Bettina was standing at the entrance to the stall.

"Thank you so much!" Bettina gave the man a bright smile as he looked up from his task to acknowledge her words.

"Are you together?" He glanced from Bettina to Pamela and then back.

"Why, yes," Bettina said, directing an admiring glance from beneath a shadowed eyelid. "And I'm wondering if we'll even be able to fit that thing into my little Toyota to get it back home."

"I could give you a hand." His gaze wandered back to Pamela, who once again had gripped the dress form by the waist and was tugging at it.

"That would be wonderful!" Bettina smiled even more brightly. Just then Pamela gave a mighty tug and the dress form came free. She teetered backwards, still clutching the dress form. She would have landed on her back on the floor with the dress form on top of her if the friendly man hadn't caught her with one arm and used his other hand to push the dress form away.

Ten minutes later the dress form, with its post and base detached, had been stowed in Bettina's trunk,

area below. To the right was another partition, also featuring a doorway with no door.

"It seems bigger up here than below," Pamela observed.

"It is," Bettina said. "The groom's quarters are attached to the stable and carriage room, and this is the attic for the whole thing."

Tables held piles and piles of old magazines. There were copies of *Life* magazine, the Kodachrome that had captured the brightly made-up faces of actresses sadly faded and the paper fly-specked. There were copies of *Time* magazine, with covers depicting men whose crisp shirt collars and carefully knotted ties testified to the wearers' seriousness. There were copies of *National Geographic*, with the unmistakable golden-yellow spines. A few people hovered over the magazines, leafing through copies here and there.

"The Farthingales and Wentworths must never have thrown *anything* away," Penny said, staring in amazement at the sight. She picked up a copy of *Life*, commenting, "Magazines were bigger back then."

An elderly man turned toward them, a copy of *Life* with a photo of Elizabeth Taylor as Cleopatra on the cover. "It was all about the photography," he said. "No Internet then."

Penny nodded and he went back to his magazine.

Pamela wandered past the magazine-laden tables and set out down a zigzagging aisle that cut through heaped-up boxes, trunks, rolled-up rugs, and furniture. Halfway down, a small trunk had been tugged from the jumble that surrounded it and someone had investigated its contents, tossing aside doll clothes, a battered straw hat decorated with cloth flowers, and several stained and frayed dishcloths.

Pamela wandered on and found she had made a complete circuit of the room without catching sight of anything that beckoned her to examine it further. Bettina and Penny still lingered among the magazine tables, smiling together over something they'd found in an issue of *Life*.

Penny held the open magazine out as Pamela came near. The pages showed a fashion show—couture from the sixties to judge by the sleek pants and tunics, the patent-leather boots with chunky heels, and the models' dramatic makeup and eyebrow-skimming bangs. "Laine and Sybil will love the clothes in these old magazines," Penny said. "I've found a whole bunch."

"I'm sure Pierre will be happy to get rid of as many as you want to carry away," Pamela said as she took the magazine and flipped through a few more pages. The show had also featured models in dresses that seemed pieced from huge squares of stiff fabric in primary colors, like ambulatory paintings in a geometric style.

Pamela handed the magazine back and pointed toward the doorway that led to the section of attic over the stable. "I'll be in here," she said.

That room featured a window at one end, in the triangular wall formed by the roof's sloping sides. It was thus brighter, and Pamela felt more inclined to excavate its jumbled offerings. Her eye was drawn to a large wicker hamper, interesting in its own right. She lifted the top, and discovered that the contents were interesting too. The hamper contained carefully folded tablecloths. The first one she unfolded had a charming allover print of oranges, lemons, and limes, and a wide border in which citrus foliage and blossoms intertwined with more of the same fruits.

"Forties for sure," she murmured to herself, "or even older." Pamela loved vintage tablecloths and a quick survey of the hamper's remaining contents told her that she'd found many additions to her collection. Soaking in a mild bleach solution would make quick work of the yellowing that some had suffered with age.

She returned everything to the hamper, closed it, and pulled it free from the crush of objects around it. As she did so, she dislodged a small leather suitcase that had been wedged behind it—very nice quality, like something a wealthy young woman might have owned in an era when elegant luggage was an essential mark of status. *Penny might like this*, she said to herself, as she set it flat on the dusty wooden floor. She clicked open the latches on either side of the handle and tipped the top back.

She'd expected to find . . . what? Maybe more vintage tablecloths. Pamela herself had an old suitcase in her attic, and it provided a useful storage space for a favorite quilt, two sets of curtains no longer in use, and the animal-print sheets that had made up Penny's bed until she turned ten. But the contents of this suitcase were quite different.

As she gently sifted through the items, it seemed she had come upon a suitcase packed for a journey many decades ago and never unpacked—perhaps never even opened after the journey was completed. She came upon light dresses suitable for hot weather, with simple scoop-neck bodices and gathered skirts—like styles that teenagers had worn in the 1950s. Beneath the dresses she found underwear—decidedly unglamorous panties, bras, and slips (slips!) in sensible white cotton. Tucked here and there were flats, in white leather and black patent, and a pair of sandals, all carefully wrapped in tissue.

Pamela checked the outside of the suitcase to see if she had overlooked any identifying tags, but there was nothing. Nor did she find anything inside the suitcase that would give a hint of its owner. The process of removing every single item and examining it closely, however, led her to an interesting discovery. A small clutch purse lay at the very bottom of the suitcase, white straw with a metal frame. Pamela snapped it open.

Inside was a handkerchief, white lawn, trimmed with delicate lace. No initial—that would be too obvious! But something—or rather some *things*—were wrapped inside. Pamela could feel small lumps through the cloth. She slowly unfolded the handkerchief, not wanting anything to land on the floor, with its gaps and uneven surface. Then a small circlet of beads appeared, cupped in the palm of her hand and cushioned by a layer of white lawn. Half the beads were plain white, but the others spelled out a word, one letter to a bead: W-E-N-T-W-O-R-T-H.

Chapter Ten

Pamela had seen such things before. When she gave birth to Penny, the mother-daughter connection had been marked by simple plastic bands on babies' and mothers' wrists. But she'd once looked through the old baby book in which her mother's parents had preserved mementoes of their daughter's birth and childhood. Bead bracelets were indestructible, sanitary, and easily personalized, and until the fifties and a bit beyond, babies had worn them until taken home by their parents. Or by someone with a rightful claim to them.

Pamela suspected that she was looking at the only souvenir Millicent's mother had been able to salvage of the baby who grew up to become Coot. She'd taken the suitcase with her to Texas on the visit to the aunt, the excuse for her sudden disappearance from Timberley. The dresses had fit for a while, then maternity garments had been supplied, no doubt. Preparing to return home, she'd packed the dresses she came with and the sad reminder of why she'd gone to Texas. But she hadn't had the heart to revisit anything about the trip by unpacking at the other end. So the suitcase had gone to the attic and there it had stayed.

"Hey, Mom!" came an eager voice from somewhere on the other side of the crowded space. "Look what I found!" As Penny rounded a corner bearing three large, flat books, Pamela wrapped the bracelet back in the handkerchief and tucked it into the pocket of her jeans.

"Awesome old suitcase," Penny observed when she reached Pamela's side. "What's in it?"

"Nothing much," Pamela said, tapping on it to make sure it was closed securely. The clothes had definite vintage appeal, but the idea of Penny wearing the outfits in which Millicent's mother had awaited the birth of the child she had to give away was just . . . *disturbing.* "What do you have there?" she asked to change the subject.

"Yearbooks from Morton-Bidwell. This is 1953." Penny held the top one toward Pamela. The book was bound in navy with the words *Morton-Bidwell* in Gothic lettering on the front and on the spine. "The boys all look so old, with their hair short and combed just so. And the girls' hair looks like they must have spent a lot of time on it. And they all wore uniforms. But the girls' uniforms are kind of cute—plaid skirts and blazers." Pamela thumbed through the yearbook. "Somebody who lived here must have gone there," Penny said.

"Lots of Wentworths and Farthingales went there, I expect." Pamela closed the yearbook and handed it back. "They were those kinds of families." Morton-Bidwell was the fancy private school where Charlotte taught.

"I found two more," Penny said. "From 1954 and 1956. But there's no 1955. I wonder what happened to it."

Pamela was pretty sure she knew why there was no 1955. Millicent's mother would have been visiting her aunt in Texas when the yearbooks came out that year.

The suitcase and its interesting contents would have to be reported to Bettina, but Pamela wasn't sure she wanted Penny to be part of that discussion. Of course Penny knew that people who weren't in a position to raise children sometimes produced them anyway. But Penny had been upstairs when Charlotte told Knit and Nibble about the woman with the DNA claim on Millicent's estate. And she had been far away talking with Wilfred when Coot introduced herself to Pamela and Bettina. Pamela was reluctant to have her daughter involved any more deeply than she already was in the mystery of who might have killed Millicent and why. So she decided to wait until she and Bettina were alone before she brought out the little bead bracelet.

"I think I've seen enough in here," Penny said, "and I'll leave these old yearbooks for someone else." She set them atop the nearest pile.

"Where's Bettina?" Pamela asked as she picked up the hamper.

"Still out in that big room." Penny pointed toward the opening in the partition. "She found some old pottery."

When Pamela and Penny reached her, Bettina was sitting on a wooden box a little ways away from a huge dresser topped with a looming heap of men's suits and shoes. She was surrounded by an assortment of garden pots, glazed ceramic in various shapes and sizes. Most were still grimy inside, with a film of dry soil left from some long-discarded plant that had brightened a patio or porch.

"There are boxes and boxes of these," Bettina said. "Won't they look nice on my patio this summer, with geraniums? Or I could plant herbs like you have, for Wilfred's cooking. I just have to decide which ones to take."

"They *are* nice." Pamela picked up a large pot with a fluted edge and a colorful geometric pattern that evoked Mexican tile.

"Take some," Bettina urged. "For your herbs."

"Take the ones you like first," Pamela said. "You found them. I'll browse around a little more, and when you're through I'll pick out a few."

Penny knelt next to Bettina to help as she began to fit smaller pots inside larger ones. A box that Bettina had emptied sat ready to receive those selected for a new life on an Arborville patio.

Pamela wandered back toward the front of the large room, picking her way around open boxes tugged from their piles, then abandoned, and people who halted without warning to examine something that suddenly seemed interesting. When she reached the magazine tables she veered off toward the partition that marked off the section of attic above the groom's quarters.

A doorway with no door led to another overcrowded space, divided into smaller spaces by partitions with rough shelving built into them. Most of the shelves visible from the doorway held books, old hardbound books with dark, solid-color bindings, as if at some point the space had been designated a library, perhaps overflow from a grand library in the main house. But other shelves held random objects, like hatboxes and a tangle of mousetraps.

Hatboxes could contain old hats, not that Pamela could imagine herself in a vintage hat, but a stylish old hat in its own old hatbox could be a fun thing to take home, or at least show to Penny, who had been amused by the formal grooming of the Morton-Bidwell students in the 1950s.

The wooden floor creaked as she made her way along the rank of shelves closest to the doorway, aiming for a particularly attractive hatbox several feet away. But she paused as she got closer. Yes, the floor was creaking, but she heard something like a sneeze. She closed her eyes in an effort to focus her hearing.

The sneeze came again, a mighty sneeze. Then a voice that sounded like Pierre said, "This dust is killing me."

Pamela heard a sound like someone blowing their nose, then another voice, a woman's voice but muffled, saying "I love you so much. I can't wait for our love to no longer be secret." The words were followed by a sneeze more delicate than the previous one, and the voice—made husky by the sneezing—spoke again. "Our future is taking shape, and then you will be all mine." The words were punctuated by sniffles. "Darling, come here!"

A clunk followed. Pamela pictured lovers sinking to the dusty floor, disarranging piles of odds and ends as they embraced.

When they stepped back out it had begun to snow, tiny flakes that drifted straight down in the still, chilly air. The bare earth around the entrance to the carriage house was no longer mud-colored, but dusted white, as was the cushion of dead leaves under the bare trees. For a moment the scene seemed unreal, as if it was a stage set and ballerinas would come dancing through the woods at any moment to music from *The Nutcracker.*

Light as the dusting of snow was, it seemed to mute the sound of their feet as they made their way along the gravel path that led to the road. The dress form had already been stowed, along with the box of yarn and knitting supplies, Penny's vintage clothing finds, and the engraving. But Penny and Bettina each carried a large cardboard box filled with ceramic planters nested within one another, and Pamela carried the hamper and Penny's magazines.

Penny spoke out as they neared Bettina's car. "There could have been an old rifle up there," she said suddenly. "In all that junk . . . stored away long ago by Millicent's grandfather—or *great*-grandfather."

"You're right!" Pamela exclaimed. "Hunting was definitely a part of people's world back then, people who lived in mansions like that. They probably went out into the woods in tweeds and high boots and served venison haunches at their grand dinners in their grand dining rooms."

"The Wentworth mansion does have a grand dining room," Bettina chimed in.

"The homemade bullets too," Pamela said. "Custom-made perhaps—not that he made them himself. Then let's say he dies. A hundred years ago, and his widow orders that all his hunting equipment be stored in the attic."

Bettina took up the idea. "But Pierre knew about the rifle, and the bullets, because Millicent started months ago trying to create some kind of order up there." She paused and added in an aside, "You can see how hopeless it was."

They had reached the car. The hamper and the magazines and the boxes with the ceramic planters all fit on the back seat, leaving just enough room for Penny's slender self. Bettina twisted her key in the ignition, her windshield wipers swept away the snow, and a bit of wintry light filtered in.

"Oh, dear," Bettina sighed as the Toyota came to a stop in her driveway. "Wilfred is coming out and he'll want to help with our boxes. I don't want him to know about the engraving—it's to be a Christmas present."

Indeed, Wilfred had stepped onto the porch, jacketless. Behind him was Woofus, pressed nervously against his master's leg.

"I'll hide it under the seat," Pamela said, leaning over to slip the engraving out of sight. "It can stay here until you have a chance to take it to the framing shop."

"That will be this afternoon, and I'll beg them for a rush job. Christmas is just five days away." Bettina pushed the car door open and swung her feet onto the asphalt, now lightly powdered with snow. The snow was still falling, but no more heavily than before.

Wilfred and Woofus reached the car as Penny climbed out. Wilfred greeted them all with a genial smile and peered into the back seat. "It looks like you had a successful adventure," he said. "What shall I carry where? I'm yours to command."

"Those boxes are mostly mine," Bettina said. "Pots

for the patio this summer, but Pamela is going to take a few."

"The hamper is mine," Pamela said. "The magazines are Penny's. And the trunk is full of things that Penny and I found."

Wilfred opened the trunk and surveyed the contents. "Your friend looks a little chilly," he observed. "Of course, with no head maybe she doesn't notice."

Penny laughed. "We got her a cape." She pointed at the loosely folded heap of black velvet lying atop the other clothes.

"I'm starving," Bettina said. "And you look cold, Wilfred. Let's eat something before we do anything else. Pamela and Penny—please come in and we'll all have lunch. Then we can sort out our goodies."

"Lunch it will be, dear wife!" Wilfred closed the trunk. "How do Co-Op sausages on Co-Op bakery buns sound? With Co-Op deli coleslaw? Woofus and I had a walk uptown this morning."

Woofus had waited on the porch looking uncertainly at the falling snow. Now he lingered there as the four of them filed through the front door, Wilfred bringing up the rear. When they were all inside, Wilfred leaned back through the doorway and urged, "It's okay, boy. Come on in."

Rollicking across the living room carpet came two kittens, a ginger one and a black one. Woofus had been coaxed indoors but suddenly bounded up the stairs to the landing.

"Is that Midnight?" Pamela asked, leaning toward the black kitten, which was lying on its back using all four paws to fend off an attack from the ginger kitten.

"Yes . . ." Bettina's lips shaped a rueful smile. "Woofus was having enough trouble adjusting to

Punkin, but having Midnight here too has pushed him over the edge."

"Wilfred Jr.'s boys really are allergic then?" Pamela's expression matched Bettina's own.

"Looks like," Bettina said. "They both have terrible rashes."

"I can take Midnight back." Pamela stooped and held out a hand to the kitten, who batted at her fingers then began to test his teeth on them.

"They're having so much fun together though," Bettina said. "And Ginger and Catrina have each other. Let's give it a few more days."

Penny's jacket and scarf had been deposited on the sofa and she and Wilfred had proceeded to the kitchen. Now Pamela tossed her jacket and scarf next to her daughter's and Bettina added her pumpkin-colored coat. Woofus watched them from the landing as they left the room, abandoning him to his fate with the lively kittens.

In the kitchen, Wilfred had tied an apron over his overalls. A large skillet waited on the stovetop. Nearby, a square of white butcher's paper had been folded back to reveal four sausages, deep pink and marbled with fat, and so plump that the membranes containing them were stretched to a glossy sheen.

Four of Bettina's sage-green pottery plates sat ready on the counter that separated the cooking area of Bettina's spacious kitchen from the eating area. A crusty oblong bun was centered on each plate, and Penny was setting the pine table with napkins and silverware.

"What can I do?" Pamela asked.

"The coleslaw is in the refrigerator in a deli container," Wilfred said. "And there's mustard. And people might want mayonnaise. I do."

Pamela joined him in the cooking area and opened the refrigerator. In a moment, Bettina was at her side, reaching into a cupboard for a serving bowl that matched her sage-green pottery. As Pamela spooned the slaw, glistening with creamy dressing, into the bowl that nearly matched the slaw's color, the sausages began to sizzle.

Bettina sliced each bun in half and spread mayonnaise on the cut surfaces. The sizzles emanating from the sausages grew louder, and the tantalizing smell of pork seasoned with garlic and spices rose from the skillet on waves of vaporized fat. Wilfred prodded the sausages with a long fork, rolling them one way and then another.

Pamela carried the bowl of slaw and the pot of mustard to the table. "Do you want something to drink?" Bettina asked from the counter where she was working on the buns. "Beer is so good with sausages. A small glass each?"

"Very small," Pamela said, "but yes." She glanced at Penny. "I know, you're in college now, so okay."

"I declare them done," Wilfred announced triumphantly from the stove.

Soon they were seated around the pine table, and after the first few bites of sausage, the conversation was reduced to variations on *mmmm* and *yummm*. No one spoke a complete sentence, or even an intelligible word, for at least five minutes. Then it was to commend Wilfred's selection of excellent sausages, and his cooking of them, and to remark how perfectly the coleslaw, with its creamy dressing, complemented the spicy pork.

"I've got to start thinking about Christmas Eve," Bettina said, after the glories of the meal had been sufficiently rehearsed. Christmas Eve fell on Tuesday, and Tuesday was the usual night for Knit and Nibble to meet. Bettina had proposed a potluck party at her house instead, with knitting left at home but spouses invited. And since it was her party, the guest list would include the Frasers' Arborville son, Wilfred Jr., and their Arborville daughter-in-law, Maxie, as well as their Boston son and his wife. And Richard Larkin. "It's not really a dinner," Bettina added. "That will be the next day, for family—and you and Penny."

"I'll make deviled eggs," Pamela said. "Everyone always likes those."

"I certainly do," Wilfred chimed in.

"And I'll bring a loaf of my poppy-seed cake."

Bettina nodded. "And I'm going to order one of those cheese balls the Co-Op does, with nuts on the outside. We'll have crackers—lots of different kinds—with it. And the Co-Op makes those nice fruit trays. I know Nell will want there to be healthy things."

"And we'll have wassail," Wilfred exclaimed, his eyes bright and his ruddy cheeks aglow. "Christmas punch. And beer and wine for the less adventurous."

Chapter Eleven

"There's no more snow," Penny moaned as Wilfred opened the front door. They were all bundled in jackets and coats now, including Wilfred, and they stepped out onto the porch. The sky was still lead-colored and the clouds heavy, as if with a pending storm. But no flakes drifted down and the film that had dusted the driveway had vanished into the asphalt.

"We have to have snow for Christmas," Bettina said. "It just won't feel right otherwise."

Wilfred opened the trunk of the Toyota and pulled out the cardboard box with the yarn and knitting supplies. "I can carry that," Pamela said and held out her arms to receive it.

"And I'll take those clothes." Penny reached into the trunk and gathered up the pile of clothing topped by the velvet cape.

"I'll get your hamper and the magazines," Bettina said, opening the front door on the passenger side of her car.

"Many hands make light work," Wilfred observed. "And I will escort this headless lady to her new home." He set the dress form's stand on the driveway and then gripped the dress form's torso by its waist to lift it from the trunk. He tinkered for a moment to make sure the torso had slipped securely onto the stand, and then set off across the street, bearing the dress form in front of him.

Pamela, Penny, and Bettina followed him. As they neared the opposite curb, Pamela noticed a small box sitting on her porch, right below where her mailbox was anchored to the clapboard of her house. It was the season for boxes, of course, but Pamela was expecting one particular delivery and from the size of the box, she suspected this was it.

Wilfred climbed the steps to Pamela's porch, set the dress form down, and stooped to retrieve the small box. He held it toward Pamela as she ascended the steps. With her hands full, she could only glance at the address label, but she smiled with satisfaction. "Yes," she said. "Just in time for my baking."

Wilfred held Pamela's boxes, large and small, as she unlocked the front door. He waited until everyone else was inside, and then followed and deposited the boxes in Pamela's entry.

"My poppy seeds are here," Pamela announced as she picked up the small box. Every year she ordered a pound of poppy seeds from a company that sold them in bulk. Her poppy-seed cakes required a whole cup of poppy seeds for every two loaves, and it took several of the small grocery-store jars, at nearly five dollars each, to make up that amount. So when a neighbor told her about mail-order poppy seeds, the information had been welcome. "I'll get busy baking this weekend," she added. She headed for the kitchen with the small box.

When she returned to the entry, the dress form was standing in the corner wearing the long black velvet cape. Even without a head, the dress form made a commanding figure, nearly six feet tall.

"We'll have to adjust her to your size," Pamela said to Penny, "if we're to use her to hem the cape up."

Wilfred reached for the doorknob. "I'm off to unload your patio pots, dear wife," he said. "Make hay while the sun shines. Shall I put them in the garage with the other gardening supplies?"

"You don't need to do that now, sweetheart." Bettina laid a hand on Wilfred's arm. "And a few of them are Pamela's. We'll sort them out first."

"In that case"—Wilfred made a courtly bow—"I'll leave you ladies and return to my basement workshop."

"I have a little errand." Bettina addressed Wilfred, but with a wink at Pamela. "So I'll see you in an hour or so."

Wilfred nodded. "No time like the present," he observed, and then he was out the door.

Pamela fingered the little bead bracelet in her jeans pocket. She was longing to show it to Bettina, but Penny lingered in the entry. She'd tossed her jacket aside and was sitting on the floor paging through one of the magazines she'd come away with.

"I'll go with you." Pamela spoke suddenly. "To Meadowside. I need some wrapping paper, if you don't mind stopping at the hobby store."

"Of course not," Bettina said. "You can help me decide on just the right frame."

Meadowside was next to Arborville, reached by driving south. Bettina turned right at the top of Orchard Street, and they cruised past the grand houses, some of the oldest in Arborville, that faced each other along that stretch of Arborville Avenue. Pamela had retrieved the engraving from under her seat and held it on her lap. "There's a party store right next to the frame shop," Bettina said. "Would that be okay for your wrapping paper?"

Pamela laughed. "I don't really need wrapping paper. I have a whole drawer full. I just wanted a chance to talk to you without Penny listening."

Bettina took her eyes off the road and turned to study her friend. Pamela met her gaze, in which curiosity blended with concern. "Shall I pull over?" she asked.

"It can wait till you get to the frame shop," Pamela said, "but I have something interesting to show you." Pamela was a kind person, but she occasionally enjoyed the slight feeling of power that came from having a secret to share.

Bettina's lips, which today were a shade of deep orange that matched her coat, curved into a tiny smile that acknowledged she knew she was being strung along. She shifted her gaze back to the road and five minutes later pulled into a parking space just a few doors down from the frame shop.

"Okay," she said, unbuckling her seat belt and turning to face Pamela. "Spill!"

Pamela had reached under her jacket and pulled the bracelet from her jeans pocket as they drove along. Now she extended her hand, fist clenched around her prize, and slowly unfolded her fingers to reveal it. "Can you imagine that Coot was ever tiny enough for this to fit around her wrist?" she asked as Bettina tentatively picked up the little circlet of beads.

"I know what it is," Bettina said. "Wilfred's mother

saved his for him. The beads on his are baby blue—it's so cute. But how do you know this was Coot's?"

Pamela described the suitcase and its contents, and added Penny's discovery of the three Morton-Bidwell yearbooks, 1953, 1954, and 1956, with 1955 conspicuously missing. Then she said, "It might not be Coot's, but the bracelet and the suitcase together establish that Millicent's mother went away and gave birth to a child while she was still in high school and was still a Wentworth."

Bettina nodded. "I can't see any other interpretation. And if what Coot claims about the DNA is true . . ."

Pamela nodded, then she twisted her lips into a puzzled knot. "But all this doesn't make her the murderer. If Coot thinks the DNA will prove her case, why would she have to kill Millicent?"

"She wouldn't," Bettina said.

Outside, people hurried along the sidewalk in either direction, past shop windows made festive with delicate strings of white lights, miniature Christmas trees, and stacks of gaily wrapped packages.

"But Pierre would," Pamela said. "We already know he and Jeannette are wild about each other. A divorce would have freed him, but if Millicent could be gone and he could end up with her estate, that would be all the better."

"He's so slick." Bettina shuddered.

Pamela described the conversation she overheard. "What else could that mean?" she added. "'Our future is taking shape, and then you will be all mine.' Jeannette knew what he was up to . . . so of course she gave him an alibi."

* * *

"Are you sure you won't need help with the tree, Mom?" It was Saturday morning. Pamela had dawdled over toast and coffee, chatting with Penny and laughing at the antics of Catrina and Ginger, but the countdown to Christmas had begun. Today's task was to pick the perfect tree from the Aardvark Alliance lot and deck it with as many ornaments as its branches could accommodate. Sunday would be baking day. A plastic bag containing the mail-order poppy seeds, looking like a small black pillow, waited on the kitchen counter—along with the yellowed and smudged card that held the handwritten recipe for Pamela's Christmas poppy-seed cake.

"I'll be fine," Pamela said, because Penny had made plans with her friend Lorie Hopkins. "The lot attendants will tie it to the top of the car and you can help me bring it in the house when you get back from the mall. We'll get out those old Christmas LPs that Grandma gave us and play them like we always do, and we'll decorate it together."

"You really don't mind?" Penny's gaze was particularly intense, as if determined to make sure Pamela hadn't been nurturing a vision of mother-daughter togetherness in the Christmas-tree lot.

"Really!" Pamela said. "Lorie Hopkins is your best Arborville friend and I know you miss each other when you're both away at college."

The doorbell chimed as Penny was slipping into her violet jacket. She looped Pamela's violet mohair scarf around her neck, greeted her friend, who popped over the threshold to say hi to Pamela, and they were gone.

* * *

Pamela prowled among the bristly trees, enjoying the fantasy that she was actually in a small forest, inhaling the nose-tickling spiciness of the dark-green foliage. She needed a dense tree with sturdy branches and plenty of them. Christmas-tree ornaments, especially vintage, were one of her weaknesses, and garage sales over the years had allowed her to build a collection that filled several boxes. She stepped back to get a better look at a likely candidate, a lush fir that appeared a bit over six feet tall.

It seemed symmetrical, and suitably bushy. A small tag wired to one of the branches read *$50*. The price was reasonable, and the proceeds did go to the high school. She stepped a bit farther back and surveyed the tree again.

Then she heard a pleasant male voice say, "Pamela?" and Richard Larkin's head and shoulders appeared in the gap between the upper branches of the tree she'd been considering and its neighbor.

Pamela had been focused on the tree's very tip, wondering if it looked substantial enough to receive the star that had topped Paterson Christmas trees ever since the first Christmas she and Michael spent together. But she had to raise her eyes a bit farther to meet Richard Larkin's eyes. "Oh, hello," she said, mustering her social smile.

"Hello." He wasn't smiling, but was studying her with the intent look he sometimes got. "I guess you're looking for a tree," he added. He was hatless, despite the cold, and the chilly breeze was ruffling his shaggy hair.

"It *is* that time of year," she answered, feeling foolish the minute the words were out of her mouth. For some reason, she was suddenly aware of her heartbeat. If only Bettina would stop stressing how eligible Richard

Larkin was, Pamela was sure chance meetings like this, or chatting when they happened to be in their driveways at the same time, wouldn't seem so awkward. "I guess you're buying a tree too," she added.

"A wreath," he said. "There's no point in putting up a tree, with Laine and Sybil out in San Francisco—and I'll be at my sister's on Long Island for Christmas dinner. Our parents are coming up from Washington, D.C."

"Oh." Pamela nodded. "Definitely no point in a tree then."

"No point. Exactly."

The conversation was taking place through the gap between the upper branches of the two trees, Richard Larkin's body from the chest down hidden by the more expansive lower foliage.

"There's Le Corbusier too," he said, a slight smile softening his strong features. Richard Larkin had adopted one of Catrina's kittens when Pamela faced the challenge of the cat's surprise pregnancy and the six offspring that resulted. "Kittens and Christmas trees can be chancy."

Pamela laughed. "You're right. I was lucky last year. Catrina was newly adopted and still on her best behavior."

They regarded each other, the conversational thread exhausted. After a moment, he said, "I guess I'll pick out my wreath then." He turned and she watched him lope away, his blond head bobbing above the tips of the trees.

"Is it going to be this one, then?" Pamela turned to see a lanky young man in a down jacket and with a knitted cap hiding his forehead and ears. "An excellent choice," he added. "The firs are our most popular trees."

Pamela dipped a hand into her purse and came up with her wallet. "I'll take it," she said.

The young man thrust an arm through the bristly foliage and clapped a gloved hand around its trunk. As Pamela backed out of the way, he plucked the tree from its neighbors and, with Pamela following, bore it along the well-trodden path that led to a canvas shelter near the entrance to the lot. She handed over fifty dollars to an older man and watched as the tree was detached from the crisscrossed staves that had enabled it to stand upright and fed into a sheath of plastic netting.

As Pamela turned onto Orchard Street, with the Christmas tree—tamed by its plastic netting—tied securely to the roof of her car, she caught sight of Richard Larkin farther down the block. He was striding along with a large balsam wreath, unadorned by ribbons or glittery ornaments, slung over one arm. A minute later, she drove past him, and she was climbing out of her car by the time he reached his house.

He waved and disappeared behind the tall hedge that separated her lot from his. But then he reappeared, back out on the sidewalk but without the wreath. "I could give you a hand with the tree," he said, then added quickly, "not that I think you couldn't manage it yourself. I don't mean to imply . . . that is, you look very strong . . ." He stopped in confusion and shifted his gaze from her face to the tree.

"Penny was planning to help me," Pamela said.

"Oh. Of course." Richard edged back a few steps, onto the strip of faded grass that separated the sidewalk from the street. "So you won't need—"

Me, she imagined he was going to say, but before he could finish the thought, he took another step back and lurched to the side as that step took him off the curb. He teetered briefly, then straightened up with a shrug and an embarrassed smile.

"But Penny's at the mall right now," Pamela heard herself say. "So, yes, I could use a hand."

The tree was lashed to Pamela's car with lengths of thick twine. Pamela untied the front one, and Richard untied the back one, rolled the twine into a neat circle, and handed it to Pamela. He grasped the tree, slid it off the car roof, and easily swung it upright. Despite the fact that his awkward retreat moments earlier had nearly toppled him into the street, he was actually quite graceful, Pamela found herself thinking, and certainly muscular. Suddenly the image of Richard Larkin at work in his yard the previous summer popped into her mind. He'd been wearing faded jeans and a T-shirt that left no question about his fitness.

"Where to then?" he asked, sounding more confident.

The question startled her and the image fled. "The house," she said. "I'll get the door." Her purse was over her shoulder, but her keys had been in her hand. Then she untied the tree, and now she held two rounds of twine. Where were the keys? She looked around, puzzled.

"In your pocket, I think," Richard said.

Of course. She dipped into her jacket pocket and there they were. She climbed the steps and unlocked the door, standing back as Catrina and Ginger fled and Richard steered the tree, base first, into the entry. The dress form had taken up residence in the laundry room the previous evening.

"Penny and I can take it from here," Pamela said as he lowered the tree onto the entry carpet. "The stand is still in the attic with the ornaments and lights." The room was already infused with the sharp, spicy scent of the tree.

"It smells like Christmas," Richard said.

"Yes. Yes, it does," Pamela agreed. Catrina and Ginger had ventured back to investigate this curious new phenomenon, prowling along its length and sniffing it warily. Both humans watched them. A few moments passed.

"Well, then." Richard shifted his gaze from the animals to Pamela's face. "I guess I'll head home."

Pamela nodded. "Thank you for helping with the tree. Penny will be glad that task is out of the way."

Richard reached for the doorknob. "I'll see you Christmas Eve . . . at Bettina and Wilfred's."

"Christmas Eve." Pamela nodded. And then he was gone.

Chapter Twelve

It wasn't really time for lunch. But after a breakfast of only coffee and toast, the tree-buying adventure in the chilly air—almost like a walk in the woods really—had awakened Pamela's appetite. There was just enough oxtail stew left for one serving, and while it heated on the stove, Pamela repaired to her office to check her email.

There were no emails bearing attachments from her boss at *Fiber Craft*, and in fact no emails from her boss at all. Her mind at ease, Pamela ate her oxtail stew. Then she went to the chest in the living room and opened the deep drawer where she stored her collection of wrapping paper and ribbon.

Penny would be choosing yarn and a pattern for the promised sweater and would find a generous check from Pamela under the tree on Christmas morning. But all during the year Pamela kept her eyes open for perfect gifts for her friends and relatives. Presents for her parents and siblings had been wrapped and mailed long ago. But upstairs on Pamela's closet shelf there waited a book for Wilfred about the settlement of the Hudson Valley, a hand-woven tablecloth and

napkin set from a craft show for Bettina, and a whole
box full of miscellaneous treats for Penny.

Pamela sorted out the Christmas wrap from odds
and ends bought for birthdays, wedding showers, or
gifts for new babies. She preferred Christmas wrap
that was recognizable as being for Christmas, not abstract patterns in wild colors, but Santas or wreaths or
partridges in pear trees rendered in Christmassy colors
like red and green. She carried a few rolls to the dining
room table, along with a huge spool of red satin ribbon
that had been a garage-sale find. Then she fetched the
gifts for Wilfred and Bettina and Penny from her closet
shelf and set to work, wrapping and taping paper
around variously shaped objects and finishing off each
job with a few twists of red satin ribbon and a bow.

When the packages were finished and sat in a cluster on the living room carpet, she retrieved from under
the mail table the small cardboard box Penny's Paterson grandparents had sent and the larger one from
her own parents. She sliced the tape that sealed the
small box. Michael Paterson's parents remembered
Pamela and Penny every Christmas with a gift and a
check for Penny and a gift for Pamela. Indeed the box
contained two smaller boxes, prettily wrapped, that
Pamela suspected contained jewelry. The tags read "To
Our Dear Penny" and "To Our Dear Pamela." There
was also an envelope with Penny's name on it.

The larger box contained four boxes. Two wide,
flat boxes were likely new pajamas, a set each for
Penny and Pamela. Pamela's mother understood the
difficulty of predicting a young woman's (Penny's)
taste in clothes, and she knew that Pamela knit her
own sweaters and was otherwise not very concerned

about fashion. But a person could always use a new pair of pajamas. A small box was probably jewelry for Penny, and a heavy box, with a tag that read "Pamela" felt like a book. An envelope addressed to each hinted at the likelihood that—if pajamas, jewelry, and books didn't thrill—a post-Christmas shopping trip funded by the enclosed check could make up the deficiency.

Pamela added the gifts from the Patersons and her own parents to the group that she had wrapped, and surveyed what was becoming an impressive pile. Catrina and Ginger wandered in to investigate this new feature of their environment. Catrina batted experimentally at a particularly luxurious bow on one of the gifts from Pamela's parents, while Ginger attempted to reach the top of the pile by hopping from one gift to another.

Pamela gathered up the cardboard boxes and the crumpled newspaper that had cushioned their contents and headed for the front door, en route to the recycling bins at the side of her house. But the front door opened before she touched the knob. She stepped back, the door opened farther, and in walked Penny, bearing a large shopping bag from the mall's fanciest store.

"It looks like you had a successful outing," Pamela said with a smile.

"It looks like you did too." Penny nodded toward the Christmas tree, which stretched across the entry carpet, its dark green branches still contained by the netting sheath. "The mall was mobbed," she added, "but it was fun to hear the Christmas music and see that huge tree they put up." She set the bag at the foot of the stairs, slipped out of her jacket, and unwrapped the violet mohair scarf from her neck.

"I'm going to make a meatloaf for tonight," Pamela said. "If you're hungry now there's cheese and apples."

"Lorie and I had lunch at the food court. Besides"—Penny's pretty mouth shaped a smile—"I have presents to wrap."

"There's Christmas wrapping on the dining room table," Pamela said.

"Some of them are surprises." Her smile became teasing.

"You can take the paper to your room."

After Penny had retreated upstairs, shopping bag from the mall and wrapping paper in hand, Pamela settled back at the dining room table for another Christmas chore. A partial box of Christmas cards featuring an angel from an antique tapestry sat before her, along with stamps and a holiday-themed batch of address labels that had come unbidden in the mail. She'd written cards on and off all month, ever since the cards from early-bird friends started drifting in. But there were still names on her Christmas-card list that hadn't been checked off.

She liked to take her time and include a little bit of news, so for the next hour she added notes to the greetings already contained in the angel cards, notes to her college roommate, Michael Paterson's aunt Joan, a high-school friend who had never left the town where she and Pamela grew up, and an old professor who had kept in touch over the years. When the cards were finished, she set them on the mail table.

The tree stand and ornaments had to be fetched from the attic, but that could be Penny's chore. Somehow it had gotten to be five o'clock and there was meatloaf to be made. In the kitchen, cat and kitten were prowling expectantly around the bowl they shared. Pamela served them several spoonfuls of chicken-fish combo from a fresh can and emptied and refilled their water bowl as they took delicate nibbles from their dinner, which looked rather like a paler sort of meatloaf.

Pamela wasn't certain how glad she was that her brain had made that connection, but she unwrapped the pound of ground beef that had been thawing on the counter and placed it in her favorite mixing bowl, the caramel-colored one with three white stripes circling it near the rim. She set to work chopping an onion and added it, with an egg and bread crumbs, to the ground meat. Next came salt and pepper and a dollop of catsup and a sprinkling of dried herbs. Soon the resulting mixture, kneaded by hand and pressed into a loaf pan, had been set in the oven to bake. Next to it sat two potatoes, their tops patterned with holes from the tines of a fork lest they explode while baking.

The meatloaf and baked potatoes would be served with a salad of cucumber slices and mini-tomatoes. Making do with grocery-store tomatoes in months when growing her own was impossible, Pamela had found that the smaller ones had a concentrated flavor that the larger ones, promising as they often looked, lacked. Dessert would be cookies from the vintage cookie tin.

The larder had gotten quite bare, but it would be replenished on the following day. Penny would come to the Co-Op too, so there would be twice as many hands to handle the canvas grocery bags.

Pamela was in the dining room arranging place-mats, napkins, and silverware on the table when she heard Penny's feet on the stairs. Through the arch that separated the dining room from the living room she watched as Penny entered and added her own offerings to the growing pile of festively wrapped packages, two large boxes and two small.

"Can you bring down the Christmas-tree stand and the boxes full of ornaments?" Pamela called. "They're all together in the back corner, to the left when you go up, and the boxes all say 'Christmas.'"

"Sure," Penny said, and she was off and up the stairs again.

After dinner, to the accompaniment of Christmas carols, Pamela and Penny spent a pleasant evening choosing their favorite ornaments from Pamela's collection and adding them, with lights and garlands, to the tree, which perfumed the entire downstairs with its sharp, piney scent. They finished off their work by topping the tree with the decades-old star and arranging the carefully wrapped boxes beneath. Then Penny retreated to her room and Pamela settled on the sofa to watch a British mystery and put the finishing touches on the ruby-red tunic.

Pamela leafed through the Sunday *Register* wondering whether any new tidbit in the Millicent Farthingale case had provided an opportunity to fill a few column inches. Penny had not come down yet and Pamela sipped her coffee in silence as she pored over news of national and state doings in the paper's first section and then moved on to the Local section. Very dramatic local events—like murders—often started out in Part 1 but then migrated to Local after the initial drama had subsided.

But there was no mention anywhere of Millicent's murder. Apparently the police had satisfied themselves that Pierre was not guilty, though at present he resided at the top of Pamela and Bettina's list of suspects. Presumably they'd interviewed Coot too—Pierre must have told them about her arrival from Texas (coincidentally?) just a few days before Millicent's death and her claim to a share of Millicent's inheritance. But perhaps they had asked themselves, as Pamela and Bettina had, why, if Coot thought DNA would prove her claim, she would have had to kill Millicent.

Penny arrived then, her dark curls still tousled from sleep and her expression still dreamy. "Did they do anything to the Christmas tree?" she asked before even pouring coffee, as Catrina and Ginger strolled across the floor.

"It looks okay," Pamela said. "I checked when I came down, and they've been in here the whole time I've been sitting at the table. So far so good. I don't want to have to shut them into the laundry room every night."

Penny slipped two slices of whole-grain bread into the toaster, then tipped the still half-full carafe over the cup Pamela had set out for her. She added a spoonful of sugar from the cut-glass sugar bowl on the counter and helped herself to cream from the carton in the refrigerator. Held in place on the refrigerator door by a magnet in the shape of a mitten was a list for that morning's shopping trip to the Co-Op Grocery.

"I'll just have the toast and this one cup of coffee," Penny said, "and then I'll get dressed and we can go."

"Sure." Pamela nodded. She herself was still in her robe and pajamas. She held out her cup. "Will you fill mine again, please?" she asked her daughter, and Penny complied. Satisfied that she hadn't missed any updates on the murder case and with a fresh cup of coffee, she put Part 1 and the Local section aside, moved on to Lifestyle, and continued sipping coffee.

Half an hour later, Pamela and Penny were en route up Orchard Street, bundled in jackets, scarves, and woolly hats, each carrying two empty canvas grocery bags. Overnight, a gusty wind had replaced the slight breeze of the previous day, and the wind had blown away the low clouds that on Friday had yielded a brief dusting of snow. Today the sky arched high overhead, cloudless and a startling shade of blue. When they reached the corner of Arborville Avenue, Pamela detoured through the parking lot of the stately brick apartment building to check behind the wooden fence that hid the building's trash cans, but no treasures had appeared since her last walk uptown.

Despite the cold wind, a few people were clustered in front of the bulletin board on the Co-Op's façade. One of those people was Marlene Pepper, a friend of Bettina and—tangentially—Pamela. She was very eager to learn how Penny had been faring since her horrid experience of the previous Monday (not even a week ago!) and it was some minutes before Pamela and Penny were able to escape through the Co-Op's automatic door—one of its few concessions to modernity—claim a cart, and proceed with their shopping.

Pamela took her shopping list from her purse. That evening they would have fish, maybe salmon, depending on what the Co-Op fish counter offered. But then the leftover meatloaf would suffice for the next two nights—especially since they wouldn't want much to eat before setting off for Bettina's Christmas Eve party. It wasn't to be a dinner, Bettina had explained, but with so many people contributing to the menu, Pamela was sure there would be plenty of food. Then on Christmas

Day they would join Bettina and Wilfred for what Pamela was sure would be a feast worthy of the season.

But everyday supplies were low, like coffee and the whole-grain bread that was a Co-Op specialty, and cheese and apples and cucumbers and mini-tomatoes. And she'd buy something green, maybe kale, to serve with the fish. And she needed eggs, lots of eggs—for the deviled eggs she'd promised to bring on Christmas Eve and for the poppy-seed cake, the making of which was on the agenda for that afternoon. "Butter too," she murmured, consulting her list, "two pounds. And milk for the poppy-seed cake."

They made a circuit of the small store, pushing their cart down narrow aisles laid out in an era before automobiles and huge refrigerators made it possible to carry home and store a week's worth of food at once. In the produce department, Pamela tucked an exuberant bunch of curly kale into a plastic bag and set it in the cart. A bag of apples followed, then she and Penny stopped at the fish counter for salmon, continued on and checked more items off the list, and wound up at the bakery counter. Pamela resisted the intoxicating aroma of sugary goodies, knowing that those aromas would be wafting through her own kitchen in a few hours. She limited her request to a loaf of whole-grain bread, sliced, and added it to the cart.

All three checkers were busy, scanning items as varied as bottles of furniture polish, cellophane bags of hard candy, and bunches of leeks, and transferring them to the counter where they waited to be bagged. Penny and Pamela staged their cart at the checkout station whose conveyor belt held the smallest number of items. As they waited for their turn, Penny stared

idly through the large windows that faced Arborville
Avenue while Pamela took out her wallet.

Suddenly Pamela heard Penny exclaim, "There
goes the scarf. A guy wearing the scarf Bettina gave
Millicent."

Pamela looked up, purse gaping and wallet in hand.
Standing at the corner, apparently waiting for the light
to change, was the young man she'd seen on Wednesday. Wrapped jauntily around his neck was the red
scarf with three green stripes at each end.

"I'll catch him," Penny exclaimed. And then she was
gone, darting around the bank of checkout stations
and through the OUT side of the automatic door. For
a minute Pamela was too stunned to move. Then she
thrust her wallet back into her purse, stepped away
from her cart, and headed in the same direction. But
before she reached the door she was intercepted by
the cheerful woman who had been bagging groceries
at the checkout station nearest the automatic door.

"You're abandoning your cart, ma'am," the woman
said. A sparkly Santa pin adorned the bib of her Co-Op
apron.

"I have to." The words came out in a rush. "My
daughter . . . she's . . . run away." Pamela pointed
toward the corner where the young man had been
standing. The light to cross Arborville Avenue was
green now and no one was there.

"I understand," the woman said comfortingly. "Of
course you want to go after her. These little mother-
daughter tiffs can be so distressing—especially at a
time of year that's supposed to be happy. Shall we
return your selections to inventory or would you like
us to hold them for you until you can return?"

"I . . . I don't know." Pamela felt so breathless she
was amazed the words came out at all.

The woman went on. "Of course, that's assuming you won't be gone too long. Or you don't have perishables. Do you have any perishables? Like fish?"

"Fish," Pamela said. "Yes, I have fish. But please"—she heard her voice start to crack—"just let me go. I'll come back. And if the fish is spoiled I'll pay for it anyway."

The woman was standing between her and the door but Pamela edged a few steps to the left. "I'm a good customer," she bleated. "I've been shopping here for two decades." And then she sprang toward the door. It swung open and she bolted onto the sidewalk. But by the time she reached the corner, the light had turned red again.

Frantically, Pamela scanned the sidewalks on both sides of Arborville Avenue, looking to the right, toward the small concentration of shops that formed Arborville's commercial district, and to the left. There was no sign of Penny or the young man in the red scarf.

The young man had been waiting for the light to change, and presumably he'd continued on his way when it did, with Penny on his trail. So when the light turned green, Pamela hurried across the intersection. Borough Hall was just in front of her. She'd tracked him into Borough Hall on Wednesday—perhaps he had ongoing business there. She climbed the half-flight of steps leading to the entrance, approached the wreath-bedecked door, and tugged at the door pull. Nothing happened.

She took a step back and studied the hours on the building's brick façade. Of course! Today was Sunday and Borough Hall wasn't open on Sunday. She retreated down the steps and scanned the sidewalk once again. To the south, Arborville Avenue became completely residential and, unless the young man had been on his way home or to visit a friend, she couldn't see what errand would have taken him in that direction. But to the north were shops and restaurants, and people bustling here and there.

Pamela returned to the corner and waited for the green light that would give her permission to cross the busy street that crossed Arborville Avenue. Then she hurried along, hardly breathing, past the bank and the dry cleaner's. Both were closed, but the liquor store, which was next, was open. She paused and leaned toward the patch of window that wasn't hidden by the large sign encouraging people to stock up on wine and champagne for their holiday parties. The store's interior was dim compared to the clear brightness of the day, but she could see only one customer and it wasn't the young man in the red scarf.

She hurried on, anxiety and exertion making her heart surge. Though it was Sunday, the hair salon was open—perhaps because of the upcoming holidays. She gazed through its large window, but the only males visible were two of the stylists. Just past the hair salon, a narrow passageway led from Arborville Avenue to the parking lot shared by the library and police department. Pamela stopped and peered down its shadowy length. The library might be open, and the young man might have been headed there. But she'd continue along Arborville Avenue before following up that notion.

Just after the passageway came Hyler's Luncheonette, an Arborville institution with its worn wooden tables and booths upholstered in burgundy Naugahyde. A huge plate-glass window looked out on Arborville Avenue and allowed solitary diners the entertainment of watching the passing crowd. They also allowed passersby to easily see who was lunching or having coffee at Hyler's.

And, in fact, as Pamela took a few steps past the entrance to the passageway and glanced toward the window, she was riveted by the sight that met her eyes. Sitting at a table for two, positioned just at the middle of the plate-glass window, was Penny. Her violet jacket was open and draped over her chair back, and the violet mohair scarf had been removed to bare her pretty neck. One of Hyler's heavy cream-colored coffee cups sat before her on the scarred wooden surface of the table. She was smiling a flirtatious smile that revealed her perfect teeth. As Pamela stared, Penny began to laugh and her cheeks grew pink.

Sitting across from her was the young man Penny had darted from the Co-Op to pursue. He had removed his jacket too, as well as the red scarf with green stripes at the ends. It was dangling from his chair back, one end on the floor.

Chapter Thirteen

Pamela was hardly aware of what she was doing. One minute she had been outside, looking through Hyler's window. The next she was inside, standing behind her daughter's chair and facing the young man.

"Where did you get that scarf?" she blurted.

Penny twisted her neck to stare at her mother. Her merriment had vanished and a frown creased her usually smooth brow. "He found it, Mom," she said. "It was tangled up in a pile of dead logs down in the nature preserve." She paused, glanced at the young man, turned back to Pamela, and added. "This is Aaron, Mom."

In acknowledgment of the introduction, the young man half rose and then sat down again. "Penny told me about finding the body," he said. "I feel bad now. It belonged to your friend . . ." He lifted the scarf from the chair back and held it out.

Pamela studied him. He was definitely the same young man she'd seen on Wednesday. Closer inspection confirmed the raffish good looks she'd noted then. Dark hair that was slightly too long topped a face with well-sculpted cheekbones, piercing blue eyes, and an expressive mouth. His eyes had met hers as he gazed over the roof of his car and he'd given her a smile that seemed slightly flirtatious. But now there was no sign that he recognized her. Was there some reason that he didn't want to acknowledge the previous encounter—or was she fooling herself to think he'd paid enough attention to her to remember her even ten minutes later, let alone four days?

Without taking the scarf, she stepped around to where she could face Penny. "There are groceries to carry home," she said sternly. "I can't manage four bags all by myself."

Looking chastened, Penny scooted her chair back, murmured "Thanks for the coffee," and grabbed her jacket and scarf. Pamela nodded at Aaron and strode toward the door. Penny followed along, tugging on her jacket as she went.

"What on earth were you thinking?" Pamela asked as soon as they were outside and hurrying back in the direction of the Co-Op. "First of all, to just vanish like that!"

"The scarf is a clue, Mom," Penny said breathlessly as she struggled to keep pace with her long-legged mother.

Pamela realized that she'd passed up the opportunity to reclaim the scarf, and her annoyance deepened. "Yes," she exclaimed. "It *is* a clue. And that means that your new friend . . . *Aaron* . . . could be a murderer." She wasn't sure what she'd meant to convey by the emphasis on his name. Scorn that Penny had been so willing to befriend someone who could be a killer? Just because he was cute?

They'd reached the corner. The light to cross Arborville Avenue was green, and Pamela launched herself off the curb. But Penny stayed behind, panting helplessly. Sensing her daughter wasn't following, Pamela returned to the sidewalk. "He's not a murderer," Penny insisted between pants. Her face was flushed from the effort of keeping up with her mother. She'd draped the violet mohair scarf loosely around her neck instead of knotting it, and the chilly wind tossed the ends to and fro. "He's very nice."

And very cute, Pamela added to herself.

Penny went on. "He found the scarf in the nature preserve and thought it was pretty and rescued it." Pamela regarded her skeptically. "I believe him," Penny said firmly, her chin at a defiant tilt.

The light turned green again. "I still have to pay for my groceries," Pamela said and she was off.

As soon as they entered the house, Penny deposited her share of the groceries in the entry and hurried up the stairs. Pamela heard her bedroom door close with a resolute thud. Pamela continued on to the kitchen with her own grocery bags. The first thing she noticed when she stepped through the doorway was the mouse lying in the middle of the kitchen floor.

It wasn't a real mouse. It was a fanciful creature Penny had made at school many, many years before. The body was a small pinecone and the head a whole pecan in the shell. The tail and ears were felt, the whiskers bits of broom straw, and the eyes dots of black marker. It had hung on every Christmas tree since Penny brought it home one December.

The sight elicited a small gasp. Pamela quickly set her bags on the table and retraced her steps to the entry and thence to the living room. In her mind, she

pictured the Christmas tree lying on its side as if
the victim of a zealous lumberjack, ornaments strewn
here and there, the fragile ones in gleaming metallic
shards. And a puddle of water on the carpet from the
overturned tree stand.

But—she sighed with relief—it still stood. A few
other ornaments had been batted loose, then abandoned when they apparently proved unsatisfactory as
playthings. The cats were nowhere in sight. Usually
they wandered into view when they sensed that their
mistress had returned from whatever errand had
taken her away. Had they felt guilty after their spree?

They need more toys, Pamela realized, as she collected the ornaments from the rug and found spots
for them among the glittering and curious objects that
adorned the fragrant branches. Catrina and Ginger
had been making do with a few balls of yarn to meet
their entertainment needs. They would get presents
too, she resolved, an assortment of toys chosen for
their aesthetic and educational value.

On her way back through the entry, Pamela collected the grocery bags abandoned by Penny. In the
kitchen, she picked up the pinecone mouse and set it
on the table. She put the apples in the wooden bowl
at the end of the counter—except for one, which
she quartered and ate with a few slices of the newly
purchased Swiss cheese. Then she stored the other
food in the cupboard and refrigerator and left the
house again.

Bettina answered the door dressed in leggings and
a tunic-length Christmas sweater. It was bright red with

a large, sequined Rudolph on the front. "I thought you'd be baking," Bettina said with a welcoming smile. She stepped back and pulled the door open farther. "Come in." Woofus was napping on the sofa, but raised his head apprehensively as Pamela stepped inside. "It's okay, boy," Bettina assured him in her most soothing voice.

"I'm going to be," Pamela said. "I went to the Co-Op this morning for the rest of the ingredients. But I had to talk to you first."

Bettina grabbed Pamela's arm. Her eyes widened. "You have something to report." The words came out in a swift stream.

"I saw the scarf again," Pamela said. "On the same young man."

"What nerve he has!" Bettina kept her grip on Pamela's arm and led her to the sofa, where they squeezed in next to the slumbering Woofus.

"That's not the worst of it," Pamela moaned, and she described seeing the young man through the window of the Co-Op, Penny's dash from the store, her own frantic search for her daughter, and the discovery that Penny had met and befriended the young man. "He told her he found it down in the nature preserve, tangled up in a pile of dead logs," Pamela concluded. "And she believes him."

"Oh, dear." Bettina shook her head, setting her earrings in motion. They were large pendants of glass, striped red and green and fashioned to resemble hard candies. "He could be telling the truth, or . . ."

Pamela echoed her. "Or . . ." She bit her lip and frowned. "Penny was smiling at him like he'd made quite an impression."

"Oh, dear." Bettina shook her head again. "I told

Clayborn when you had that first sighting at the Christmas-tree lot, but he said you can't arrest someone for wearing a scarf and there was no way of knowing if it was even the same scarf. But I'll tell him again. And now I have a name, a first name anyway."

Back at home, Pamela set about baking the special poppy-seed cakes that had been a Christmas tradition since the early years of her marriage. The recipe had come to her from a friend, on the handwritten card that—much the worse for wear—was now propped up on the counter before her. On the card, the recipe was identified as "Liza's Ukrainian Poppy-Seed Cake," though the friend who had given it to her was neither Ukrainian nor named Liza.

The first step was to start the butter softening. She was doubling her recipe in order to produce four loaves at once, so her largest mixing bowl was called for, even larger than the caramel-colored bowl with the white stripes. A huge pale green bowl resided in a cupboard in the laundry room, brought out once a year for Christmas baking. She fetched that bowl and took the four butter quarters out of their box and unwrapped them. Then she held each butter quarter over the pale green bowl and whittled away at it with a knife, letting the butter chunks accumulate at the bottom of the bowl. Butter and sugar had to be creamed together for the recipe and smaller chunks would reach a consistency that her mixer could manage sooner than whole quarters would.

The next step was to blend the poppy seeds with milk. Pamela tugged at the bag's zipper seal and the seal parted, releasing the rich, slightly nutty fragrance of the tiny, dark seeds. She measured two cups of seeds into a saucepan, added two cups of milk, and set the saucepan over a low flame. The seeds wanted to float, so she stirred the mixture with a wooden spoon to make sure they were all submerged. The milk wasn't to boil—only nearly so. So Pamela watched the surface carefully. When the tiniest bit of steam began to rise from it and the tiniest bubbles formed around the edges of the saucepan, she turned the heat off and left the seeds and milk to sit. They were supposed to sit for an hour.

As she turned away from the stove, Pamela realized something was missing—the Christmas music that Christmas tasks required. The old LPs had been brought out for the tree-trimming. Now she stepped around into the living room, picked up the LP whose cover showed a festive but much faded Christmas wreath, slid out the glossy vinyl disk, and set it to spinning on the turntable.

The butter and seeds needed to sit a bit longer and email hadn't been checked since that morning. Pamela's boss seemed never to rest and liked her communications to be speedily acknowledged, even though the deadlines she gave were usually quite reasonable. So Pamela climbed the stairs as the lush sounds of a chorale singing "The Holly and the Ivy" surged from the speakers. On the second floor, the door to Penny's room was still closed. Pamela hesitated for a moment but then continued on to her office.

Her inbox contained nothing of note, and ten minutes later she was back in the kitchen. It was time to butter and flour the pans for the poppy-seed cake—loaf pans, four of them. And once they were lined up on the kitchen table with an even dusting of white on sides and bottom, she turned on the oven, setting it to 350 degrees. It came on with a whoosh.

The recipe called for white flour or whole wheat flour or half of each. Pamela liked the poppy-seed cakes with half of each, so she sifted two cups of white and two cups of whole wheat into a small bowl, along with salt and baking powder, and set the bowl aside. Then she took out six eggs and proceeded to separate the yolks from the whites. She tapped each egg sharply on the side of another small bowl and eased the globe of yolk and the translucent white back and forth between the eggshell halves until all the white slithered into the bowl. The yolks, which had been left nestled in their half shells, were tipped into a third small bowl. She beat the whites until they were stiff and set them aside.

The chunks of butter in the pale green bowl were soft enough now to proceed with the recipe. She fit the beaters into her electric mixer and set to work. The mixer whirred and growled, the beaters clanked against the bowl's sturdy earthenware surface, and gradually the chunks of butter became a yellow mass teased into waves and peaks by the action of the beaters. Sugar would be blended in next, and then egg yolks.

The recipe also allowed the cook leeway in the choice of sugars: white or brown or a combination of both. Pamela had made the cakes with both sugars in various proportions but liked the result best with half of each. Thus she filled a two-cup measure with white sugar and another with brown sugar (packed down, like the recipe said) and set them nearby.

She added the brown sugar, a little at a time, to the butter in the pale green bowl, mixing as she went. She followed with the white sugar. When the butter and the sugars had been blended smooth, she tipped the small bowl with the yolks over the large bowl and let one yolk slip out. The beaters captured it and spun orange streaks through the pale butter-sugar mixture. She tipped another yolk, and then another, and soon the small bowl was empty.

By this time it had been an hour since the poppy seeds were set to soaking in their warm milk bath. Pamela set the mixer aside for a moment and picked up the saucepan. Using a rubber spatula to capture every last one, Pamela coaxed the seeds, which now had absorbed much of the milk, into the pale green bowl, along with the remaining milk. She dribbled two teaspoons of vanilla over the dark pile of damp seeds and set to work again with the mixer.

When the seeds and vanilla had been thoroughly blended with the butter-sugar-egg-yolk mixture, and the whole now had a soupy consistency, she added the dry ingredients a half cup at a time, and beat the batter smooth. Then with the spatula she scooped the egg whites from their bowl, spread them on top of the batter like a moist white cloud, and gently folded them in.

As she worked, she noticed that something was different. She'd been humming along to one carol after another, but now she wasn't—because the house had become silent and there was nothing to hum to. That was the problem with LPs! She rinsed her hands and wiped them on a dishcloth and a minute later was standing by the stereo in the living room turning the glossy black disk to side two. She returned to the kitchen to the strains of "Good King Wenceslaus."

Filled with a double recipe of batter, the pale green

bowl was too heavy to lift and tilt. Pamela used a giant soup ladle to portion the batter out into the four buttered and floured loaf pans, tipping the bowl at the end to coax out the last dribbles with the spatula. When the four loaf pans had been arranged on the middle shelf of the now-hot oven, Pamela set about cleaning up the inevitable mess that her project had created.

Twenty minutes later, the sounds of Christmas drifting in from the living room were augmented by an appeal to another of the five senses. The distinctive aroma of sugary, buttery things baking had begun to fill the kitchen. Pamela had just closed the dishwasher and was rinsing her hands again when Penny's voice said, "They smell good, Mom."

Pamela turned and studied her daughter's face. What she saw there looked like contrition. "I made four of them," she said. "Some are to give away, so I might make more."

Penny had been standing in the doorway between the kitchen and the entry, but now she crossed to the kitchen table and picked up the Christmas-tree ornament that Pamela had discovered on the kitchen floor. "My mouse," she said. "Why is it in here?"

"Ask Catrina." Pamela smiled. "Or Ginger."

"They put it here?" Penny wrinkled her nose in puzzlement.

"It was on the floor," Pamela said. "I assume it didn't wander in by itself."

"How old was I when I made this?" Penny fingered the creature's long felt tail.

"Second grade, I think." Pamela's gaze shifted from her daughter to the threshold between the kitchen and the back hall. "Uh-oh," she said. "What do we have here?"

Standing in the doorway were Catrina and Ginger, the larger inky-black cat a few (cat-sized) paces ahead of the smaller butterscotch-striped kitten. Catrina edged farther into the room. Her amber eyes flickered back and forth between Pamela and Penny.

"You have been a bad cat," Penny said, squatting before Catrina and displaying the pinecone mouse on an outstretched palm. "Very bad. And you know that."

Catrina stared fixedly at the mouse. She flattened her supple body until her belly was barely an inch from the floor. Lingering off to the side, Ginger imitated her mother.

"You will not do this again." Penny's voice was stern. She shifted her attention a foot to the right and addressed Ginger. "And you neither. Do you understand?" Pamela bit her tongue to keep from laughing, but Ginger flattened her body even further and raised her eyes warily to Penny's face.

Penny stood up. "I'll put this back on the tree," she said and skipped from the room. Cat and kitten relaxed.

"I suppose you're hungry," Pamela observed as they waited uncertainly in the doorway. She fetched a fresh can of cat food from the cupboard, opened it, and spooned a dinner-sized serving for two into a clean bowl. As she refilled their water bowl, they ventured across the floor with an occasional glance upwards, as if wanting to make sure that they were back in the good graces of at least one of their mistresses.

It was time to test the poppy-seed cakes for doneness, by sticking a wooden toothpick into them.

Pamela slipped on an oven mitt, shook a toothpick from the toothpick box, and opened the oven door, squinting at the blast of hot air. She carefully slid out the middle shelf, heavy with its freight of baking goodies, and plunged the toothpick into the closest one. The toothpick came out clean. The tops of all the cakes were rounded and firm and a nice golden brown, but she tested the other three to make sure that different positions on the oven rack hadn't affected the rate of baking. She grasped a potholder in the hand that wasn't wearing the mitt and transferred the loaf pans, one at a time, to the stovetop, from whence the aroma of their baked sweetness filled the little kitchen.

Pamela had wondered if Penny would return to the kitchen after the errand to rehang the pinecone mouse. Perhaps her plan had been to retreat back upstairs and commune with her smartphone until she was summoned to dinner. But suddenly Penny was skipping back through the doorway asking, "What can I do, Mom?"

"Get the kale ready to cook?" Pamela suggested.

Soon Penny was standing at the sink, tearing the frilly dark green leaves into bite-sized pieces and dropping them into the plastic basket of Pamela's salad spinner. At her side, Pamela measured brown rice and water into a saucepan. As she worked, she mulled over the conversation she wanted to have. When she felt she was ready, she said, "I trust you to do the sensible thing, you know."

Penny's hands paused in midair, a whole kale leaf with its exuberant ruffle in one, and the other empty.

"As in not chasing strange men down Arborville Avenue?" she asked without turning her head.

"I was very worried." Pamela addressed the saucepan. "He was wearing the scarf that Bettina gave Millicent Farthingale right before Millicent Farthingale was murdered."

"That's why I chased him," Penny said. "It was a clue. But he turned out to be very nice."

"And very cute." Pamela felt her lips tighten in a disapproving way. Was she upset that her daughter had been so obviously *attracted* to an attractive man? Penny was a young woman, after all. Pamela made an effort to relax her lips. She turned to her daughter and smiled. "So I expect you to be sensible. I know I can trust you."

Nordlings had kept in touch with Pamela and Penny ever since Michael's death. While they were in Timberley, they planned to stop at the fancy Timberley yarn shop so Penny could choose the yarn for the sweater Pamela was going to make her.

Catrina had waited patiently in the hall while Pamela detoured into her office. When she emerged, the cat scurried toward the stairs, anticipating the morning breakfast ritual. Ginger was nowhere in sight, nor was there any sign of Penny—evidently both were still dozing in Penny's bed. But Pamela and Catrina proceeded to the kitchen, where Pamela spooned a small serving of cat food into a clean bowl and set water boiling for coffee. While the water boiled, she darted out into the cold to collect the *Register*.

Back inside, she slid the newspaper from its plastic sleeve and spread it out on the table. A quick search of the first section and then the Local section turned up no articles about the murder case. But Bettina often met with Detective Clayborn on Monday mornings and Pamela hoped she might have something to report when she arrived.

The kettle began to whistle and Pamela put the newspaper aside and hastily ground the beans for coffee. While the boiling water was dripping through the freshly ground beans and a slice of whole-grain bread was toasting, Penny arrived with Ginger at her heels. Soon mother and daughter were sitting at the table sharing breakfast while Ginger took delicate bites from the kitten-sized serving of cat food Pamela had added to the communal bowl.

* * *

Chapter Fourteen

Pamela's boss had been busy before Pamela even rose from her bed. Now, at eight a.m. on Monday morning, and still in her robe and pajamas, Pamela checked her email to discover a message with ten attachments, already lurking in her inbox. *No need to rush on these—I know it's holiday time*, the message read, *but please evaluate them for publication and get them back to me before next Monday.* Above the message, the titles of the attached documents appeared, each accompanied by a miniature Word icon. Pamela skimmed the list: something about embroidery, something about Etruscans, something about knitting, and many more somethings . . . But she had a week to read them, and today was a day for Christmas errands. Bettina was coming on the outing too, and would be arriving about eleven.

The first stop would be the Arborville post office, where Pamela would mail one of her poppy-seed cakes to her boss at *Fiber Craft*. Then a poppy-seed cake would be delivered to old family friends, the Nordlings, in Timberley. Michael Paterson and Jud Nordling had been friends and collaborators for years, and the have been, and I had to admit I didn't know." Bettina took a sip of her coffee.

"He's got a point," Pamela said. She picked up the spool of red satin ribbon and began to loop ribbon around the second loaf. "Does he know about Coot?"

Bettina nodded. "Pierre told him. Clayborn talked to her. She doesn't have an alibi but he doesn't see why she'd have to kill Millicent if she thinks her DNA will prove her right to a share of her mother's estate."

"He's got a point about that too." Pamela nodded. "And he accepts Pierre's alibi, so I suppose telling him everything we know about his carryings-on with Jeannette Thornton wouldn't have done any good."

She finished her wrapping job with a neat bow. "Those were our three leads," she said, shaking her head mournfully.

"Millicent was a wonderful person." Minus her customary smile, Bettina looked twenty years older. "And her shop was such a boon to local craftspeople."

"I hate to think her murder might just go unsolved." Pamela set the second loaf next to the first one.

"Such a loss." Bettina's voice quivered. "It will be a miracle if Nadine can keep the shop going." She consoled herself with a long sip of coffee.

A cheery voice roused them from their gloom. "We can go any time," Penny said as she bounced around the corner, wearing jeans and the turtleneck Pamela had knit for her when she went off to college. It was fashioned from ombre yarn that shaded from green to indigo to violet and back again, and her pretty face looked all the prettier, framed by the sweater's high-rising neck and her dark curls.

"I'll use one of those boxes you can buy at the post office to send this off to my boss," Pamela said, picking up one of the wrapped loaves. "And the other will be delivered to the Nordlings in person."

The visit to the Nordlings began with a festive holiday brunch and ended with hugs all around and good wishes to Penny for her coming semester at college. At the yarn shop, Penny picked out a blend of silk and merino wool in a delicate shade of lilac. The gift project was to be a loose tunic with flowing sleeves, worked in a complicated stitch that looked like lace. Pamela thought it seemed an old-fashioned style for a modern young woman, but she was looking forward to the challenge of trying a stitch unlike any she had done before.

"The craft shop is right here," Bettina said as they stepped out onto the sidewalk. "Let's stop in and see how Nadine is doing on her own."

"I'll take a walk down the block," Penny said. "There's a consignment shop that has designer things in Timberley. Laine and Sybil told me about it."

Nadine was not doing well. That was clear as soon as they entered the shop. The tiny woman was cowering in the shop's farthest corner, peeking out from behind a huge construction seemingly formed from driftwood. "Oh," she murmured in her tiny voice, blinking rapidly. "It's you." She edged around the jagged chunks of driftwood. "When I saw the door open, I wasn't sure . . ."

"Well, you poor thing!" Bettina bustled across the shop, narrowly missing a display of art pottery. "Here all on your own like this." She turned briefly to give Pamela a rueful smile then pulled Nadine into a hug.

"That man was here again," Nadine said. "He said he was here last Monday, so now I know who it was that got Millicent so upset." Bettina loosened the hug but Nadine clung to her, like a tiny colorless sparrow nearly lost in Bettina's bright orange plumage.

Nadine went on. "He was waiting outside when I came to open the shop. He said now that Millicent is dead he wondered if I'd be interested in carrying his work." Bettina made eye contact with Pamela and her own eyes widened.

Blinking frantically, Nadine clung even tighter to Bettina. "I was horrified," she said, her voice squeaky. "I . . . I called him a *ghoul* and he got really angry and I told him I'd phone the police if he didn't leave that instant."

"Did he?" Pamela and Bettina asked in unison.

Nadine nodded. "He said he had to go anyway. He had another engagement."

Bettina's eyes grew even wider and she let go of Nadine, nearly pushing her away. "And you didn't think to find out more about him when you had the chance?" she asked, her pitch rising. Nadine criss-crossed her arms over her meager breast and lowered her chin as if she was trying to shrink even smaller.

Pamela tried to keep her tone soothing. "Did he say anything else, anything at all that might make it possible to track him down? He could be the person who killed Millicent."

"Oh, dear." Nadine raised a slender-fingered hand to her mouth. "Yes, you're right. I should . . ." Her voice trailed off and she began to blink. "All I know is Millicent called him the tentacle man. The Haversack tentacle man. And something about colleges, like Wendelstaff? Or Collages? Or something . . ."

* * *

Penny was standing by the car when they came out. She flourished a small bag.

"Good luck at the consignment shop?" Pamela asked, feeling cheerful again.

"Cat toys," Penny said with a grin. "There's a pet shop a few doors down. Maybe they'll leave the tree alone if they have toys of their own."

Bettina had her gloves off and her phone in hand before she even climbed into the passenger seat. Pamela looked at her curiously. Bettina wasn't one of those people who couldn't go ten minutes without communing with her mobile device.

"You might as well start driving," Bettina said in answer to the unspoken question. "Arborville and Haversack are both in the same direction."

As Pamela maneuvered her car out of the parking space and turned right and right again to head south, Bettina's busy fingers danced about on the tiny keyboard. "College," she murmured to herself. "Haversack college . . . craft . . . artist . . . collage . . . tentacle . . . Haversack collage . . ."

"What's she doing?" Penny asked from the back seat.

"Someone wanted Millicent to carry his work at the shop," Pamela said, "and he got angry when she refused."

"Tentacles!" Bettina shouted. Pamela gave a start, her hands twitched on the steering wheel, and the car swerved. She was grateful that they had left the traffic of Timberley's commercial district behind and were on an unbusy section of County Road.

"Tentacles?" Penny spoke up again. "I can see why she wasn't interested in him."

"His name is Geoff Grimm," Bettina explained.

"This has to be the guy. Here's what his website says: 'Horror movies and comic books inspire Geoff's fantastical monsters, and his own vision elaborates them into a world that wraps you in tentacles of wonder. Work is available for purchase in Geoff's studio/gallery, open Monday through Friday from noon to five.'"

Pamela laughed. "Sounds intense."

"He's got some samples of his work up on his site." Bettina held out her phone.

"I'm driving," Pamela said. "But anyway we'll see them in person soon enough."

"I thought you'd say that." Bettina turned to her friend with a satisfied smile. Then she consulted her phone again and read off a Haversack address.

From the back seat, Penny spoke up. "I'll look at them," she said. Bettina passed the phone to her. The next sound they heard was "Ugh!"

Geoff Grimm's studio/gallery was on a side street off what the residents of Haversack still called "downtown," though its heyday had passed long ago when the first mall opened in the county. Shopping and dining possibilities now consisted mostly of pawnshops, discount stores, and restaurants with takeout counters and a few mismatched chairs and tables. A half-hearted attempt had been made to celebrate the season by garlanding the lampposts in tarnished tinsel.

Pamela poked along for a few blocks, maneuvering around double-parked cars and erratic pedestrians until Bettina said, "Turn here." Then, "It's just a few doors down. Grab this parking space." A meter had to be fed, then they walked past a storefront church and a shop whose window displayed a collection of dusty crystals. A sign offered psychic readings. The front window of Geoff Grimm's studio/gallery was painted black.

Just past the window was a faded wooden door with a hand-lettered sign that read GEOFF GRIMM GALLERY ENTER AT YOUR OWN RISK. For all her eagerness to follow up on the lead Nadine had given them, Bettina hung back when it came time to reach for the door handle. So it was Pamela who entered first.

"Greetings, earthlings," a deep voice intoned. "You have entered the realm of Geoff Grimm." The words came from a skinny man sitting on a tall stool behind a drawing board, evidently at work on some kind of project. His eyes were large and dark. They seemed all the larger in that his skin was pale and his face so bony it was almost skeletal. His hair was jet black and fell in oily strands to his shoulders.

What to say? They hadn't discussed that. Obviously *Did you kill Millicent Farthingale?* wouldn't be a good opening gambit. It was Penny who came to the rescue. She stepped boldly across the floor and bent toward the project on the drawing board. "It's a collage," she said. "Your website mentions that as a medium you work in."

"Why, yes." His thin lips stretched into something like a smile. "It's out of fashion now. But I've never been fashionable . . . so why not?" He turned to Penny. "Are you interested in art?"

Penny nodded. "I sketch and paint a bit, and I took art history last semester. I'm home from college for Christmas, and I saw your website . . ." She bent closer. "You're using newspaper," she said, "just like the Dadaists."

Pamela and Bettina had been creeping closer as this conversation unfolded. With one final step, Pamela reached her daughter's side. What she saw laid out on the drawing board made her shudder and suppress a gasp. Bettina noticed the shudder and edged closer.

Geoff Grimm was indeed using newspaper for his collage creation. In fact he was using the article that had appeared in the *Register* the day after Millicent's murder, complete with the headline: "Timberley Woman Found Dead in Arborville Nature Preserve."

Trying to sound calm, Pamela said, "Millicent Farthingale owned the craft shop in Timberley. Is there some particular reason you're using this article for your project?"

Geoff Grimm sat up straighter and focused his large, dark eyes on Pamela, then on Bettina, then on Penny. "You would understand," he said to Penny, and then concentrated his gaze once more on Pamela. "It's *art*," he intoned. "It's not *life*. In my *life*, Millicent Farthingale rejected me. And that rejection *hurt* me. Then *someone* hurt her, and that became the substance of my *art*." His eyes grew larger and darker. "And just this morning I was rejected again, in my *life*. So who knows what form that will take in my *art*? Got it?"

He picked up a long strip of green paper that had been cut in undulations with a taper at one end, like a tentacle. With his other hand he reached for a glue stick. "You're welcome to look around," he said as he stroked the glue stick along the length of the tentacle.

He was obviously very prolific. Paintings and collages covered every inch of the walls, from floor to ceiling.

More were staged along the edges of the floor, leaning against one another in groups of five or six.

The horror movie and comic book influences were obvious. Heroes in futuristic garb confronted giant creatures modeled on octopus or squid. Flailing tentacles wove complicated patterns against skies whose violent orange and purple tints hinted at apocalypse. Some of the heroes fended off the creatures with their bare hands, tying tentacles in knots. Others brandished swords, lopping off tentacles, which quickly sprouted tentacles of their own. But some of the heroes seemed to hail from a less fantastic world. They were dressed in camouflage hunting gear and they had been provided with rifles to vanquish their slithery foes.

"These look quite realistic," Penny observed. Pamela and Bettina had retreated to a spot near the door and were scanning the gallery's offerings from there, but Penny was circling the small room, pausing to crane her neck upwards or stoop to examine a canvas leaning against the wall.

"I sketch from life," Geoff Grimm replied, without looking up from his intense gluing.

"The creatures?" Penny asked. "Do you go to an aquarium?"

"Not the creatures," he said. "I *do* have an imagination, you know." He leaned closer to his project and used a delicate finger to nudge something into place. "The rifles, of course. I sketch the rifles from life. So many little details, and I want to get them right."

Pamela and Bettina looked at each other, and Bettina said, "I think we should go now."

Geoff Grimm looked up from his work and mustered a disconcerting smile. "Thank you for dropping in," he said, addressing his words to Penny. "I'm on Facebook. I have 698 followers. Maybe you'd like to follow me. It's Geoff Grimm@TentacleMan."

Pamela pulled the door open and they stepped out into a gritty wind.

"Merry Christmas," Geoff Grimm called as the door closed behind them.

Chapter Fifteen

Once back in the car, they sat in silence for a few moments. The sidewalk was livelier than it had been. People bundled in nondescript jackets and caps and carrying flat cardboard boxes and white plastic bags emerged from a small restaurant that advertised an "early-bird pizza and soda combo" and scurried off in various directions, squinting against the wind.

Penny was the first to speak. "I thought he was kind of interesting," she observed. "Weird, but interesting."

"He sketches rifles from life," Bettina said. "So he must have access to rifles. Millicent was killed with a rifle."

Pamela nodded. "And that newspaper article! He cut it out and saved it and now he's making it into a collage."

Penny's voice came from the back seat. "It was *art*, Mom. He was making it into art."

Pamela sighed. "He had to explain it *somehow*." Was speaking in italics catching? she asked herself, but she went on. "He didn't expect people who knew Millicent to show up right while he had the article in front of him. So he thought fast—and that's what he came up with."

"He really was making it into a collage," Penny said.

"But why that article? Maybe it *was* art . . . or something . . . but he could be making it to *celebrate* the fact that he murdered her." Pamela twisted the key in the ignition and stepped on the gas. The engine rumbled to life.

"I'm certainly going to tell Clayborn about Geoff Grimm," Bettina said firmly. "First thing tomorrow."

When they got back home, Penny gave Catrina and Ginger their new toys. "After all," she said, "they don't know that Christmas is any different from any other day, so there's no point in waiting." One toy was a weighted ball with a cluster of feathers sprouting from it. The ball rocked from side to side, but always righted itself, with the cluster of feathers sticking straight up. The other was a yellow bird sewn from felt and filled with catnip. Catrina seized the catnip bird immediately. She rolled onto her back in the middle of the living room rug and writhed ecstatically as she used both front paws to rub it against her cheeks and then position it within range of her darting pink tongue.

The next day Pamela was in her office finishing up a note recommending "Seventeen Ways of Looking at a Poppy: Stylized Flowers in Ukrainian Folk Embroidery" for publication. She was thinking about going downstairs for lunch when Penny knocked at the door. Pamela called "Come in," and Penny stepped into the room. She was wearing her usual jeans, topped with the golden-yellow sweater Pamela had knit for her the previous Christmas. It wasn't an unusual outfit, but she had finished it off with a scarf that blended gold, green, and blue in an abstract design, and the chic knot that anchored the scarf in place looked like the result of considerable calculation. She was also wearing earrings, small opal pendants that had been a birthday gift from Bettina.

"You're quite dressed up for a day lazing around at home with your mother," Pamela commented. "Shall we have some lunch?"

Penny smiled and seemed to blush. "I have a date for lunch," she said.

Pamela swiveled her desk chair around to face her daughter. "With Lorie Hopkins? It's great that you're getting to see so much of her."

The blush intensified. "It's a *date*, Mom, as in with a guy."

"Anyone I know?" Pamela asked.

"Okay . . ." Penny looked away, and then she turned back toward Pamela and met her mother's gaze. "It's Aaron," she said.

Pamela forced herself to pause before she spoke. In raising Penny she'd always depended on the content of her words to make her point, not the volume at which they were uttered. At last she said, calmly, she hoped, "We talked about it maybe not being a good idea to cultivate that friendship."

"He *found* the scarf, Mom." Penny did not speak calmly. "He didn't kill Millicent Farthingale."

"But, Penny"—Pamela half rose from her chair and the chair responded with a squeak—"you promised me."

"You said you trusted me to be sensible," Penny said. "In my mind going to lunch with Aaron is sensible."

From downstairs came the sound of the doorbell chiming. Pamela groaned. "You told him where we live?"

"He wanted to pick me up." Penny smiled and blushed again. "He's very gentlemanly." She turned to go out into the hall.

"I'm coming down too." Pamela stood up. "Don't go anywhere where it's just the two of you alone," she said firmly. "And be back by the time it gets dark, if not sooner. And remember, we have Bettina's party tonight."

By the time Pamela reached the bottom of the stairs, Aaron had just stepped over the threshold, bundled up against the cold but minus the red scarf with green stripes. He wasn't too tall, Pamela noted—she'd only ever seen him sitting down or from a distance. But he had the confident manner of someone who knew he was attractive, with his blue eyes and his cheekbones and his expressive mouth. He greeted Pamela pleasantly, calling her "Mrs. Paterson," and then helped Penny on with her jacket.

Pamela stood in the doorway and watched him lead her daughter toward the car he'd been climbing into at the Aardvark Alliance Christmas-tree lot. She watched until the car pulled away from the curb, then she closed the door.

Mothers have to set their daughters free at some point, she told herself. Penny was sensible, and she was probably right about Aaron. He found the scarf and thought it was too nice to abandon to the elements. And no obvious motive for Aaron wanting to kill Millicent had come to light.

At least Penny hadn't accepted a lunch date with Geoff Grimm, Pamela reflected. He'd seemed interested in Penny too, and why wouldn't he be? She was a pretty young woman and she'd acted interested in his art.

This thought caused Pamela's heart to give an extra thump. With her interest in the arts, who knew what kinds of men Penny was meeting in college? Artists and strange bohemian men, and Penny was so sweet and innocent . . . *Oh, dear.* But Pamela had deviled eggs to make for Bettina's party. Cooking would take her mind off things, and soon Penny would be home. It was only a lunch date. Pamela had a quick bite to eat and fed cat and kitten. Then it was time to work on the eggs.

Pamela went first to the cupboard in her laundry room where she kept her collection of deviled-egg platters. Her favorites were the ones whose decoration linked them to the very purpose for which they were designed. She selected one made of glazed green pottery on which a pleased hen surveyed an oversized egg, and another, a cream-colored one, that featured a whole cluster of hens with plumage rendered in a riotous assortment of colors.

She had boiled a dozen eggs the night before. Now they were waiting in a bowl on the counter. She set out salt and pepper, powdered mustard, and tabasco sauce, then opened the refrigerator to retrieve the mayonnaise. As she lifted the jar from the shelf, she realized it felt very light, and when she looked inside she discovered that there was barely a tablespoon left. Penny must have been garnishing her lunchtime sandwiches quite liberally with mayonnaise.

Fortunately she'd decided to start on the deviled eggs early enough that she could fit in a walk to the Co-Op—and a little exercise would be a good idea anyway. But while she was exploring the refrigerator she took out a jar of pimento-stuffed green olives. Green olive halves with their little red pimento centers would be the perfect topping for deviled eggs on a Christmas Eve buffet table.

In the entry Pamela tugged on her heaviest jacket,

wrapped a scarf around her neck, pulled a wooly hat down to her eyebrows, and slipped her hands into her warmest gloves. Canvas grocery bag in hand, she opened the front door and set off for the Co-Op. The wind was strong, and bitter, and brooding, dark gray clouds were massing at the edge of the no-color sky.

Blinking against the wind and with head bowed, she hurried along Arborville Avenue, barely glancing to the right or to the left. Soon she was passing Borough Hall, heading for the big intersection where traffic lights controlled the cars flowing north and south along Arborville Avenue and east and west to and from the George Washington Bridge ramps.

She raised her head to check whether the seconds counting down on the "Walk" signal would allow her to make the green light—or would she be doomed to freeze through a red light before she could plunge across the street and take shelter in the cozy environs of the Co-Op? The Arborville Avenue traffic had paused for a red light, and a green light invited pedestrians to cross, with fifteen seconds remaining. She sped up, blinking through the harsh wind. She was focused on the "Walk" signal and the seconds rapidly expiring, but then something else caught her attention.

A figure stood near the Co-Op, waiting to cross the busy street that ran east and west, a small figure wrapped in a dark coat and with hair hidden by a dark cap. But a bright touch enlivened the somber outfit— a red scarf. The wind was playing with its long tails, each of which sported three green stripes at the ends. Even from across Arborville Avenue, it was clear that one of the stripes was not quite the same shade of green as the others. The figure turned its head to display what was clearly the delicate profile of a young woman.

Pamela reached the corner and started across Arborville Avenue. At that same moment, the young woman in the dark coat and red scarf apparently lost patience with waiting for her light to change. She stepped off the curb, glanced in both directions, and scurried to the other side of the street. By the time Pamela reached the spot where the young woman had been standing, her quarry had darted along the side of the bank that anchored that corner and vanished around the back of the building.

Ignoring for the moment both the cold and her Co-Op errand, Pamela followed the path the young woman had taken, across the street and along the side of the bank. Behind the bank was a small parking lot that opened out into a larger lot used by patrons of Arborville's shops and restaurants. The right-hand edge of the lot backed up against the yards of a few small houses that hadn't yet fallen to developers of commercial property. Ragged fencing with gaps here and there marked that boundary, along with a few dumpsters that served the shops on the east side of Arborville Avenue.

The young woman was nowhere in sight.

As Pamela made her way down one of the Co-Op's narrow aisles toward the section where mayonnaise could be found, she pondered what she had just seen. She also asked herself what she had planned to say if she had caught up with the young woman. Would the young woman have been able to vouch that, yes, Aaron had really *found* the scarf? And then he had given it to her? (And what would that mean in light of his interest in Penny?)

Or was there a more sinister explanation? The young woman had come by the scarf first, in a less benign manner than simply *finding* it. And she and Aaron were now sharing it. (Again, what were the implications of that for Penny?) And Aaron had merely *said* he found it because he didn't want to give away the dark secret of how it actually came into the young woman's possession.

Pamela was so occupied with these thoughts that she almost walked out of the Co-Op without claiming her mayonnaise or the change that the cashier tried to hand her.

Back at her kitchen counter, Pamela reapplied herself to the deviled-egg project. The first steps would be freeing the eggs from their shells, slicing each egg in half, and removing the cooked yolks. She took a medium-sized bowl from the cupboard and set it nearby to receive the yolks. Then she picked up an egg and tapped it on the counter, turning it this way and that, until the whole shell was patterned with fine cracks. She pried at one crack until the shell began to peel away from the glistening hard-cooked white and then pulled the rest of the shell off in a few jagged pieces.

After all twelve eggs were peeled, Pamela cut each in half lengthwise, revealing the golden rounds of the yolks. She held each egg half over the medium-sized bowl and squeezed gently to pop the half yolk out. When the twenty-four yolk halves lay in a heap at the bottom of the bowl, she mashed them with a fork, adding mayonnaise until the mixture became a smooth golden paste. She flavored it with salt, pepper, powdered mustard, and a dash of tabasco sauce, tasting as she went.

After many years of making deviled eggs, she had only recently discovered that the secret to returning the mashed and flavored yolks to the whites in an elegant swirl was to use a cookie press. She had spooned most of the yolk mixture into the cookie press's cylinder and was using a rubber spatula to collect the last bits of it from the bowl when she was interrupted by the doorbell.

It wouldn't be Penny, she told herself as she balanced the spatula across the top of the bowl, because Penny had her own key—though if the date had been only for lunch, Penny should be home soon. But as she reached the entry, she immediately recognized her caller, even through the lace that curtained the oval window in the front door. Bettina's bright pumpkin-colored coat stood out against the bleakness of the wintry afternoon.

"I have a million things to do to get ready for the party"—Bettina started speaking as soon as Pamela opened the door—"though Wilfred, bless his heart, has been as busy as a bee all day." She stepped inside, slipped off her coat, and explained. "I had to let you know about my meeting with Clayborn."

"I'm making the eggs," Pamela said by way of greeting. "Come on back in the kitchen."

Bettina's voice followed her as she led the way. "He wasn't very interested in Geoff Grimm—*at first.*" Bettina stressed the last two words as if foreshadowing a dramatic revelation to come. They reached the kitchen. Pamela stood near the counter but didn't pick up the waiting spatula. "He said tentacles are not a recognized murder weapon outside of horror movies and comic books." Bettina twisted her brightly painted lips into a zigzag shape signaling annoyance and went on. "I said 'I know that, but Geoff Grimm is a very weird and sinister person.'"

Pamela frowned. "Detective Clayborn probably has a point about tentacles. I think octopuses are really rather intelligent and benign creatures. But it wasn't just the tentacles that made Geoff Grimm so sinister. It was the newspaper clipping—and then he said he sketches rifles from life. So he must own at least one rifle. And he admitted he was angry and hurt that Millicent wouldn't carry his creations in her shop."

"I told him about all that," Bettina said, "and that's when he got interested. Of course he wanted to know how we happened to be visiting Geoff Grimm. I explained that we'd dropped by the shop to talk to Nadine and she'd told us the person who got Millicent so upset the morning she was killed had come back. He didn't like it that we tracked Geoff Grimm down on our own. But he said he'd interview Nadine about her conversation with him and follow up if it seemed warranted."

"I should certainly think it *will* seem warranted." Pamela nodded sternly. "But here it is Christmas Eve, and tomorrow's Christmas, and so I suppose nothing will happen. And meanwhile Nadine could be in danger from Tentacle Man."

"I'll call her," Bettina said. "I'll tell her to be sure to lock her doors and windows."

Pamela had been so caught up in what Bettina had to say that she'd forgotten she had something of her own to report. Bettina started for the entry, again invoking the party details that awaited, but Pamela's voice called her back. "I saw the scarf again," she said.

Bettina turned "On that young man? Aaron?"

"No." Pamela shook her head. "Penny went out to lunch with him and he showed up wearing no scarf at all."

Bettina's lips parted and she opened her eyes so wide Pamela could see white around the irises. "You let her go out with him?" Bettina's voice rose through several notes of the scale. "And he came here? So he knows where you live?"

Catrina and Ginger, who had been milling about in the kitchen as Pamela worked on the eggs, scurried toward the back hallway.

"Penny's in college now," Pamela said. "I have to trust her to be sensible." She tried to sound confident, but she could feel her forehead puckering with worry.

"I guess I can't trust *you* to be sensible though." Bettina tightened her lips into a firm line.

"Do you want to hear about the scarf?" Pamela asked. Maybe talking about the most recent sighting of the scarf would help sort out whether the scarf had anything to do with who was guilty of killing Millicent.

Bettina nodded, though it was clear she was still upset. Cat and kitten had ventured back and were prowling around Pamela's feet.

"A young woman was wearing it this time," Pamela said. "An attractive young woman in a dark coat. She was waiting to cross at the intersection where the Co-Op is and I was on the other side of the street, and before I—" Pamela stopped because her eyes had shifted from Bettina's face to the doorway. Penny was standing a little behind Bettina, staring at Pamela with a tragic expression on her face. They hadn't heard her come in, but she had apparently overheard the last minute or two of their conversation.

"How was your date?" Pamela asked, feeling a twinge in her throat at Penny's distress.

Penny seemed to droop. "He's very nice," she said. "At least I thought he was." She turned away and a moment later they heard her feet on the stairs.

"A womanizer, I suppose." Bettina's irritation with Pamela had found a new object. "Playing with Penny's feelings, and sharing his clothes with another girl. And who knows what else? Shameful. But at least Penny came home safe."

"Maybe the scarf is actually the young woman's," Pamela said. "I mean, she came by it somehow and his story about finding it in the nature preserve is just that—a story."

Bettina shrugged and twisted her lips into a zigzag again. "What would that mean?" she asked.

Pamela echoed the shrug. "I don't know," she said.

Bettina turned and stepped toward the entry. Pamela followed her. As Bettina slipped back into the pumpkin-colored coat, she mustered a smile. "Richard Larkin isn't a womanizer," she observed. "So I hope you will wear something attractive to the party tonight—Christmassy and special, and some sparkly earrings, and for heaven's sake put on some makeup for a change."

After she had seen Bettina on her way, Pamela resumed her deviled-egg project. She eased the last dabs of the mashed egg-yolk mixture from the spatula into the cylinder of the cookie press, screwed the top on the cylinder, and pumped the lever to fill each egg-white half with a graceful swirl of golden yellow. She divided the completed eggs between the two deviled-egg platters, nestling each into one of the oval hollows around the rim. Then she spooned twelve olives from the jar of pimento-stuffed olives, cut each in half crosswise, and topped each egg with a festive touch of red and green. When all was complete, she covered each platter with plastic wrap and slid the platters into the refrigerator.

She decided that since she was doing kitchen things, she might as well arrange the poppy-seed cake on a platter for the party. Two of the loaves remained. She'd keep one for holiday nibbling at home, but she freed the other from its foil and set it on a wooden cutting board. She fetched a platter of her wedding china from the cupboard and set it nearby. The butter, whole-wheat flour, and brown sugar in the recipe made the poppy-seed cake very dense and rich, so small portions were in order. She cut careful, narrow slices and then cut each in half, down the middle. Finally, she arranged the slices on the platter in overlapping rows. She covered the platter with plastic wrap but left it out on the counter.

Bettina had invited everyone for seven, and it was only three p.m. Eight articles of the ten that had arrived the previous morning still remained to be read. She had until Sunday night to do them, but Pamela hated to waste time. So she climbed the stairs to her office.

En route, however, she paused outside Penny's bedroom. The door was closed. No sound emerged from within, so Penny wasn't crying. Nor was she on the phone with a friend lamenting the fact that her new romantic interest apparently already had a young woman in his life. On an impulse, Pamela tapped on Penny's door.

A little voice replied, "Come in, Mom."

Penny was lying on her bed. "What will you wear tonight?" Pamela asked brightly.

Penny sat up, a faint smile taking the place of her dour expression. "You sound like Bettina," Penny said. "You didn't really come in here to ask me that, did you?"

"Are you okay?" Pamela studied her daughter's face.

"Yes, I'm okay." Penny sat up straighter and wiggled backwards until she was leaning against her headboard. "It was silly of me to think that one conversation at Hyler's and one lunch date meant anything serious."

"But you like him," Pamela said.

"He's *nice*, Mom." Penny's voice became more assertive. "And he's smart. He goes to Wendelstaff. He's majoring in political science. We ate at a Mexican restaurant in Haversack and he spoke to the waiter in Spanish."

Pamela took a few steps and sat on the edge of the bed. "What was he doing in Arborville on Sunday?" she asked.

"He lives here." Penny nodded. "Arborville isn't that far from Wendelstaff. He lives in one of those houses behind the big parking lot."

"It's just a scarf. It doesn't necessarily mean what we think it means. And anyway, you'll be back at college and he'll be here and . . ." Pamela's voice trailed off.

"I'm going to wear the red dress you bought me for that Christmas party when I was still in high school," Penny said.

"And my black high heels?"

Penny smiled, for real this time. "Do you mind?"

* * *

In her office, Pamela read two more of the *Fiber Craft* submissions. She gave an enthusiastic thumbs-up to "Waste Not, Want Not: Repurposing Fast Fashion," but she hesitated over "Knitting as Meditation." The premise was certainly valid. She often found herself transported to a state of near bliss by the rhythmic motions of her knitting needles and the soothing caress of yarn against her fingers. But the article included very little about knitting and a great deal about meditating. She pondered the form her rejection should take, though she realized that her boss wouldn't necessarily relay it to the author verbatim. Finally she wrote a brief note suggesting that the author might revise and resubmit.

As she clicked on Save to store the file, she heard Penny's voice at the door. Then the doorknob turned and the door opened a crack. "Are we going to eat?" Penny said.

"Meatloaf sandwiches." Pamela clicked on Exit and watched as Word vanished from her computer screen and a display of icons took its place. She swiveled her desk chair around to face the door. "There will be plenty of munchies and goodies at the party, but I don't think we want to go with empty stomachs." She stood up. "And I'm sure the cats are ready for their dinner."

An hour later Pamela stared into the long mirror on the inside of her closet door. An unfamiliar version of herself stared back at her, a tall, slim woman with shoulder-length dark hair wearing a glamorous red tunic. True, the black pants with which the tunic had been paired were quite pedestrian—not nearly as sleek as the tunic deserved. But the tunic itself was stunning, and flattering in the extreme. The rich ruby red made Pamela's skin glow and her eyes seem dark and mysterious. The high neck called attention to the pleasing angles of her face. The long sleeves that nevertheless left her shoulders bare were illogical, of course, but they emphasized her graceful slenderness.

She'd bought the yarn for the tunic at the fancy yarn shop in Timberley the previous June and it had been her knitting project through the summer and fall. The yarn—and the pattern—had been suggested by the yarn shop's owner. Pamela had carried her purchases back to her car in a kind of daze, not sure how she had been persuaded into such an extravagant project. "A charming look for après-ski," the woman had said, as if Pamela moved in circles for which that was a wardrobe category. "Or holiday parties," the woman had added.

Well, she was dressing for a holiday party. Pamela hated waste, and if she wasn't going to wear the tunic now, when would she? But the sparkly earrings Bettina had recommended? And makeup? Simple silver orbs and a bit of lipstick were the best she could do.

Chapter Sixteen

Bettina's porch light beckoned from across Orchard Street, and the festive wreath that had marked the season since the beginning of December. The still, cold air hinted at snow to come. Pamela had considered just tossing on her warmest jacket—after all, the journey would last two or three minutes at most. But in deference to the occasion she had pulled her good coat from the closet. She set off down her front walk with a long-legged stride, but Penny's advance was slowed by the high heels. Pamela lingered at the curb and they crossed the street side by side, caught in the headlights of a car nosing into a spot in front of Bettina's house. Pamela was carrying the two platters of deviled eggs and Penny the platter of poppy-seed cake.

Four people emerged from the car. "We picked up Nell and Harold," Holly Perkins exclaimed as she recognized Pamela.

"Otherwise Nell would have walked," Harold said, and he added, in a good-natured imitation of Nell's voice, "No point in polluting the atmosphere just to go a few blocks."

Harold had opened the trunk and now he stepped around the side of the car bearing two large plastic containers and a white bakery box. "Lots of goodies," he announced.

Nell stood on the sidewalk, wrapped in her ancient gray coat. "Sugar." She sighed. "I suppose it's inevitable at Christmas. I hope there will be some takers for my vegetable plate."

"Mine isn't sugary," Holly protested. "I made little sandwiches."

They proceeded up the driveway, Holly and Nell leading the way.

A burst of Christmas music greeted them as Wilfred pulled the door open wide, looking like the very spirit of the season with his white hair and ruddy cheeks. Behind him, lights on the Frasers' Christmas tree twinkled, reflected by gleaming ornaments. "Welcome, welcome!" Wilfred boomed. "Come in!" He'd traded his everyday coveralls for dark slacks topped by a bright red flannel shirt. He stood aside as six people filed past. Harold was last, with the two plastic containers and the bakery box, and Wilfred quickly took them from his hands. A cheerful fire blazed in the fireplace.

Wilfred and Bettina's sweet-faced daughter-in-law, Maxie, had appeared at his elbow. She reached out a hand for the deviled-egg platters as Bettina hurried in from the dining room. Bettina greeted Pamela with a quick hug and freed Penny of the poppy-seed cake. She was dressed in head-to-toe green, the color of emeralds—a scoop-necked velvety dress that hugged her substantial curves, matching pumps, and necklace and earrings of glittering dark green stones. The effect was striking with her scarlet hair. She started toward the dining room but paused to survey the newly arrived crowd, doing a quick count with a raised finger.

"The Boston children"—her term for her younger

son and his wife, residents of Boston—"are in the kitchen," she said. "So now we're just waiting on Roland and Melanie, and of course Richard Larkin. Karen and Dave are at home with little Lily—but everyone is doing well, and Charlotte called to say she has a school party tonight so she won't be here." Wilfred, Bettina, and Maxie headed for the kitchen with the food.

Pamela unbuttoned her coat. No sooner had she begun to slip it off than Holly caught sight of the ruby-red tunic. "You finished it!" she cried. "Let's see the rest!" Pamela obeyed, feeling her cheeks flush, as Holly grabbed her husband's arm. "Isn't this color just perfect on her?"

Holly and Desmond Perkins were hair stylists who owned a salon in Meadowside, and both looked the part. Desmond was all in black, with a dark stubble beard and clean-shaven head. Holly often enlivened her dark hair with flamboyantly colored streaks. Tonight, red and green streaks and bright red lipstick added a touch of color to a dramatic black dress with an asymmetric neckline, paired with thick-soled black lace-up boots.

"Very flattering," Desmond said with a smile.

Wanting to offer a compliment in return, Pamela commended Holly's seasonally appropriate coiffure.

"Well," Holly said, with a shrug and a laugh, "when your name is Holly, what else can you do?"

Wilfred returned from the kitchen to collect the coats, gathering them into an unwieldy bundle. Then the doorbell chimed, and since Pamela was nearest the door and had her hands free, she opened it. Roland and Melanie DeCamp stood on the porch, Roland in a handsome navy wool coat and a paisley cashmere scarf and Melanie in a lambskin coat with a wide collar that folded back to reveal creamy fur. Melanie carried a flat tray covered in aluminum foil and Roland a white box with a fancy label and a magenta bow.

"Merry Christmas," Pamela said. "Come in!"

They stepped inside, to be greeted again by Wilfred. The door was nearly closed when from the yard came a cheerful voice. "One more," it called. Pamela peered through the gap between door and doorframe to see a tall figure loping up from the street. Then Richard Larkin appeared in the pool of brightness cast by the porch light.

Pamela stepped back and pulled the door open wide. He entered in a burst of chilly air that seemed to energize the space around him. He stood motionless for a second, as if trying to get his bearings. "Pamela," he said at last. "You look—" He stopped.

"Cold?" she suggested, self-conscious about the illogical bare shoulders.

"No. I—" He looked around rather desperately and flourished a paper bag that obviously held a bottle. "Is Wilfred here?"

"Indeed he is," boomed Wilfred's jolly voice from the stairs. The coats, including Roland's and Melanie's, had been borne away to wait out the party on the bed in the guest room. "And I suspect that bag contains the crucial ingredient for my wassail."

Richard pulled a shapely bottle filled with amber liquid from the bag. "Will Courvoisier do?" he asked.

Wilfred hopped down the last few steps and greeted Richard with a hearty handshake. "Perfect!" he said.

Somehow Pamela ended up holding the brandy.

Wilfred helped Richard off with his coat and sped upstairs again. Pamela was trying out various conversational gambits in her mind when Bettina bustled in from the dining room, gave Richard a hug, and bore him away. "You come along too," she called over her shoulder, "and bring that brandy. Everyone is clamoring for wassail."

The holiday music had shifted from medieval carols to a more contemporary sound. At the moment, Elvis was singing about having a blue Christmas, though the words were nearly drowned out by the laughter and chatter emanating from the dining room.

Bettina's dining room table had been pushed to the side to serve as a buffet, and covered with a white damask cloth. Red candles flickered in Bettina's muted silver candleholders with their sleek Scandinavian lines. In the place of honor, surrounded by platters of party food, sat Bettina's huge cut-glass punch bowl, filled with steaming cider speckled with spices and waiting for a dollop of brandy to make the wassail complete.

The cheese ball Bettina had promised, an impressive dome encrusted with chopped nuts, sat to the left of the punch bowl. A few nibbles had already been carved from one side, revealing a tempting cheddary interior streaked with the rich red of port wine. Crackers—square, round, and oval—surrounded the cheese ball, and two cheese paddles waited to assist in the transfer of cheese to crackers.

"I think we'll have enough food," Bettina commented, as Wilfred occupied himself with the wassail, adding a generous amount of brandy to the punch bowl and ladling servings into the punch cups that waited nearby. "There's beer and wine too," he advised. "And soft drinks, of course."

Wilfred Jr. stood in the doorway that led to the kitchen. "I'm your man if you want something besides wassail," he said.

Bettina went on. "The Co-Op did a great job with the cheese ball. And I put both your egg platters out to start—I didn't want people to think there were only twelve eggs and be shy about eating them. She pointed to a plate heaped high with what looked like mini-drumsticks, glazed with a tawny sauce. "These are like buffalo wings," she said. "Maxie made them. She disjoints the wings so they're easier to eat."

"Who brought these yummy-looking onion tarts?" Pamela asked. Next to the mini-drumsticks sat a tray of golden-brown puff-pastry rounds. In the center of each was a glistening tangle of caramelized onion slices.

"Melanie," Bettina said. "And she brought sugar-plums from a fancy candy shop in Timberley."

"And the—what is it—hummus?" Pamela pointed at a bowl containing a substance the color and texture of putty.

Bettina nodded. "The Boston children. Very health conscious."

Nell had just accepted a cup of wassail from Wilfred and edged over to join Pamela and Bettina. "I hope someone eats my vegetables," she said, nodding toward a platter where cucumber spears, carrot sticks, celery, and baby tomatoes were arranged in careful rows.

"I'm sure they will," Bettina assured her. "I can name at least two people who will for sure."

"My goodness!" Nell leaned close to examine another offering. "I haven't seen these in decades." A tray held what looked like a black-and-white checkerboard made out of bread, alternating squares, each speared with a toothpick sporting a cellophane frill.

"Those are my sandwiches." Holly spoke up from over Nell's shoulder. "I found the idea in my 1950s cookbook. People made such amazing things back then. I wish I'd been alive."

"Oh, my dear." Nell turned. "You really don't." She softened the comment with one of her gentle smiles. "Things are so much better now, for young women. For everyone really."

"I can see that," Holly said with a dimply answering smile. "But the food was just so awesome."

As they talked, people had been milling about, arranging their choices from the buffet on the small plates that Bettina had provided and accepting cups of wassail from Wilfred or other drinks from Wilfred Jr.

"Go ahead," Bettina urged. "Nell, Holly, Pamela. Have some food." She stepped toward the middle of the dining room to survey the crowd.

Pamela took a small plate and added an onion tart, a mini-drumstick, one of Holly's little sandwiches, and some carrot sticks. She didn't want to eat her own eggs until everyone had had a chance at them. Wilfred was no longer serving wassail, but a few full cups sat near the bowl. Without an extra hand, eating and drinking at the same time would be impossible, at least if one wanted to remain standing. Deciding to concentrate on eating for a while, Pamela joined Bettina.

Having served themselves food and/or drink, most of the guests had migrated to the living room. Some had solved the problem of not having three hands by perching on the sofa or in one of Bettina's comfortable armchairs and setting plates and drinks on the coffee table. The medieval carols were back, with a sweet rendition of "The Cherry Tree Carol."

Richard Larkin stood off to the side, near the Christmas tree. But Penny had stationed herself near him and they were having a lively conversation. Richard was holding a bottle of beer and Penny a cup of wassail. Pamela was sure the wassail was potent, with the hard cider and brandy. She hoped that was Penny's first and would be her only cup.

The red dress, with its flirty skirt and close-fitting bodice, set off Penny's pretty figure, and the high heels—Pamela's high heels—gave the outfit a more grown-up look than when Penny first wore it to a high-school Christmas party.

Penny *was* grown up. Pamela knew that, though the realization always brought a little pang. Only two more Christmases after this before Penny was out of college and on her own. And she meant to be on her own then. Penny had made that clear. But she'd worked in Manhattan the previous summer, so maybe Manhattan would exert its pull and Penny would end up not too far away.

Satisfied that her guests were provided with food and drink, Bettina filled a plate at the buffet and joined Pamela at the edge of the living room. "Richard Larkin looks handsome tonight, don't you think?" she said, tilting her head and glancing at Pamela from under an eyelid shadowed with a green that matched her dress.

"I really hadn't noticed." Pamela tried to sound offhand. But he did look handsome, in a pair of dark wool slacks and a dark V-neck sweater that revealed a crisp white shirt collar.

Bettina resumed gazing at the crowd. "I wish the

Boston children would mingle more," she said. "It's true they hardly know anyone outside of the family, but they could make an effort."

Bettina and Wilfred's younger son, Warren, and his wife, Greta, stood near the foot of the stairs, making occasional comments to each other. Warren resembled a smaller, thinner Wilfred Jr., but his sandy hair was longer and shaggier—befitting his career as a college professor. Greta was nearly the same height as her husband and was wearing an austere garment that appeared to be made of some undyed natural fiber. Pamela thought it might be hemp. She had recently edited an article for *Fiber Craft* on the burgeoning market for artisanal hemp products.

Everyone else seemed to be mingling just fine. Harold, Wilfred, Desmond, and Roland were standing near the fireplace, Roland looking a bit incongruous as the only man wearing a suit and tie. Snatches of conversation suggested Harold and Wilfred were attempting to interest Desmond and Roland in joining the Arborville historical society. Both were responding with sociable interest.

Nell and Holly were sitting side by side on the sofa, and Maxie had pulled up a low hassock. The three were comparing recipes for homemade granola. Melanie DeCamp was sitting in one of the armchairs and Wilfred Jr. in the other, leaning toward each other and deep in conversation. It was hard to make out what they were talking about, but Wilfred Jr. seemed charmed by Melanie's blond elegance and her ready smiles.

Pamela took a closer look at what Melanie was wearing, then she nudged Bettina and pointed. Roland must have been so eager to have his wife show off to his knitting group the sweater he had knit for her that he presented his Christmas gift a day early. Pamela had been amused at the notion that the ultra-sophisticated Melanie would find a place in her wardrobe for a pink angora sweater. But paired with white silk slacks, caramel-colored shoes, and glittery chandelier earrings it made a pretty holiday ensemble.

Wilfred stepped away from the group he'd been talking to. "We're due for another round of wassail," he declared and headed for the dining room.

"And please refill your plates," Bettina urged, stepping to the side as Wilfred passed by on his way to the kitchen.

Pamela moved aside too, as the sofa and armchair people rose and began to file through the arch that separated the living room from the dining room. Along the way, Holly greeted Penny, and Penny joined the pilgrimage to the buffet, followed by Harold, Roland, and Desmond. Warren and Greta brought up the rear. Richard Larkin lingered near the Christmas tree, until Bettina swooped out to wrap an arm around his waist and lead him through the arch.

A happy hubbub ensued as people once more arranged crackers spread with port-wine cheddar (or hummus) on their plates, along with deviled eggs and caramelized-onion tarts, mini-drumsticks, or sandwiches from Holly's checkerboard creation.

"Have some of the raw vegetables," Nell insisted to anyone who would listen.

"I'm eating them," Greta said. "Lots of them. I appreciate having a choice of something *healthy*." To judge from her plate, besides the raw vegetables she apparently deemed the deviled eggs healthy, and her own hummus, but not much else.

Wilfred had borne the wassail bowl off to the kitchen. Now he appeared in the kitchen doorway, under the sprig of mistletoe, and announced, "Wassail is ready but the bowl is hot. I'm serving from the counter—and I have fresh cups."

Chapter Seventeen

Several people responded to Wilfred's invitation, carrying full plates with them. Pamela followed, setting her empty plate aside and accepting a brimming cup of wassail. When she stepped back into the dining room, she found herself standing next to Richard Larkin. For a few moments, he seemed preoccupied with the decision of what to eat next from the assortment on his plate. Then without choosing anything he leaned toward her.

"You . . . got the tree up okay then?" he asked.

Pamela had just taken a potent sip from her wassail cup, so at first she just nodded. Then she managed a quick, "Yes, yes." He studied her with that serious look he often had. "And your daughters are having a good time in San Francisco?" she added.

That comment provoked a smile. "Penny has heard more from them than I have," he observed. "But, yes, I think they are."

They were distracted by a giggle coming from the doorway that led to the kitchen. Wilfred Jr. had discovered the mistletoe and surprised his wife with a kiss as she emerged bearing a cup of wassail. Then more distraction came in the form of Bettina, who stepped up with Warren and Greta in tow. "I know you know Pamela," she said. "But I don't think you've met our neighbor Richard Larkin."

Pamela mustered her social smile. Richard extended his hand and Warren and Greta each shook it. For some reason, he seemed more comfortable talking to his new acquaintances than to her, so Pamela was happy when Melanie DeCamp appeared at her elbow.

"The sweater turned out beautifully," Pamela said.

Melanie smiled. "He's very proud of it, and he enjoys the knitting group so much." As if making a gesture that had become automatic, she pushed up the sweater's left sleeve and they continued chatting. But the sleeve began to droop again and soon the narrow sheath of pink angora extended nearly to Melanie's carefully manicured fingertips. "It's just the one sleeve," she observed with a little laugh. "The other one is exactly the right length. Isn't it, darling?" she added as Roland strolled up bearing fresh cups of wassail for himself and his wife.

From the kitchen doorway came another giggle, but not from the kisser or kissee this time. Harold had bent down to give Nell a hearty kiss, much to the delight of Holly. Holly held up her cheek for a peck from Harold, and Nell joined Pamela and Melanie. Richard, Warren, and Greta seemed to have run out of conversational topics—Richard had lived briefly in Boston, so that had provided an entrée—and the three now gazed blankly at each other. But ever the perfect guest, Melanie spoke up.

"I understand you have a new baby," she said. "A little girl. How sweet! I love pink!"

Even had her expression mirrored Melanie's encouraging smile, Greta—with her unstylish garment and unstyled hair—would have appeared the very antithesis of Melanie. But Greta furrowed her untended brows and fixed Melanie with a pitying stare.

"We're raising an ungendered *child*," she announced. "Not a *girl*. They will make the decision about gender when they are older."

"Twins?" Melanie said, puzzled. "I thought there was just the one."

The stare became even more pitying and Greta explained. "The English pronoun system does not allow for gender fluidity in the singular."

Roland had been following the conversation with considerable interest. Now he spoke up. "But aren't babies just . . . what they are, usually. I mean, you can kind of tell by looking at . . . looking at . . ."

"Not always." This came from Nell. "People can be one thing on the inside and another on the outside." She offered Greta one of her gentle smiles. "What you're doing sounds fine to me, dear. The world is changing." With the light from the kitchen doorway behind her making her corona of white hair resemble a halo, Nell looked, Pamela realized suddenly, like a superannuated angel. Or maybe I'm just getting a bit tipsy, she said to herself. The wassail really was quite potent.

Roland took a long swallow from his cup of wassail and mustered a smile. Pamela suspected that had this been a regular Knit and Nibble session, he'd have been happy to press his point. He and Nell had certainly clashed on other occasions, since Roland tended toward conservatism in all things. But it was Christmas Eve and he was apparently resolved to be sociable no matter what the provocation.

Pamela realized she hadn't seen Penny for a while

and hoped her daughter wasn't feeling the effects of
the wassail. But just then Penny bounced in from the
living room and began to inspect the dessert offerings
on the buffet.

"Yes!" Bettina clapped her hands and looked around.
"Don't be shy! Everyone! Please have some dessert."

The sweet things occupied the space to the right of
where the wassail bowl had been. Slices of poppy-seed
cake waited on the platter of wedding china. Next to it
was a plate containing small dome-shaped cookies
dusted with powdered sugar.

"Pfeffernuss," Nell explained. "Harold drove all the
way up to the German bakery in Kringlekamack for
them. He has to have his sweet goodies at Christmastime."

"So do I," Melanie said, reaching for one, though
her sleek and well-toned body suggested such treats
were carefully rationed.

"And who brought these cute yummies?" Holly gazed
at a platter of gingerbread men. Their chubby bodies,
with outstretched arms and legs, were an appealing
shade of gingery brown, and their eyes, smiles, and
buttons had been provided by artful touches of white
icing.

"They're Wilfred's handiwork," Bettina said.

Holly turned her gaze to Wilfred, who hovered at
the edge of the crowd that had once again gathered
at the buffet. The candles had burned down considerably, but they still cast a flattering light that accented
Holly's bright eyes and the perfect teeth that her dim-
pled smile revealed. "You are amazing," Holly crooned.
"If I catch you under the mistletoe, I'll give you a
Christmas kiss."

"I can share him!" Bettina laughed good-naturedly.

She went on, "The fruit tray is my contribution—well, the Co-Op's really. And these adorable sugarplums are from Melanie."

The fruit tray added a lively touch of color to the dessert assortment. Pineapple chunks, kiwi slices, orange segments, and slivers of honeydew formed undulating rows, interspersed with grapes—delicate green, dusky rose, and deep purple. Ruby-red pomegranate seeds provided a bright accent, and long toothpicks for spearing sat ready to hand. The sugarplums were arranged in a tempting cluster, chocolate truffles embellished with flourishes of red and green icing and furnished with lollipop sticks striped like candy canes.

More small plates waited at this end of the buffet, and soon people were busily browsing among the offerings. Some then sought out the sofa and armchairs to focus on their goodies. Others stood around in the dining room, nibbling on poppy-seed cake, pineapple chunks, and pfeffernuss—with the powdered-sugar smudges on fingers and mouths to show for it—or decapitating gingerbread men.

Penny, Holly, and Maxie had found an out-of-the-way spot at the edge of the arch that separated the dining room from the living room and were discussing something that provoked gales of laughter. Warren Fraser had latched onto his brother for a chat.

Still others had drifted back into the kitchen, perhaps in search of the last few ladles of wassail. But soon it became apparent that another beverage was on offer. The luxurious aroma of brewing coffee began to drift through the kitchen doorway, all the more tempting to Pamela because of the silky sweetness that lingered from the sugarplum she had just consumed.

It occurred to Pamela that she could help with cups and cream and sugar, and coffee would be a welcome antidote to the unfamiliar condition of being slightly tipsy. Besides, the people who remained in the dining room at this point—Nell, Harold, and Greta—were talking quite seriously about something political and she didn't want to interrupt them by joining their group. She hadn't taken a plate, but had contented herself with a gingerbread man and a sugarplum, so her hands were free as she turned toward the kitchen doorway.

A cheerful buzz came from within, Bettina's voice rising above the rest to say, "If you're going out there, please let people know about the coffee."

The next second, Richard Larkin appeared in the doorway. He caught sight of Pamela and paused, his eyes widening slightly. He didn't retreat or advance, but ducked his head and seemed to lean in her direction. Bright voices sang in harmony about three kings, but a rushing sound in her head drowned out the jaunty carol.

The sprig of mistletoe dangled above his blond head. Pamela took a step forward and started to lift her face toward his. He ducked farther, but then he backed up and stood aside. "Excuse me," he said. "I almost ran right into you."

Pamela closed her eyes. Her cheeks were bright red, she was sure, to judge by the warmth that had suddenly suffused them. "Y-yes," she stuttered. "Or, no . . . I . . . it's okay. Really."

She fled toward the kitchen counter where Bettina was setting out cups and saucers from her sage-green pottery set. Grateful for the diversion, she listened to Bettina lament that she didn't have enough sage-green cups for everyone who might want coffee.

"Lots of people don't like caffeine at night," Pamela murmured comfortingly. She half heard Bettina ponder whether the tea drinkers could make do with cups and saucers from a different set, as she recalled that Richard Larkin always ducked when he went through doorways, because he was so tall.

The party venue shifted to the kitchen now, as people accepted cups of coffee and helped themselves to cream, sugar, spoons, and napkins. Some indeed demurred, and Bettina's sage-green cups and saucers sufficed for everyone who wanted caffeine. Bettina's Dutch Colonial house was the oldest house on the street, but its kitchen had been updated and enlarged, and it featured a modern cooking area separated by a high counter from a spacious eating area furnished with a well-scrubbed pine table and four chairs. Sliding-glass doors opened out to a patio.

Now a few people, Nell among them, stood at the counter chatting with Wilfred, who had prepared a cup of tea specially for her. Richard Larkin, Harold, and Wilfred Jr. had stationed themselves along the doors that led out to the patio. Melanie, Holly, Penny, and Maxie took their coffee to the pine table. Pamela was hovering near Bettina, hoping that her cheeks would soon return to their normal color.

"It's snowing," Harold announced suddenly. From where Pamela stood, the view through the sliding glass doors was of nothing but deepest night. But Penny jumped up from the table and joined the men.

"It is," she cried. "A lot has piled up already."

Desmond joined Holly at the table, laying gentle hands on his wife's shoulders. "Shall we think about heading up the hill?" he asked. "The roads might be getting slippery."

"I'm ready to call it a night." Harold turned from the view of the yard and took a few steps toward the table.

"It's been a lovely party," Nell said, a gentle smile crinkling the skin around her faded blue eyes. "Bettina, Wilfred, and—" She paused to survey the room. "And everyone, Merry Christmas!"

Over the next few minutes, coffee cups were drained and lined up on the counter. Wilfred disappeared upstairs and returned with a giant armful of coats and scarves. Wilfred Jr. hurried outside and, as the first departures commenced, it appeared he had shoveled a narrow path from the porch to the driveway and down the driveway to the street. From the front door, the falling snow was a dramatic sight, with the whirling flakes caught in the cone of light cast by the streetlamp, and the ground, all white, seeming to glow.

"Does anyone need to borrow boots?" Bettina asked, but overlapping voices answered with versions of "We'll be okay," "We don't have to go far," and "We can dry our shoes when we get home." Roland, however, insisted on saving Melanie's shoes by carrying her to where his Porsche was parked. As people bade their good-nights, Pamela hung back, mortified at the thought that after her obvious bid for a kiss, Richard Larkin might think she was timing her departure so she could walk with him. Penny stood nearby, bundled in her coat and scarf and ready to brave the snow.

When everyone but Pamela and Penny—and Warren and Greta, who were staying in the guest bedroom— had been seen off, Bettina turned to Pamela with a happy sigh. "It went very well, don't you think?"

"It was perfect," Pamela said, hugging her friend. "Merry Christmas!"

She opened the front door and peered out. There was no sign of Richard Larkin, so she pulled on her own coat, took Penny's hand, and they set out into the scattering swirl of flakes. At the end of the path that Wilfred Jr. had shoveled, they reached a street covered with a few inches of snow.

"You're sure you don't want boots?" Bettina called from the doorway.

"We'll be okay," Pamela called back. "We don't have to go far."

Pamela wasn't concerned for her own shoes, nor for the high heels that Penny had borrowed. So they set off, holding on to each other and taking the longest steps they could manage, blinking against the flakes that dusted their faces with icy pinpricks. The snowfall was deep enough that a swoosh of snow instantly blanketed Pamela's instep. By the time she and Penny reached their own front walk, Pamela's feet felt numb—and also wet, from the dribbles of snow melt that had seeped into her shoes.

"I can't stand it, Mom," Penny said, darting ahead. "My feet are freezing."

As Pamela watched Penny negotiate the snowy steps leading to the front porch, she heard a voice from behind her say, "Pamela!" The voice was familiar—a nice voice, as she had noted the first time she heard it a little over a year ago. She turned to find Richard Larkin standing in the pool of light cast by the street-lamp, snowflakes dancing around his head and a snow shovel in his hands.

"I'm getting a head start on my sidewalk," he said, glancing down at her snow-covered feet. After a moment he raised his head and words tumbled out. "I thought you were already home. I looked for you . . . before I left Bettina's."

"I . . . I was helping Bettina." Pamela felt her cheeks flush again, though the sudden burst of warmth in that part of her body did nothing for the state of her feet.

"Well, you're . . ." Richard looked at the ground again. His gaze wandered from the patch of snow he stood on—in sturdy boots, Pamela noticed— back to the icy mounds that covered the toes of her shoes and her unprotected insteps. "You're freezing. I won't keep you. I just . . . I didn't get to tell you Merry Christmas."

"Merry Christmas to you," Pamela said, and she turned away and headed up her front walk.

Chapter Eighteen

It was tempting, especially at holidays, to imagine a past in which joy had been unalloyed. But Pamela knew she'd been happy about some things, worried about others then too, just like now.

Yes, in the past she would have awakened on Christmas morning next to her beloved husband. They would have laughed to each other to realize that it was not yet light but their excited daughter was already hopping down the stairs, eager to see what Santa had brought. Today she awoke to find a cat perched on her chest, busily kneading the bedclothes and watching her with amber eyes. Clear light was streaming through the white eyelet curtains at the windows and a glance at the clock told her that it was past eight a.m. It had been a few years since the excitement of Christmas cost Penny any sleep.

Pamela sat up, stretched, swiveled around, and lowered her feet to the rag rug at her bedside. She pulled on her fleecy robe and slid her feet into her furry slippers. Catrina preceded her into the hall and scurried down the stairs, though in anticipation of breakfast rather than the discovery of Christmas bounty. Pamela glanced at Penny's closed door and listened. No plaintive meows came from behind it. Apparently Ginger had chosen to sleep late as well. Pamela followed Catrina to the kitchen.

The first order of business was to scoop a breakfast-sized serving of cat food into a fresh bowl for Catrina. As Catrina took delicate bites and her tail expressed her pleasure by twitching this way and that, Pamela measured water into the kettle for coffee. Then she headed for the entry. The fleece robe would be protection enough for a quick dash down the front walk for the newspaper, but recalling the frozen feet of the previous night, she opened the closet to retrieve the boots she wore for all but the dressiest winter occasions and traded the furry slippers for them.

When she opened the front door, however, she discovered that the boots would not have been necessary. Her front walk had been shoveled, as well as the stretch of sidewalk that passed in front of her house. In addition, the steps leading up to her porch and even the porch itself had been cleared of snow.

Such nice friends, Pamela mused to herself as she studied the scene—the unbroken sweep of white, almost blindingly so even in the cold light of a winter sun. Wilfred or Wilfred Jr. must have been up and busily shoveling while she was still deeply, deeply asleep.

The snow must have continued quite late. At least four inches had fallen, to judge by the height of the snowy cliffs at the edges of the path carved by the shoveler.

The kettle was whistling when Pamela returned to the kitchen carrying the newspaper. She quickly slipped a paper filter into the plastic cone that balanced atop the carafe, added freshly ground coffee, and poured the boiling water through. As the smell of brewing coffee filled the little kitchen, she slid the newspaper from its chilly plastic sleeve and laid it out on the table. She was relieved to see that nothing had happened in the Millicent Farthingale murder case dramatic enough to make it onto the front page, so she could enjoy undisturbed the many pleasures that the day promised.

The arrival of Ginger, who proceeded directly to the now-empty cat-food bowl, suggested that Penny was awake and on the move too. Pamela added a few small scoops of cat food to the bowl and straightened up to find Penny standing in the doorway.

"Toast and coffee?" Pamela asked. "And then the presents?"

Penny nodded. "I put the Christmas-tree lights on," she said. "But I forgot the music."

She darted back through the doorway, and in a moment Pamela heard the familiar strains of "The Little Drummer Boy."

Penny busied herself at the counter, slipping two slices of whole-grain bread into the toaster as Pamela poured two cups of coffee. Penny added sugar and a dollop of cream to hers. Soon mother and daughter faced each other across the table, nibbling on buttered toast, sipping coffee, and passing sections of the *Register* back and forth.

The LP had ended by the time they moved to the living room. Penny turned it over, and as a jaunty chorus sang about Good King Wenceslaus, she plucked a large, festively wrapped box from under the tree and presented it to Pamela. "You have to open this first," she said, joining her mother on the sofa.

Pamela delicately untied the ribbon, which would be saved and reused. (As Wilfred would say: waste not, want not.) Then she unfolded the paper to reveal a box from the fanciest store at the mall. She lifted the lid to find tissue paper, expertly deployed to swathe . . . something very grand. She folded back the enveloping tissue to reveal a handbag—made of glowing, supple leather in a dusky shade of blue. She picked it up with a sigh of pleasure. It was simple and elegant, something she'd definitely use, a nice size and with a long strap that could go over the shoulder to leave hands free.

"It's beautiful!" she exclaimed.

"It was time, Mom," Penny said with a laugh. "That one you've been using saw its better days long ago."

"I suppose so." Pamela echoed her laugh. "Have you been conspiring with Bettina to improve my wardrobe?"

Penny shrugged and laughed again. "Not exactly."

"Now you open something," Pamela suggested. "The little one with the partridge-in-the-pear-tree wrapping is for you."

Penny slipped off the ribbon and peeled away the paper. Under the paper was a small wooden box incised with ornate designs.

"I found it at a tag sale," Pamela said. "But there's something inside."

Penny tipped back the hinged cover, pushed aside a twist of tissue, and lifted out a necklace made of bold glass beads, each patterned like an image seen in a kaleidoscope.

"The beads are Venetian," Pamela said. "Very old. *Fiber Craft* was one of the sponsors for a craft show in the city, and one of the exhibitors was a woman who collects beads from anywhere and everywhere and makes them into jewelry."

"I love it!" Penny held it up to the light, then clasped it around her neck. Framed by the collar of her fleecy robe, it glowed against her skin.

Ginger had discovered the tangle of red ribbon that Penny had cast aside and was stalking it as if it was particularly fascinating prey. She pounced, tossed it in the air, and resumed stalking, her small tail lashing frantically to and fro.

More gifts were unwrapped, both thoughtful and amusing. Among them were gold and pearl earrings for Penny from the Paterson grandparents, along with a generous check. The two wide, flat boxes from Pamela's parents turned out, indeed, to be pajamas—flannel, with a print of kittens for Pamela and snowmen for Penny. But the smaller box for Penny contained an antique silver bracelet, along with a note that it had belonged to Penny's great-grandmother. And Pamela had been correct in her suspicion that the heavy package from her parents was a book. She peeled back the wrapping to find a lavishly illustrated volume dealing with vintage kitchen equipment.

Soon just one package remained unopened—aside from the gifts for Bettina and Wilfred that would be delivered that evening. It was wide and flat too, and the tag read "To Mom."

"More pajamas?" Pamela asked, as Penny delivered the package to Pamela's lap.

Penny smiled. "You'll see."

But the box was heavier than pajamas would be. Pamela untied the ribbon, freed the box from its paper, and lifted the lid. Inside, cushioned by crinkled tissue, was a plate with twelve oval-shaped depressions around the rim—a deviled-egg platter. But in place of the usual chicken-themed decoration, this one sported pink roses. Garlands of them embellished its scalloped edge, along with a delicate tracing of gold, and a huge bouquet of them filled its center.

"It's not quite your wedding china," Penny said, "but you didn't have any with flowers. I found it at a thrift store near the campus."

"I love it!" Pamela lifted it from the box. "It's perfect!" Across the room, Catrina and Ginger were tussling over the red ribbon.

Pamela and Penny sorted through the discarded wrappings, saving what could be saved and putting the rest in the paper-recycling basket. They neatly staged the opened gifts under the tree and they fetched one of Pamela's canvas bags to stow the gifts to be delivered that evening. Soon they'd restored the room to its previous state of neatness. Penny put another LP on the turntable and with a surge of choral voices "I Saw Three Ships Come Sailing In" filled the room. Mother and daughter stood for a moment admiring the tree, with its lights and gleaming ornaments bright against bristly dark green boughs.

After a lunch of cheese omelets, Penny retreated to her room to commune with friends via her smartphone. Pamela settled onto the sofa with her new knitting project—the lilac tunic with flowing sleeves that was to be one of Penny's Christmas gifts, though it certainly wouldn't be completed before Penny left to go back to school. The pattern created an unusual lacy effect and required careful counting of stitches. Pamela worked enough rows to see the delicate shell shapes and eyelets taking form, then set her knitting aside and invited Penny to go for a walk.

* * *

They returned, invigorated, just as the sun was setting. At the west end of Orchard Street it blazed red-orange through the crisscrossing tree branches and it stained the glazed surface of the snow the palest pink.

The invitation to Bettina's was for five p.m., so it was time to think about getting dressed. The black-and-white checked wool suit from the estate sale had turned out to fit Penny just right, even the skirt, and she'd gotten the stain out of the front. But the skirt was too long to be chic and too short to be purposely long, and the jacket—with its nipped-in waist and rickrack-trimmed black velvet collar and cuffs—was the really striking part of the suit anyway.

Pamela promised to help her hem the skirt up before she went back to college—though what college occasion would call for the suit Penny wasn't sure. For Bettina's Christmas dinner, she paired the jacket with black pants.

And what would Pamela wear? She stood in front of her closet studying the possibilities. The ruby-red tunic was definitely Christmassy, but it had already made an appearance. She finally settled on the Icelandic-style sweater with the white snowflake pattern. The natural brown wool (from Icelandic sheep!) wasn't the most festive color, but the snowflakes were seasonal. The sweater looked best with jeans and boots, but for this occasion she imagined her good black pants and black shoes would elicit less of a scolding from Bettina.

Down in the kitchen, Catrina had rediscovered the catnip-filled bird that had excited her so much when it was first introduced. Ginger was sitting in the corner where food was accustomed to appear. Even the smell of the dinner that Pamela scooped into the communal bowl didn't distract Catrina from her catnip session, but content that a generous portion of cat food would remain even after Ginger ate her fill, Pamela and Penny slipped on their coats and set off across the street. Penny bore the canvas bag with the gifts. They'd added small treats for all three of the Fraser grandchildren.

Chapter Nineteen

As Bettina's front door swung back they were greeted by the strains of "God Rest You Merry, Gentlemen" and a spirited greeting from Wilfred. He'd swapped the red flannel shirt of the previous night for a shirt of red-and-green plaid but looked no less festive. His grandsons, Willy and Freddy, bobbed against his legs, curious to study the new arrivals.

"You know Pamela and Penny," Wilfred assured them, bending down to the level of the littlest one and offering an encouraging pat on the head.

No sooner were Pamela and Penny ushered inside and freed of their coats than Bettina appeared in the arch that separated the living room from the dining room. She was wearing bright red tonight—a jersey wrap-dress not exactly the same color as her hair, and red suede pumps. She'd tamed the look a bit by accessorizing it with pearls, a three-strand pearl necklace and earrings with dangling pearl teardrops.

"Welcome!" she exclaimed with a broad red-lipsticked smile.

"Santa's here!" Penny offered the gift-filled canvas bag.

"We have things for you too," Bettina said. "Shall we open gifts after dinner?"

"I'll put them under the tree." Penny swiveled around and busied herself arranging the packages she and Pamela had brought among the ones that already waited beneath the branches.

As Penny worked, Bettina continued talking. "The Boston children are upstairs. They'll be down in a while, but Morgan was getting fussy. A house full of people is a lot of excitement for somebody who's not even one yet. Woofus is hiding in the basement. And the kittens are in the utility room. The allergy, you know, and I thought the little boys would be sad if they could see Midnight but couldn't play with him."

Penny had arranged the presents to her satisfaction and now joined them. "And don't you look chic!" Bettina clasped her hands before her. Her nails were the same bright red as her dress and lipstick.

"It's the suit—part of it anyway—from the estate sale," Penny said.

"Come on back here." Bettina reached out both arms and escorted Pamela and Penny to the kitchen, where tantalizing aromas hinted at the splendid meal to come. The Fraser grandsons were crouched near the pine table eating crackers dabbed with cheese and playing with small wheeled objects. Wilfred was standing at the high counter between the cooking area and the eating area. A cluster of gleaming wineglasses sat before him, as well as open bottles of red and white wine. Wilfred Jr., festive in a red-and-green plaid shirt of his own, stood a few paces away with his wife.

Seeing father and son reminded Pamela that she had thanks to convey. "I was so surprised to find my walk shoveled when I opened the front door this morning," she said, "and I suspect the good deed was done by one of you."

Wilfred and Wilfred Jr. looked at each other, the younger face mirroring the older face's puzzlement.

"I can't take credit," Wilfred said, and his son echoed the denial.

Bettina had been lingering near the pine table, where the remains of the previous night's cheese ball and a fresh supply of crackers had been set out to accompany the wine. Now she looked up from the cracker she was spreading with cheese.

"I bet I know who did it," she offered in a teasing lilt.

Pamela suddenly realized that she knew too. Trying to keep her expression neutral, she turned toward Bettina. "Go ahead," she murmured. "Say it."

"Your neighbor to the east." Bettina giggled. "He liked the red tunic. I could tell by the way he was looking at you all night."

"Bettina . . . please," Pamela groaned. She turned back toward Wilfred. "Yes," she said, though he hadn't asked. "I'd like a glass of red wine."

Penny took a glass of red wine too and joined Bettina at the pine table. Warren and Greta appeared, announcing that Morgan had fallen asleep—and would probably wake up at an inopportune moment. But they had apparently resolved to act more sociable. Or perhaps this party's smaller, mostly family guest list had made them more at ease. Greta was wearing a pretty coral shirt and pants outfit in a silky fabric, and she made a beeline for Pamela with an admiring comment on the Icelandic sweater. Soon they were engaged in a conversation about the many advantages of natural fabrics.

Meanwhile, Maxie, Bettina, and Penny sat around the pine table, trying to convince the little boys that they would enjoy their dinner much more if they didn't eat quite so many crackers and cheese before it was served. Wilfred and his two sons labored in the cooking area of the kitchen. "Oh, yes," Greta confided to Pamela, "Warren does the cooking at home. Domestic tasks shouldn't be as gendered as they often are."

The aromas emanating from the cooking area were becoming more seductive by the moment. Buttery and cheesy smells blended with olive oil, garlic, and something spicy, all overlaid with the irresistible aroma of sizzling meat. A timer buzzed and conversation ceased as all eyes turned toward Wilfred. He stooped, opened the oven door, and lifted out a baking pan that held a magnificent rib roast—its surface glazed a crusty dark brown and the protruding bone ends slightly charred at the tips.

"Now this will rest," he announced, "while we have our first course. Please be seated."

After a scramble to get everyone settled at the dining room table, with cushions on the chairs for the little boys, Wilfred and his helpers delivered small plates on which were arranged servings of jumbo shrimp—pink, shiny with oil, and speckled with flakes of red pepper.

"They like spicy things," Maxie assured Pamela as each little boy raised a shrimp to his mouth. "They eat their dad's cooking all the time."

"Heavenly!" Bettina moaned with pleasure. "Just the right amount of heat, and such a clever change from always dipping them in that red cocktail sauce." Plates were soon empty and Warren cleared while Wilfred and Wilfred Jr. hurried to the kitchen.

The rib roast arrived first, Wilfred bearing it in on Bettina's largest sage-green platter. He lowered it to the table with a chuckle of satisfaction. Next came Wilfred Jr., wearing oven mitts and carrying a round casserole. He set it on a trivet that had been prudently included in the table setting. Within the casserole thin slices of potatoes overlapped around and around till at the center there was just one slice. The potatoes looked buttery and cheesy and had been baked till their edges were just starting to brown.

Wilfred Jr. set off for the kitchen again as his father began to carve the rib roast. Plates were passed to the head of the table and Wilfred settled a lovely rare chop with rib bone attached on each one.

"Will you do the honors with the potatoes?" Wilfred asked Greta, who was seated next to him. "The casserole is too hot to pass."

As they worked, Wilfred Jr. returned with an oval bowl containing slender green beans, glistening with olive oil and fragrant with garlic.

"I knew I smelled garlic," Maxie commented.

Wilfred Jr. nodded happily. "I added a pinch of red pepper flakes too. And see how bright the color of the beans is? It doesn't do to overcook them. I just blanch them lightly and then sauté them with the garlic and pepper flakes."

"The wine!" Bettina exclaimed and jumped up from her chair. She returned with two bottles and set one in a wine coaster. Then she made her way around the table with the other, pouring dark red wine into the elegant wineglasses she brought out for special occasions.

The plates proceeded from Wilfred to Greta and then to Wilfred Jr., as scoops of potatoes and then servings of green beans were added to the chops.

"The boys can share a chop," Maxie advised Wilfred.

Willie, the oldest, spoke up. "I want the half with the bone."

"You can have the bone," Maxie said, directing a

sweet smile across the table at her son, "but the chops won't be finger food tonight. This is a fancy meal."

"Okay." He drew the word out uncertainly but nodded, watching with expectant eyes as the plate destined for him made its way from hand to hand.

Soon everyone was served. After a few minutes in which the only sound was tableware clinking against pottery plates, voices joined one another in chorus to congratulate the cooks. Even Greta chimed in with praise for the rib roast, though she made sure to remind everyone that she and Warren seldom ate meat.

"What a pleasure to have our family and our best friends all here together," Bettina said with a happy sigh. At the opposite end of the table, Wilfred raised his wineglass and everyone joined in except the little boys, who had been provided with milk as they were being settled onto their cushions.

Pamela was content to focus on her meal as conversations sprang up around her. Ever the conscientious host, Wilfred had made sure Greta knew that Penny went to college in Boston, and the three were engaged in a lively discussion of free entertainment available in that city, especially outdoor theater in good weather. Across from her, Warren and his sister-in-law Maxie were comparing notes on adjusting to life with children, or a baby in his case. Bettina was lavishing attention on her two grandsons, one to her left and one to her right.

But suddenly Pamela heard her name. She turned to find Wilfred Jr. looking apologetic. "I didn't mean to startle you," he said.

"No . . . you didn't," she insisted, nevertheless feeling startled. She'd been concentrating so hard on the food, and the hum of conversation around her had been so soothing. "Please, go ahead."

He smiled, still apologetic. "I just wanted to say, I'm sorry about the cat. I know you had six of them to find homes for. I hoped we could do our part and the boys were so excited to have a pet. Then the itching started, right away."

"Are they okay now?" Pamela glanced toward where Willy and his younger brother, with Bettina's help, were finishing up their dinners.

Wilfred Jr.'s lips shaped a puzzled twist. "Not really," he said. "I suppose it will take a while for the rashes to clear up, even though the cat has been gone for almost a week."

Willy touched Pamela on the arm. "Are you talking about Midnight?" he asked in his high-pitched little-boy voice.

Bettina answered before Pamela could. "Yes, sweetie," she said, stroking his back tenderly. "It was sad that Midnight had to come and live with Grandma and Grandpa instead of you, but we can't have you itching all the time."

He nodded sadly.

"It's odd though." Pamela spoke up. "Before they got Midnight, the boys played with Punkin when they visited you and Wilfred and there was never any itching."

"It *is* odd." From the other direction, Wilfred Jr. agreed. "But I guess when a person is around a cat all the time, and living in the house where the cat lives too, there's just so much more exposure to the cat dander."

Across the table, Freddy had been listening. He was the mirror image of his brother, though at four years rather than five, he was a slightly smaller version. "Will we ever get to have a pet?" he asked.

"Maybe a dog, a big furry dog just like Woofus," Bettina suggested as Wilfred Jr. grimaced. "You've been hugging and playing with Woofus for years and you never got a rash from him."

Nods all around suggested that the cat-allergy discussion had reached a logical conclusion. And anyway, from his end of the table Wilfred had launched a survey of who was ready for a second round . . . of rib roast, potatoes, green beans. Abundant supplies of all remained.

Voices overlapped—pleading fullness, requesting a bit more of this or that, wondering if anyone wanted to share a chop, petitioning for a refill of wine. So another twenty minutes elapsed before Wilfred Jr. and his brother rose to clear away Bettina's sage-green dinner plates, slick with olive oil, dabbed with buttery-cheesy potato smudges, and bearing a cargo of rib bones. Several trips were required to clear away plates, tableware, and serving dishes.

"Do we get to eat Mom's cake now?" Freddie asked Bettina.

"Not quite," Bettina said, because next to arrive was a salad.

Wilfred Jr. and Warren had reappeared to deliver small plates on which sliced persimmons, their bright orange set off by sugared walnuts, nestled among curly greens. The greens proved to be arugula, and Pamela found their bitter tang a refreshing contrast after the rich meal. The little boys nibbled at the persimmons, which were very sweet, and the walnuts, which were sweeter.

The conversation became general as people talked

about their intentions for the lazy time between Christmas and New Year's. Greta and Warren planned to stay in Arborville for the next week, taking advantage of Bettina and Wilfred's babysitting to explore museums and see shows in Manhattan. Maxie and Wilfred Jr. would join them on a few outings. Penny confessed that her life was so busy at school she was happy to spend vacation time sticking close to Arborville and catching up with old friends.

As that conversational topic wound down, Maxie surveyed the table. "It looks like we're ready for the cake," she observed, her glance traveling over plates that now held only a few wilted strands of arugula.

Pamela started to rise. "I haven't done anything useful tonight," she said. "Let me help you."

"Wait until you see Maxie's cake," Wilfred Jr. interjected. "It's a masterpiece."

"Yes, it is." Bettina seconded his statement. "Bring it out here. Everyone has to admire it before you cut into it."

Pamela had already climbed to her feet. "I'll get coffee started then," she said, and as Bettina pushed her chair back, she added, "No, no—I can find my way around your kitchen." She followed Maxie.

The cake had been tucked away on a counter in a remote corner. As it was borne into the light, Pamela heard a sharp intake of air that was her own delighted gasp. Maxie had made a yule log. It was a cake shaped in a long roll, its chocolate-frosted surface scored to resemble bark and its ends revealing the spiral created by its construction: a long flat chocolate sponge spread with a lighter chocolate buttercream and rolled up. Mushrooms cleverly formed from marshmallows were placed here and there at its base to enhance the impression that it was a genuine product of the forest.

Pamela busied herself setting water to boil in Bettina's gleaming kettle and measuring grounds from a bag of Guatemalan coffee into a coffee filter. While she worked she enjoyed the oohs and aahs coming from the dining room as people admired Maxie's yule log. After a minute Maxie darted back to the kitchen to retrieve a stack of dessert plates.

Cups and saucers from Bettina's sage-green pottery were already waiting on the high counter that edged the cooking area of Bettina's spacious kitchen. Someone had set out the sugar bowl too, and made sure it was filled, but the cream pitcher needed cream. The kettle began to hoot as Pamela was returning the carton of cream to the refrigerator. She poured the boiling water slowly through the grounds, tilting her head aside to avoid the drift of steam.

The water would take a minute to seep through the grounds into the carafe below, so Pamela delivered the sugar and cream to the table. She paused to watch Maxie transfer a slice of the magnificent cake to one of Bettina's sage-green dessert plates, dark chocolate sponge and light chocolate buttercream alternating in a spiral, with a marshmallow mushroom tucked at the side.

When the cups of coffee had been delivered, with Bettina's help, and sugar and cream added to everyone's liking, people applied themselves to the pleasant task of demolishing their share of the yule log. Appreciation required focus: on the layers of flavor and texture represented by the chocolate buttercream filling, the tender crumb of the chocolate sponge, and the dense chocolate ganache that provided the log's bark. But as forks hunted the last morsels down and conveyed them to eager mouths, concentration was broken by a thin wail emanating from above.

Both Greta and Warren were on their feet in an instant. "I knew it was too good to last," Warren murmured with an apologetic smile.

"Morgan's schedule is all messed up," Greta added. "Too much excitement."

Wilfred Jr. and Maxie insisted on handling clean-up duties and the boys scampered off to the kitchen with their parents. Soon Greta and Warren descended the stairs with their lively child. Enfolded in her father's arms, she was no longer crying, and willing to be admired by her grandparents' neighbors before being carried off to the kitchen for a meal.

"Shall we adjourn to the living room?" Bettina asked. "There are gifts to be opened."

As Pamela and Penny settled on the sofa and Bettina sank into one of her comfortable armchairs, Pamela noticed that the engraving from Millicent's attic, now framed, was propped up on the mantel. "He loves it," Bettina said, beaming.

Wilfred slipped away to launch another round of carols, and soon voices serenaded them with "O Come, All Ye Faithful." On his way back to join the group, Wilfred detoured past the Christmas tree and selected four gaily wrapped packages.

"Yes," Pamela said, seeing his choices. "The big one with the red ribbon is for Bettina from me and the one with partridges in pear trees on the wrapping is for you from Penny."

"And here's one from us for you"—Wilfred deposited a small silver-wrapped box in Pamela's outstretched hand—"and for you." With a bow and a smile he offered Penny a larger silver-wrapped box.

After a few minutes in which the only sounds were crinkling paper, Pamela lifted the lid of a box from the mall's fanciest department store. Inside was a pair of sparkly, dangly earrings looking for all the world like miniature chandeliers.

"Too late for you to add them to your outfit last night," Bettina said with a fond smile. "But I hope you will wear them sometimes, especially with that beautiful ruby-red tunic."

"Just what I need!" Wilfred exclaimed, lifting a set of stainless steel mixing bowls from a nest of tissue paper.

"Almost indestructible," Penny explained. "And they fit inside each other, so there's every size you might ever need, but they hardly take up any room to store."

The hand-woven tablecloth and napkin set was received with equal delight by Bettina, and Penny opened the box from Bettina and Wilfred to find a wallet made of smooth leather in a bright shade of turquoise.

"Two more!" Penny jumped up and hurried to the tree, returning with the remaining gifts. Soon Bettina was holding up hands encased in Penny's gift of purple leather gloves and Wilfred was paging happily through the book on the settlement of the Hudson Valley from Pamela.

The four of them stood at Bettina and Wilfred's front door. Pamela and Penny were wrapped in their coats and ready to step outside. Wilfred Jr. and Maxie had departed, each bearing a sleeping child, and Warren and Greta had retreated upstairs with their own sleeping offspring. Thanks and final Christmas greetings had been exchanged, along with hugs.

"Could you fancy a trip to the yarn shop in Timberley?" Bettina asked suddenly.

"I suppose," Pamela said. "After all, this is a vacation week. But you still have quite a ways to go on that sweater for Wilfred, don't you? And I've barely begun the project with the yarn Penny picked out."

"I was just thinking though—" Bettina cocked her head and smiled. "Maxie was talking about learning to knit. I could give her some yarn and a pattern for something simple to get her started. Sort of a belated Christmas present." She paused and smiled again. "I do like Christmas."

Chapter Twenty

Bettina regarded the two freshly baked poppy-seed cakes cooling on Pamela's kitchen counter. "You've been busy," she commented. It was the next morning.

Pamela nodded. "I wanted to get them done before we went on our Timberley errand. I thought we could have lunch out and make an afternoon of it." She was working at the sink, rinsing the bowls and utensils she'd used to make the cakes and tucking them into the dishwasher.

"You made two," Bettina said, noting the obvious. "Who are they for?"

"I promised Penny she could take one when she goes back to school." Pamela pulled out the dishwasher's lower rack and inverted a large mixing bowl over the prongs that marked out spaces for plates. She gave the rack a gentle shove.

"And the other one?" Bettina tried to hide a teasing smile. "It wouldn't be for a certain snow-shoveling neighbor, would it?"

Pamela stooped and stared into the dishwasher's shadowy interior. Something was preventing the rack from sliding all the way back. She pulled the rack out again and a dull clank from deep in the dishwasher's interior suggested that a utensil had strayed from the silverware compartment and ended up somewhere hard to reach. At that moment the doorbell chimed.

"I'll get it," Bettina said. "You've got your hands full."

Pamela heard the front door open, then feet coming down the stairs. From the entry came overlapping voices: Bettina offering a greeting, Penny adding a cheerful hi, and a pleasant male voice acknowledging both. After a brief mumble of conversation that Pamela couldn't make out, Penny stuck her head around the edge of the kitchen doorway.

"I'm going to lunch with Aaron," she said in a voice whose tone implied that discussion wouldn't be welcome. Pamela frowned. "He *found* the scarf, Mom," Penny added. "That's all." And she hopped away.

Almost before Pamela heard the front door close, Bettina was back in the kitchen. "Penny introduced me," she said, looking stricken. "That was *him*, the person who ended up with my scarf. I can't believe you're letting her go out with him!"

Pamela sighed. "She's in college now, and who knows what kind of people she's meeting up there?" She sighed again, more deeply, and ran a hand over her forehead. "I have to trust her."

"Penny could know more about him than we know." Bettina's earlier cheer had fled. Her bright lipstick and eye shadow seemed to decorate a mask that scarcely resembled its original.

"I think she'd tell us." Pamela felt her throat tighten and the next words came out at a higher pitch. "Wouldn't she?"

"He's a nice-looking boy," Bettina said. "She's obviously smitten. I could see it in her face." She shook her head. "Penny could know *horrible* things about him. But love is blind."

Pamela turned away and bent toward the dishwasher's interior.

"I'm glad you're giving the other poppy-seed cake to Richard Larkin," Bettina added. "He deserves it."

Overnight, the snow had settled and its surface had hardened into a bright glaze that made the sunlight dazzle the eyes. Pamela and Bettina crossed Orchard Street and climbed into Bettina's faithful Toyota. Fifteen minutes later they were cruising along the street that ran through Timberley's charming commercial district, gay with its holiday decorations, looking for a place to park. The sidewalks were abuzz with well-dressed people hurrying to and fro, and they had nosed along for two blocks without encountering a single empty spot.

"Here's one," Pamela exclaimed. "Grab it. A bird in the hand is worth two in the bush, as Wilfred would say, and I don't mind a little walk."

Bettina swung into the spot and in a few moments they had joined the bustling crowds. But something brought them up short just before they reached the yarn shop. As people scurried around them, they gazed in the window of the craft shop that had been Millicent Farthingale's.

"Nobody's here," Bettina said. She turned to Pamela, concern sketching a vertical line between her carefully shaped brows.

"It's totally dark inside." Pamela nodded, a vertical line forming between her brows as well.

"Nadine can be a little batty," Bettina commented. "Maybe she's doing something in the back room and forgot to turn the lights on."

Pamela tried the door, pressing down hard on the latch, but the door didn't budge. She leaned to the side and tapped on the window. Meanwhile Bettina had launched a call on her phone. "No answer for the shop number," she announced after a few moments. She launched another call. "Nadine doesn't answer at her own number either," she said, lowering the phone from her ear. "It just goes to voicemail."

"We'll ask at the yarn shop," Pamela said. "It's right next door—surely the people who work there notice what goes on at the neighboring shops."

The stylish blond woman who had sold Pamela the ruby-red yarn for the tunic looked up from behind the counter as they entered. But something in their faces must have suggested that their quest was not solely for yarn. "Has something happened?" the woman asked, in lieu of a more conventional greeting.

Pamela and Bettina both spoke at once. Pamela's "Has the craft shop been open at all today?" overlapped with Bettina's "Do you know Nadine from next door?"

The woman pursed her lips and frowned. "Is no one there now?" she asked.

"No one," Pamela said, and Bettina added, "The shop is locked and the lights are off."

"Very strange." The woman shook her head. "The day after Christmas is an odd day to be closed, because lots of people are off work and they're in the mood to shop and some people don't like the malls. The craft shop was closed on Tuesday too—which is even more odd because the day before Christmas is when the procrastinators come out looking for last-minute gifts."

So distracted were they by this upsetting development—the apparent disappearance of Nadine—that Pamela and Bettina left the yarn shop without choosing anything for Maxie, though the shelves were piled with yarns in every shade and texture imaginable.

Back in the car, Bettina tried again to call Nadine but with no success. She thrust her phone back into her handbag and turned to Pamela, her lips quivering and her eyes wide with concern. "Are you thinking what I'm thinking?" she whispered.

"Geoff Grimm?" Pamela whispered back.

Bettina's head drooped forward. Even the tendrils of her hair seemed to sag. She nodded mournfully.

Pamela went on. "Nadine was terrified of him. When we stopped by the shop last week she was hiding in a back corner because she thought it was him coming back."

"She's dead," Bettina whispered. "Geoff Grimm came back and killed her." She raised a gloved hand to her mouth and her eyes grew even wider. "We have to tell the police."

"Let's make sure she's really dead first," Pamela said. She straightened her shoulders and tightened her lips into a determined line.

"What?" Bettina's hand darted from her mouth to Pamela's arm, where it squeezed hard. "How?"

"Well . . ." Pamela's lips relaxed into a slight smile. "Geoff Grimm might have come back, but let's at least make sure Nadine's not just hiding out at home. You know where she lives, don't you?"

* * *

The apartment building was a few blocks from Timberley's commercial district. It was an elegant brick structure suited to Timberley's stately grandeur, five stories tall and with carved stone trim. An awning-covered walk led from the sidewalk past artful landscaping, now softened by snow, to the building's imposing entrance. Just inside the heavy glass doors a doorman sat at a handsome desk.

Bettina hung back, as if afraid to hear the answer that their question might receive. So it was up to Pamela.

"We're here for Nadine Davenport," Pamela said, "in apartment 2B. Can you please let her know she has visitors?"

The doorman, a young Hispanic man, glanced up from studying a textbook open to a page of complex formulas. "She isn't here," he said.

"You've seen her though?" Bettina blurted. "She's okay?"

"She left Monday evening." One of his fingers rested on the open page, apparently marking the spot where he'd left off.

"She left?" Bettina blinked.

"In her car." He nodded. "I carried her suitcase out. I often carry things for her."

"Did she say where she was going?" Pamela asked. "Or when she'd be back?"

He shook his head no. "Sometimes they do." He shrugged. "She didn't. They don't have to. I'm just the doorman." He returned to studying the page of formulas.

At first Pamela and Bettina were silent as they retraced

their steps through the snowy landscape back to Bettina's car. The air was still, the day was bright, and the only sound was the echo of their boots on the meticulously shoveled Timberley sidewalks.

"Millicent had all the money anyone could want," Bettina said as they turned onto Timberley's main street and were once again strolling past shop fronts where strings of twinkling lights, luxuriant wreaths, and garlands of holly marked the season. "The craft shop was a hobby. Millicent loved being a patron of the arts—and she loved being able to help her old friend Nadine. She could have just given her money, but she wanted to give her a job instead . . . so Nadine didn't feel like an object of charity."

"So why would Nadine vanish?" Pamela thought for a minute and then answered her own question. "With Millicent gone, the job would end." She paused in the middle of the sidewalk and Bettina paused too. Someone jostled her elbow and a woman scurried past, aiming an irritated look in their direction. Pamela turned to Bettina and asked, "Who handled the shop's financial business?"

"Nadine," Bettina said. "Millicent had no head for numbers. She just liked artists and craftspeople, and she liked helping them find markets for their work. Nadine worked as a bookkeeper when she was younger."

"What if Nadine cleaned out the shop's bank account before she disappeared?" Pamela edged toward the nearest shop window, tugging Bettina with her, as more people jostled them in their hurry to get past. "And there were valuable things in the shop. She could have bundled up whatever she thought she could resell and made off with that too."

The series of expressions that passed over Bettina's

face—doubt, concern, then anger—suggested that she was pondering this scenario. "I liked Nadine," she commented at last. "But you're right. She must have been very worried. What would she live on with Millicent and the job at the shop gone?"

"We should go to the police," Pamela said. "The Timberley police. But first we have to get into the shop to see if things are missing."

"Pierre." Bettina sighed. "We'll have to go see him. He's the only person I can think of with a key to the shop. And he can probably get into the shop's bank account too. He was as interested in Millicent's money as he was in her—if not more so."

Pamela thumped the ornate brass knocker against the ornately carved wood of the Wentworth mansion's door. After a long pause the door swung back to reveal the slim figure of Pierre. For an instant he looked annoyed, but then his face settled into an expression more flattering to his elegant features. He nodded deferentially, invited her and Bettina to step over the threshold, and escorted them to a room where Victorian-era woodwork formed a backdrop for a sofa and armchairs upholstered in luxurious velvet, draperies of heavy silk (with tassels), and a richly patterned Persian rug. A pair of red stiletto heels in the middle of the rug—one poised on its stiletto heel, the other lying carelessly on its side—contrasted markedly with the traditional nature of the room's décor.

"Are we interrupting something?" Bettina asked as her glance strayed to the shoes.

"Not at all," Pierre replied smoothly. "What can I do for you lovely ladies?"

Pamela explained the errand and Pierre nodded as she spoke. He seemed neither surprised nor upset to hear that his deceased wife's business partner might have disappeared with the contents of the shop's bank account and some or all of its most valuable stock.

"But of course I will help you," he said when she had finished. "I just have a bit of . . . work . . . to finish up here." His glance strayed toward the shoes but he quickly focused back on Pamela. "I'll meet you at the shop in an hour, key in hand. And I'm sure I can find the password for the bank account."

He led them back the way they had come and opened the door to reveal the deep expanse of snowy yard, studded with bare trees and sloping gently to the road, that assured the Wentworth mansion its privacy.

"You know," Pierre said suddenly as the three of them clustered in the doorway, "Nadine was aware she owed that job to Millicent's charity, and I think she resented it. I know I would. Perhaps she saw that she could more easily run away with the shop's profits and whatever else she wanted if Millicent was out of the way first."

Pamela had just raised a foot to step over the threshold. Now she felt herself stumble, jolted by Pierre's words. She was saved having to speak by Bettina's response.

"Nadine knew Millicent cared for her," Bettina said. "She appreciated Millicent's help."

"But"—Pierre smiled slightly—"what you are now thinking Nadine has done doesn't make her seem a nice person. *N'est-ce pas?*"

* * *

"We have a lot to talk about," Pamela observed. She and Bettina were making their way along the slate walkway that curved away from the Wentworth mansion's entrance. The dark slabs were slick and icy, and navigating them required concentration.

"And we forgot we were going to have lunch," Bettina said.

"We forgot to buy the yarn for Maxie too." Pamela struggled to stay upright as her heel encountered a slippery spot. "We have an hour before Pierre will be at the shop," she added after she caught her balance. "We can grab a bite and get the yarn then."

But when they reached the gravel road that connected the carriage house to the road, Bettina veered left as Pamela veered right.

"The road is this way," Pamela called as Bettina picked up her pace on the gravel.

"I want to peek in on Charlotte," Bettina called back. "I'm not sure she knows Knit and Nibble is meeting next Monday. She might just think we're skipping a week because Tuesday is New Year's Eve."

Pamela reversed direction and the two friends crunched over the gravel, past the weathered façade of the carriage house with its four pairs of double doors and its peaked roof. They rounded its far corner and then turned left again. A small door and a small curtained window marked the portion of the carriage house designated as the groom's quarters.

They stepped into a most domestic scene, illuminated by lamplight. A hooked rug cushioned the wide planks of the rustic floor, and old-fashioned prints decorated walls papered with a faded but still charming flower print. In a shadowy corner were rustic stairs. Charlotte sat on a charming love seat, snug in a dark fleecy top and dark leggings, her dark hair loose. Next to her was a soft mound of sky-blue yarn.

"The perfect project for a chilly day like this," Bettina declared as she stepped across the rug. She bent over to take a closer look. "You're ripping it out!" she exclaimed. "All your beautiful work—and such a complicated pattern!"

Pamela stepped closer too. Off to one side sat two completed pieces, sleeves maybe, that had so far been spared. But it looked like Charlotte had undone most of the sweater's front (or back)—whatever she'd been working on the last time the group had gotten together to knit. As Pamela recalled, it had featured an elaborate interlocking pattern like a multi-strand braid.

Charlotte sighed and her lips curved into a sad smile. "Sometimes things just don't come together the way you expect," she said, "so you can't go on the way you planned."

"I hope you'll do something else with that lovely yarn," Bettina said, and delivered her message about the Monday night meeting of Knit and Nibble. "At Roland's," she added.

"I don't know about you," Bettina said as they followed the graveled driveway back to the side street where they had parked, "but I am starving."

Among the charming storefronts that lined Timberley's shopping street was Sara's Soup Station. Sitting at a small table in the window that looked out on the bustling sidewalk, Pamela and Bettina gratefully applied themselves to steaming earthenware bowls filled with thick split pea soup. It was after two p.m., well past time for lunch.

The demands of Pamela's stomach gradually became less insistent as she spooned the satisfying soup to her lips. With her stomach silenced, a nagging voice in her brain spoke up. She gave it her attention for a moment, noted that it had a good point, and then looked over at Bettina.

"You said Millicent had been inviting everybody she knew to help themselves to whatever they could find in the attic," she observed.

Bettina looked up from buttering a piece torn from one of the crusty rolls that accompanied the soup. "For months," Bettina said. "Starting right after her mother's funeral. She was longing to get all that junk cleared out so she could sell that huge house." She twisted her lips the way she did when she was puzzled and added, "What made you think of that now?"

Pamela spoke slowly. "If the antique rifle that killed Millicent was tucked away up there, and if Nadine accepted the invitation to help herself, she could have found it."

Bettina had gone back to buttering the piece of roll, but now she dropped the knife and it clunked against the wooden table. "No!" she squealed. "I just can't believe that Nadine could have been so ungrateful." She lowered her voice and leaned forward. "I mean, I can see why she might have done . . . what we think she did . . . after Millicent was gone. A person desperate about their future might do lots of things. But to think she's the one who *killed* Millicent? When would she even have done it?"

Pamela smiled regretfully and shook her head. "She had the best opportunity of anyone."

"How?" Bettina stared at Pamela, her eyes wide.

Pamela set her spoon down. "On the Monday morning that Millicent was killed, you visited her at her shop. You gave her the red scarf with green stripes and she gave you the vase. She got ready to go out and put the scarf on, but had to wait until Nadine got there before she could leave. Nadine came in while you were there and then you left." Pamela leaned across the table. "Think about it. Nadine could have killed Millicent and then closed the shop long enough to dispose of the body in the Arborville nature preserve—barely ten minutes away."

As Pamela spoke, Bettina's mouth had sagged. "The shop has a back door," she whispered. "People delivering things can pull up in the alley. A person could . . . take something away . . . through the back door too."

Pamela nodded. She reached across to where one of Bettina's hands rested on the table and squeezed it. "There are other suspects too," she said comfortingly. "And we still don't know whether anything's missing from the shop—or the bank account."

Bettina squeezed Pamela's hand in return. Suddenly her face brightened. "The police might have crossed Pierre off their list of suspects, but we certainly haven't. Why would he plant the seed that someone else—in other words, Nadine—might be guilty unless . . ."

"Good point!" Pamela said. "We have to keep our wits about us when we meet him at the shop. He might want to make sure we think Nadine did what we're afraid she did."

"I wonder if he'll really come up with the password for the bank account," Bettina said.

Chapter Twenty-One

Sara's Soup Station was almost directly across from the craft shop. Pamela and Bettina were just reckoning up how much to leave for a tip when Pamela noticed the striking figure of Pierre strolling along Timberley's shopping street. In his scrupulously tailored wool overcoat and dashingly deployed scarf, he could equally well have been taking the air on the Boulevard Saint-Michel. He reached the door of the craft shop, paused to look up and down the street, and then bent to unlock the door.

A few minutes later Pamela and Bettina joined him in the crowded shop. "What a great pleasure to see you," Pierre crooned, as if he hadn't just bid them farewell an hour ago. He seized Pamela's hand and bowed, then seized Bettina's hand and repeated the gesture. "I haven't spent so much time in the shop," he added, glancing around, "but everything looks the same to me."

Indeed, the towering driftwood construction Nadine had been hiding behind on Pamela and Bettina's last visit still occupied the far corner of the shop. The shelves were still laden with glassware in glowing colors, metal creations, and pottery—some useful, some purely decorative. Paintings and prints were displayed on the walls, and lengths of intricately patterned fabric hung from a rack near the entrance. A table held tablecloths and bedspreads, hand-woven by the look of them, neatly folded and stacked.

"The jewelry would be easiest to carry off," Bettina said, "and most valuable. Some of the craftspeople use gold and semiprecious stones in their work." She stepped toward the counter, dodging around a tall stand displaying fanciful teapots.

"I can't see that anything's been taken," she announced once she was behind the counter. Pamela had followed her friend through the shop. From the front of the counter she gazed down at the assortment of earrings, necklaces, bracelets, and brooches arranged on a shelf below the counter's glass top. Some combined silver and turquoise or jade. Others used materials unusual for jewelry, like polished wood or rough-textured stone. A few pieces were gold, with obviously valuable gems—in shades of pink, clear aqua, and yellow—or pearls, or amber, or opals.

Pamela and Bettina looked at each other and shrugged. "There's always the bank account," Pamela said.

Bettina shifted her eyes to where Pierre still stood near the shop's entrance. "Do you have the password for the bank account?" she asked.

"I don't have it but I know where to look for it." Pierre smiled. "I knew my late wife's habits very well."

The three of them clustered around the desk in the little office off the hallway leading to the shop's back door. A computer monitor, a keyboard, and a few piles of papers occupied the desk's surface, along with a

pottery coffee cup that still contained a few inches
of coffee.

"Millicent never concerned herself with the shop's
finances," Pierre said, "so she wouldn't have memo-
rized the password. But just in case she was in the shop
and wanted to verify that a check had cleared, for
example"—he reached for the keyboard and, with a
flourish like a magician doing a trick, flipped it upside
down—"*et voilà!*"

Taped to the black plastic of the keyboard's under-
side was a tiny strip of paper inscribed "millicent
craftshopbankaccount."

"Not a very original user name or a very strong password," Pamela observed.

Pierre took charge of bringing the computer to life.
After a brief session of beeps and chirps, the screen
displayed an assortment of icons. Pierre opened Google
and keyed in the bank's name. Once on the bank's
site, "millicent" and "craftshopbankaccount" got them
to a page that revealed a balance of $21,765.30. No
debits had been posted for over a week.

Bettina was exploring the contents of the desk
drawers as Pierre worked. Now she held up a thick
sheaf of bills. "Hundreds, fifties, and twenties," she explained, leafing through them. "Nadine must have
known about the cash. She's the person who worked
at this desk."

"So," Pamela said, "Nadine may have disappeared,
but she hasn't disappeared with anything from the
shop."

"That would appear so." Pierre nodded.

"I think we should put the money right back in this
desk drawer," Bettina said, matching her action to her
words and sliding the drawer closed. "If Nadine has

really disappeared, the police will want to investigate and every detail should remain just as she left it."

Pierre's expression was serious as he logged out of the bank's site and returned the computer to its resting state. Without the veneer of good nature that normally softened his sharp features, he looked quite wolfish.

Was he disappointed that Nadine no longer seemed a possible suspect in Millicent's death? Or had he just been hoping to pocket the cash Bettina had found?

"We're right by the yarn shop," Bettina said as they stood on the sidewalk watching Pierre lock the craft shop's door. "I might as well pop in and pick something out for Maxie since we're so close."

The stylish blond woman behind the yarn shop counter welcomed them back and listened with concern as they described their visit to Nadine's apartment building. "But it's too soon to go to the police," she said. "I can tell you that from an experience one of the other Timberley merchants had last year. The police told him they wouldn't have time to do anything else if they launched a missing-persons search every time an employee didn't show up for work." She laughed. "Not that the police have much else to do here in Timberley." Then she became serious again. "That *is* very troubling about your friend though."

Determined not to forget the purpose of their errand this time, Pamela and Bettina studied the rack of knitting-pattern books. Bettina selected one called *Simple Styles for Little Folks* and leafed through it, stopping at a page that showed two little boys wearing matching pullover sweaters.

"This pattern doesn't look too hard, does it?" she asked, tilting the page in Pamela's direction. "It's just basic stockinette stitch and there aren't any button-holes to worry about."

"And for the yarn?" The stylish blond woman stepped out from behind the counter and pulled a wooly skein of navy-blue yarn from a shelf piled high with similar skeins.

"It will have to be acrylic," Bettina said. "They're allergic to cats and so maybe wool will make them itch too."

Soon the pattern book sat on the counter next to several skeins of acrylic yarn, also navy blue, and a pair of knitting needles.

"I'll keep an eye on things at the craft shop," the stylish blond woman said as she handed Bettina's credit card back and began to slip the purchases into a bag. "If you want to leave your phone number, I'll let you know if your friend comes back and opens the shop again."

Orchard Street after a snowfall was as picturesque as a Christmas card, Pamela's house on this wintry afternoon particularly so. In her absence, a snowman had appeared in her yard. He was imposing in height, constructed of three snowballs in graduated sizes. He had twigs for arms, lumps of charcoal for eyes, and a carrot for a nose. Around his neck—the spot where the top snowball joined the middle snowball—he wore a plaid scarf.

"Hello?" she called as she pushed the front door open and stepped into the entry.

"In here, Mom," came Penny's voice from the kitchen.

The snowman wasn't the only visitor. Aaron was seated at the kitchen table, across from Penny. He bobbed up from his chair at the kitchen table and greeted Pamela as she entered the kitchen, once again addressing her as "Mrs. Paterson." Awfully polite, she said to herself. Almost too polite, like Pierre. And almost too good-looking. But she smiled in return.

Pamela's wooden cutting board sat on the kitchen table between Aaron and Penny. It bore a loaf of poppy-seed cake—minus several slices.

"It's the one you kept for us," Penny said hurriedly as Pamela's glance strayed to the cutting board. "But I won't take one of the new ones back with me if you had other plans for this one."

"It was for us to eat . . ." Pamela hoped it didn't sound like she was emphasizing the "us"—meaning only Pamela and Penny—too much. "I like the snowman," she added. "I'm glad I had carrots."

"Penny said you baked this." Aaron extended his hands toward the poppy-seed cake. "It's a fantastic recipe. Would you share it or is it a family secret?"

"Not family," Pamela said, flattered in spite of her misgivings about the flatterer, "but an old friend."

"Aaron likes to cook." Penny beamed at him across the table.

"Self-preservation," Aaron said. "When you share a house with a bunch of people, somebody has to do it. And after I sampled what my housemates came up with . . ." He laughed.

"How many of you are there?" Pamela asked. "Cooking for a crowd every night could be quite a challenge."

"Four." He nodded. "Two guys, two women. The place is huge—we each have our own room. They pay for all the food and they take turns doing the dishes. So far, it's working fine."

The young woman Pamela had seen wearing the red scarf must have been one of the housemates then. Penny had said Aaron lived in one of the houses behind Arborville's public parking lot. The young woman had hurried off in that direction the day Pamela tried to follow her.

"I think I saw one of your housemates wearing the red scarf," Pamela said. "There's no reason somebody shouldn't get some use from it," she added. "It *is* a nice scarf."

Aaron had been looking at Pamela during the conversation about cooking. Now he looked down. "After I found out what its connection was to your friend, I didn't want to wear it anymore, especially not around Arborville. I hung it in the big closet where we all keep our outdoor gear. Sometimes people just grab what's handy."

Penny spoke up. "At first he thought it was litter, Mom."

"Litter?" Pamela said. "Something as nice as that?"

"Well," Aaron said, "not exactly litter. But it's amazing what people will just *dump*—useful things that could be reused or recycled. And the nature preserve attracts a lot of dumpers. I was putting in some volunteer time for a project called The Earth Is My Home Too. Old shoes, pots and pans, furniture. It's amazing what all we've carried out of there."

Penny was watching Aaron as he spoke and Pamela was watching Penny—though Penny's expression was so adoring that to watch her almost felt like an invasion of privacy. Pamela wondered if she had stared so adoringly at Michael Paterson in the early days of their courtship.

The slice of sky visible from the kitchen window was already growing dark. Pamela retreated discreetly upstairs after saying a quick good-bye to Aaron, and soon she heard voices in the entry as Penny walked him to the door. Pamela wasn't sure what stage of physical expression the courtship had advanced to at this point, but a long silence before she heard the door open suggested that a farewell kiss had been a likely conclusion to the date.

Could she stop worrying about Aaron? she asked herself later, as she moved about the kitchen putting together a simple meal of cheese omelets and salad. The story about finding the scarf—while engaged in such a worthwhile task—was eminently plausible. And the police had said Millicent's body was dragged through the nature preserve to the spot where Penny found it. Certainly the red scarf could have slipped off along the way.

The sound of cats meowing frequently inserted itself into Pamela's dreams. The meowing would feature in curious dream plots. She'd hear it as she searched desperately for the room where a crucial editorial meeting had been scheduled, or as she toured a house in dire need of renovation that had somehow replaced her own cherished dwelling.

She was always glad when the meowing became so insistent that it woke her up. She would find a real-life cat standing on her chest, angry about a delayed breakfast, and the dream would fade away.

She opened her eyes in her shadowy room, expecting

to gaze into a pair of amber eyes in a dark, furry face. But Catrina was nowhere in sight. Yet the high-pitched squeals that had finally awakened her persisted. As the rest of the dream slipped from her conscious mind, she realized that the sound she heard wasn't the meowing of a cat. In fact a quick exploration with her left hand established that Catrina was still snuggled against her thigh. The sound was sirens.

She threw back the covers and jumped out of bed as Catrina burrowed under the cozy mound that Pamela's gesture had created. At the window, Pamela edged aside one panel of the eyelet curtains and tilted an ear toward the glass. The sirens were clearly coming from the direction of County Road.

"It could be anything," she said to herself. "Police chasing a speeder, or an ambulance on its way to the hospital." A glance at the bedside clock showed that it was nearly eight, time to start the day.

Catrina stuck her head out from under the bedclothes and watched as Pamela pulled her fleece robe over her pajamas and slipped her feet into her slippers. Satisfied that the morning ritual was about to commence, the cat hopped lightly off the bed, darted through the door, and preceded Pamela down the stairs.

In the kitchen, Pamela served Catrina her breakfast—Ginger was apparently sleeping late with Penny. Then she set water boiling for coffee and whirled a few scoops of coffee beans in the grinder. A trip outside to collect the *Register* would occupy the few minutes it took the water to boil, so she made her way toward the door. As she opened it, she caught sight of an unusual spectacle.

Bettina, usually so flawlessly groomed, was scurrying

across Orchard Street in her robe and slippers, her hair looking like it had more recently been in contact with a pillow than with a comb. "Did you hear those sirens?" she cried.

Pamela hurried down the steps. Bettina paused when she reached the *Register*, which lay on Pamela's front walk halfway between the street and the porch, and Pamela met her there, bending to retrieve the paper in its plastic sleeve.

"They could be anything," Pamela said. She paused and studied Bettina's face. "Couldn't they?" she added in a lower voice.

"It's police cars, two of them. Down by the nature preserve," Bettina said. "Wilfred was up and out early, taking his car for servicing at that place in Timberley he likes. He drove right past the turnoff for the preserve and he called me to tell me what he saw. He thought I might want to follow up with Clayborn, though it's too late to get anything in the *Advocate* for this week. In fact"—she swiveled her head this way and that to survey the street—"this week's *Advocate* should have been delivered by now."

"The nature preserve . . . again," Pamela murmured. She felt her forehead crease and her lips tighten.

"I'll call Clayborn," Bettina said. "I'll be over later." She looked down at her unconventional ensemble. "After I'm dressed of course. Make extra coffee."

Pamela hurried back to her warm house. Inside, the kettle was hooting frantically and Penny was standing in the entry rubbing sleep from her eyes. "I was worried," she said. "I didn't know why you hadn't heard the kettle. Where were you?"

"Talking to Bettina." Pamela hoped her face wasn't

still wearing the expression that had greeted Bettina's news.

"Really?" Penny said, signaling her suspicion by raising one brow. "It's kind of cold out for a chat."

"Oh"—Pamela willed her voice to sound offhand—"she just wanted to say she'll be over later and that I should make extra coffee."

Chapter Twenty-Two

Penny had finished her breakfast and retreated to her room, but Pamela was lingering over coffee and the *Register* when the doorbell summoned her.

"Pierre is dead," Bettina announced before even crossing the threshold.

"What?" Pamela stepped back, the door swung open wide, and Bettina rushed in. Pamela felt as if her brain had just been swept clean. She struggled for words and managed only to repeat the same monosyllable. Her reaction wasn't the shock that comes from hearing about the death of someone one cares for. It was more surprise. How could Pierre be dead? No theory she and Bettina had pondered about Millicent's murder had included the possibility that Pierre might be the next victim.

Pamela blinked a few times and shook her head as Bettina tossed her coat on the chair by the mail table. She'd obviously dressed quickly, in one of the leggings-and-tunic outfits she wore for babysitting her grandchildren, and hadn't bothered with makeup. "I'll tell you everything," she said. "But I need coffee."

Pamela led her to the kitchen, where extra coffee was waiting in the carafe. It just needed a gentle warming.

This was accomplished as Pamela retrieved cream from the refrigerator and Bettina helped herself to a cup and saucer from the cupboard and settled into her accustomed chair. All the while Bettina was talking.

She explained that she had called Detective Clayborn as soon as she returned to her house. She had reminded him that her reporting on police doings shaped public opinion in Arborville and, whether or not she had a pressing deadline, it was important to keep her in the loop.

Pamela served Bettina coffee, refreshed her own, and sat down across the table from her friend. "So Pierre is the body in the nature preserve?" she said.

Bettina nodded. "They think he was killed last night and then moved there."

"Just like Millicent." Pamela nodded too. "And the murder weapon . . . ?"

"He was shot," Bettina said. "The ME hasn't done her work yet, but it seems likely—this is my opinion anyway—that if she retrieves a bullet, it will be a homemade bullet like the one that killed Millicent."

"There's plenty of poppy-seed cake," Pamela said. "I just finished breakfast, but . . ."

"I wouldn't say no to a slice, or two"—Bettina scanned the counter, where two loaves of poppy-seed cake, securely wrapped in foil, reposed—"as long as you won't be cutting into the loaf that's meant for Richard Larkin."

"I won't be." Pamela laughed. "There's still some left from one of the original four." She carved two slices from the partial loaf tucked away in the cupboard and served them to Bettina on a dessert plate from her wedding china.

"I guess we can cross Pierre off our list of suspects,"

Pamela said as Bettina applied herself to a slice of poppy-seed cake. "And Geoff Grimm too. Why would he have wanted Pierre dead? His anger was directed at the craft shop. And the same person who killed Pierre most likely killed Millicent, so Geoff Grimm didn't kill Millicent, angry as he might have been."

Bettina finished the thought, a fork bearing a tidbit of poppy-seed cake poised halfway between her plate and her mouth. "And Nadine didn't kill Pierre, because she isn't even around. Therefore Nadine didn't kill Millicent."

Pamela sighed. "So who's left?" She explained her conviction that Aaron was also innocent.

Bettina shook her head sadly. "Clayborn hasn't made any progress with the case. I don't know why we thought we could figure it out."

"The only suspect we have left is Coot," Pamela said.

"Possible, I suppose." Bettina pursed her lips and wrinkled her nose.

"But if she really thinks the DNA results prove she's entitled to half her mother's estate, why would she take the chance of being charged with murder—*two* murders—to claim it?" As Pamela finished speaking, a door opened upstairs. A burst of laughter accompanied footsteps hurrying down the stairs. In a moment, Penny appeared in the kitchen doorway. She was carrying her smartphone and her face was pink with merriment.

"Geoff Grimm," she gasped, barely able to get the words out she was laughing so hard. "You absolutely won't guess—" She paused, overtaken by laughter again.

"What on earth?" Pamela rose, frowning. "You haven't been talking to him . . . have you?"

"I friended him on Facebook," Penny said, still

struggling with laughter. "I didn't mean to. Sometimes I just click on things." She paused to compose herself. "Anyway, you'll like this."

She handed her phone to Pamela, who bent toward the little screen. Bettina jumped up, ran around the table, and leaned against Pamela to study the image Penny had summoned.

"Is he trying out for a role as Dracula?" Bettina asked.

The photo in the Facebook post was clearly Geoff Grimm—spectral gaze, skeletal visage, and oily strands of hair reaching to his shoulders. But Geoff Grimm was wearing a nicely tailored tuxedo ensemble, complete with cummerbund, pleated shirt front, and impeccable bow tie.

"Look at what it says above the photo," Penny said.

Pamela read the words aloud: "'Being honored by Timberley General Hospital at their New Year's Eve gala. Guess I should dress to impress.'"

"There's a link to the hospital's site." Bettina tapped on the phone's screen and waited a moment for the site to come up. "Oh, my goodness," she murmured as her eyes scanned the screen. "Who would ever have thought . . . ?"

"So he's not really scary at all." Was there a hint of I-told-you-so in Penny's tone?

"Volunteer work at the hospital." Pamela laughed softly, shook her head, and quoted from the site: "'Also to be honored is Haversack artist Geoff Grimm. Every Monday morning for the past five years, Geoff has toured the children's wing, drawing cartoons on command and lifting the spirits of countless children.'"

"He didn't kill Millicent," Penny said.

Learning about Pierre's death had already made Pamela and Bettina cross Geoff Grimm off their list of suspects, but Penny didn't yet know that Pierre was dead. Pamela nodded though, and added, "Now we know why he always visited the shop on Monday mornings." She was pondering how to announce the fact of Pierre's death to Penny, but Penny reached for her phone and darted through the kitchen doorway before Pamela could say anything. More Facebook posts to read, no doubt, and the doings of Laine, Sybil, Lorie Hopkins, and new college friends to catch up with. Not to mention Aaron.

She'd give Penny an update on things later.

"I didn't see Richard Larkin's car." Bettina took a few steps toward the stove and lit the burner under the carafe. "My coffee got cold while we were talking," she explained.

"Probably at work," Pamela said.

"You *will* give him that loaf of poppy-seed cake though, won't you?" Bettina faced Pamela with her hands on her ample hips.

Pamela sighed. "I haven't decided yet," she said. "I don't want him to think he has to give me something."

"It's just a neighborly thing to do," Bettina said. "And you want to be neighborly, don't you?"

"I don't know how you talked me into this," Pamela said. It was Saturday morning and she was sitting at the pine table in Bettina's spacious kitchen. "You know I don't like to shop."

"The mall is fun at Christmastime." Bettina lifted another doughnut from the white cardboard bakery box on the table before her. "These homemade doughnuts from the farmers market in Newfield are amazing. Have another. And how about more coffee?"

Pamela groaned. "Two is plenty, especially if we're going to have lunch out. But I will take a refill on the coffee."

"It's still the holiday season." Bettina headed toward the cooking area of her kitchen to fetch the coffee. "You might as well enjoy yourself before your boss starts sending you work again."

"That reminds me," Pamela said. "I have a couple more articles to evaluate, but nothing's due back till Sunday night."

From the living room came a muffled bark, then the doorbell rang. Wilfred, a hint of surprise in his voice, greeted someone he apparently knew quite well. Woofus tore around the corner from the dining room and took cover under the pine table. Pamela could feel his body trembling against her calves.

Wilfred stepped through the kitchen doorway a moment later. "Absence makes the heart grow fonder," he said. "Look who's back."

He edged to the side, revealing Nadine, looking more insubstantial than ever in comparison with Wilfred's bulk. Her lips began to shape a hesitant smile, but then her face reverted to its customary expression of mild confusion. Pamela realized that she was glowering at the apparition and was thankful that Bettina was the first to speak. She herself might not have been so charitable.

"Where on earth have you been?" Bettina asked, sounding more curious than angry. "We were very worried about you."

Nadine's slight figure seemed to close in on itself. Her shoulders contracted and her hands, crossed over her chest, gripped her upper arms protectively.

Wilfred, ever the gentleman, pulled a chair out from the table and motioned Nadine to sit.

Huddled in the chair, Nadine looked from Bettina to Pamela. Apparently identifying Bettina as the more receptive audience, she fixed her gaze on Bettina and began to speak.

"The woman at the yarn shop said you were looking for me," she said in a tone that suggested she found this fact puzzling.

"Yes." Bettina nodded. "We were."

"There was no reason to worry," Nadine said. "I had the vacation days clearly marked on my calendar."

Pamela couldn't contain herself. "Vacation days!" she exclaimed. "Right after your boss had been murdered? Aside from the obvious—like weren't you curious about what the police would discover?—who did you think was going to run the shop?"

"The vacation days were on my calendar," Nadine repeated, sounding a bit more assertive. "I cleared my plans with Millicent."

"But then Millicent was murdered!" Pamela had never liked the scolding tone that she sometimes heard in her voice, and she'd worked hard to suppress it on the rare occasions when Penny had done something scold-worthy. But now she was glad to summon it from her vocal repertoire.

With an alarmed glance in Pamela's direction, Bettina jumped in quickly. "You should at least have told someone you'd be away for a few days," she said gently. "For all we knew, the same person who killed Millicent had come back to the shop to kill you."

Or for all we knew, you were the person who killed Millicent, added a small voice in Pamela's brain.

Nadine sagged forward until her face was hidden by

frowsy strands of no-color hair. "I didn't think of that," she mumbled.

There seemed nothing more to say. After an awkward silence, Bettina rose. Nadine looked startled for a moment, as if she wasn't sure what was happening, but then Bettina reached out, pulled her to her feet, and enfolded her in a hug.

"I don't know what will happen to the shop now," Bettina commented when she and Wilfred returned from seeing Nadine to the door. Wilfred headed for his basement workshop and Bettina reclaimed her chair.

"She seems pretty hopeless," Pamela agreed.

Pamela was home from the mall visit and lunch with Bettina by midafternoon, though the winter sun was already nearing the horizon. The beginnings of the lacy lilac tunic rested on the arm of the sofa, where she'd left it the previous evening. The tunic's back, the section she had started with, had grown by several inches since Christmas Day, when her cautious needles first tackled its challenging stitch. She settled at the end of the sofa and picked up the project. Soon her pulse slowed as, row by row, her hands shaped delicate filigreed shells from the lilac yarn.

She glanced up only briefly when Aaron popped around the corner from the entry to bid her a courteous good-evening and Penny waved and said she'd be home by midnight.

It was Sunday evening. As Penny entered the kitchen, Pamela looked up from the remains of her solitary meal. She'd bought groceries at the Co-Op and roasted a chicken. The thigh she'd eaten for dinner was only one of many meals the chicken was destined to provide.

"You're wearing the necklace!" she exclaimed. It was the necklace of Venetian beads that had been one of Pamela's Christmas gifts. The richly colored glass beads seemed to set Penny's complexion aglow, and Pamela found herself staring, startled at her daughter's beauty. A date with Aaron was in the works, she knew. Penny had announced earlier that she wouldn't be eating dinner at home.

"I think your holiday romance is becoming serious," Pamela said.

"Maybe." Penny suppressed a smile and looked at the floor. Pamela wouldn't have thought Penny could look any lovelier or full of life, but the bloom in her cheeks had suddenly intensified.

The doorbell chimed and Penny skipped toward the entry. In a moment, Aaron popped his head through the kitchen doorway to greet Pamela as "Mrs. Paterson" and wish her a good evening, and then they were off.

Catrina strolled in from the back hallway, followed by Ginger. They paused to see whether anything interesting had appeared in their bowl since they'd finished their own dinner, and then they were gone too.

Well—Pamela sighed—*enough procrastinating.* Christmas week had been fun and she'd been lazy. One article remained from the batch her boss had sent the previous Monday. She'd tidy the kitchen, read the article, email the bundle of evaluations off to *Fiber Craft*, and then settle down to work on the lacy lilac tunic with a British mystery unfolding on the screen before her.

Upstairs in her office, she settled into her desk chair and poked the buttons that roused her computer from its sleep. She opened the email from her boss, clicked on the attachment labeled "Symbolism," and began to read.

The article, illustrated with charming line drawings, asserted that the designs knit into garments hadn't always served purely aesthetic purposes. A common design used in Irish fishermen's sweaters, for example—cabling—was intended to protect men who spent their days at sea and ensure that they returned to shore with a bountiful catch. Other Celtic patterns were associated with attracting and keeping love. Knitting was knotting, the author pointed out, and what was the purpose of a knot but to hold fast?

Pamela stared at the line drawings accompanying this section of the article. Somehow one of the designs looked familiar. She continued reading. Now the author was talking about designs based on plant imagery, designs intended to ward off diseases that the plants themselves were believed to cure.

The article was well written and the topic would be interesting to readers of *Fiber Craft*, she believed, and she began to draft a note to that effect. But she couldn't concentrate. Her thoughts kept returning to the line drawing that had caught her attention.

Yes! she whispered suddenly, leaping from her chair.

Chapter Twenty-Three

Pamela ran across the hall to look out a window that faced the street. But then she turned away, disappointed. No lights were on in Bettina's house. Perhaps Wilfred Jr. and Maxie were hosting a family get-together before Warren and Greta headed back to Boston.

Back in her office, she reached for her cell phone. She scrolled down her list of names, selected one, and then pressed Talk. "Hi. It's Pamela," she said when she made contact. "I'm just evaluating an article for the magazine and it occurred to me that you're the one person who can help me." She summoned a laugh that she hoped didn't sound as fake as it felt. "It's kind of silly, really, but this author thinks knitting patterns can be used as charms—to remove impediments to love and cast love spells. Just a superstition, really, I'm sure you would agree. Sometimes a person has to take a more practical approach to the impediments, and if there's a weapon handy . . . combined with a charm . . . But even then, sometimes, the charm doesn't work and a person is so disappointed that there's only one thing"—a click told Pamela that the connection had been broken, but she finished the thought—"to do."

Now for the next step. Pamela hurried down the

stairs and through the kitchen to the laundry room. There, the dress form, still draped in the black velvet cape, loomed at her from the shadows. Hugging it around its waist, she lifted it into the hallway. Not even pausing to put on a jacket, she carried it out the back door and down the back steps. Thankfully Penny had supplemented Richard Larkin's shoveling with some shoveling of her own before alternate melting and freezing created an impenetrable crust.

The night was dark and cold, but still. In the faint light that reached her from the streetlamp, she hauled the dress form along the driveway. She was panting slightly now and the frigid air caught in the back of her throat. When she reached the spot where the re- cycling containers were lined up, she set the dress form down.

Then she continued along the driveway until she was within a few yards of the street. She turned and stared toward the dress form. As she'd hoped, the streetlamp behind her provided enough light to make the dress form visible, but not enough to reveal that it was just a dress form and not a human. The long cape, which in the darkness could easily pass for an all- enveloping robe, hid the fact that instead of legs, the dress form's torso stood on a metal post anchored in a heavy base. She'd been concerned that its lack of a head would be too obvious. But she was pleased to see that the effect was of someone bending slightly, as if intent on a recycling task. As she passed the recy- cling containers on her return to the back door, she flipped up the hinged cover of the one closest to the dress form.

Back in the house, she sat on the sofa, cell phone at the ready. The lilac yarn and partly finished back of the lacy tunic were within reach, but the lacy stitch was complicated, and at the moment she didn't trust herself to focus properly. Catrina joined her on the sofa, regarding her mistress curiously, as if wondering why the evening ritual of sofa plus television plus knitting plus cat was lacking two of its components.

Ten minutes passed before Orchard Street's Sunday night quiet was disturbed by the sound of a car engine. Pamela had left the light off in the entry on purpose. Now she grabbed the cell phone, rose from the sofa, and crept toward the front door, where she stooped and leaned close to the lace that veiled the oval window. There was no sign of a car and all was quiet again. She was about to return to the sofa when from the bottom of the street came the distant sound of another engine. Headlights carved bright tunnels through the darkness, making the frosty asphalt gleam.

The car drew closer, then paused at the curb in front of her house. The headlights went dark and the driver's side door opened. From around the car a figure emerged into the spill of light cast by the streetlamp. Obviously untrained in the proper handling of firearms (*Probably doesn't watch enough British mysteries*, Pamela murmured to herself), the figure carried what was obviously a rifle as if it were a mop or a broom.

But then the rifle's position shifted to horizontal. The figure crept toward the head of Pamela's driveway, pivoted, and with the rifle aiming at precisely what Pamela had hoped its target would be, began to sneak along the side of Pamela's car. She clutched her cell phone. It was time to summon the police.

But suddenly the scene became more complex than she had intended. A masculine voice shouted, "Who are you? What are you doing with that rifle?" Pamela ran to the entry's side window and pushed the curtain aside. As she had expected, Charlotte Sprague stood in the driveway, armed with a rifle, which she was aiming at the dress form. But between Charlotte and the dress form stood Richard Larkin.

A weapon, a weapon! she whispered frantically to herself. But what? A heavy thing. She darted into the kitchen, jerked open a utensil drawer, and seized the rolling pin whose most recent task had been rolling out the Christmas cookies that she and Wilfred and Bettina had decorated.

Hardly aware of what she was doing, she flung the front door open, leapt down the front steps, and crunched across the snowy stretch of lawn between porch steps and driveway. Once on the asphalt of the driveway, she slowed to a soundless creep, edging toward Charlotte, who was intent on Richard Larkin and the dress form that she still mistook for her quarry.

"Get out of my way, whoever you are," Charlotte muttered, and the rifle barrel wobbled erratically. "She has to die. You can't prevent it."

Behind Charlotte, Pamela raised the rolling pin. Richard lunged toward the dress form as if to shield it with his body. It fell over with a clunk, and Richard fell with it, just as Pamela brought the rolling pin down on Charlotte's head. With a flash and a sharp crack the rifle discharged, then slipped from Charlotte's hands and clattered to the asphalt. Pamela struck again with the rolling pin, feeling a jolt that reached her shoulder as the rolling pin connected with Charlotte's skull. Charlotte reeled for a moment then collapsed with a moan.

Pamela stooped toward where the rifle had fallen. It was barely visible, except for the slight metallic gleam of its barrel. The barrel was hot to the touch, so with the toe of her shoe, she pushed the rifle toward the edge of the driveway where Penny had heaped snow as she shoveled. Charlotte remained crumpled on the frosty asphalt.

Then Pamela turned her attention to Richard. He too was barely visible in the darkness—except for his blond hair—his clothes blending with the asphalt and the velvet cape, which had slipped off the dress form as it tipped over. Pamela knelt near his head and bent toward his ear.

"Can you hear me?" she said. "Richard?"

He lifted his head slightly and started to push himself up but sank back down with a groan. "What happened?" he asked. "What was that thing? I thought it was you. I was trying to push you out of the way."

"I'll explain everything," Pamela said. "But we have to call the police. Do you have your cell phone? Mine is in the house."

"Shirt pocket, I think." He tried again to push himself up, managed to rise to his knees, flexed both arms, and commented, "Nothing seems broken." He fumbled inside his jacket and pulled out his cell phone.

As he completed the call, Charlotte began to stir. But the thin sound of a siren was already piercing the chilly air.

"How did you happen to be in my driveway?" Pamela asked Richard as they waited. He had sagged back down onto the asphalt.

"I just got home from delivering Laine and Sybil to their dorm," Richard said from his prone position.

"They flew back from San Francisco today. I saw a car pull up while I was still outside, and I saw somebody with a rifle get out. So I watched through the hedge to see what was going on. Then I saw what I thought was you, standing by the recycling containers. And that person was stalking you. It looked like there wasn't a minute to lose before you got shot. So I pushed a couple of bushes aside and dove through the hedge."

After a few feeble motions, Charlotte had lapsed back into stillness. But now, without lifting her head, she began to speak.

"How did you figure it out?" she asked in a plaintive voice.

"The sweater you were ripping out when Bettina and I stopped by to see you the other night." Pamela had run outside with no jacket to rescue Richard Larkin, and the outfit she'd been wearing for a quiet evening at home was no match for the wintry air. But the thrill of resolving the mystery that had vexed her and Bettina for so long distracted her from the fact that she should have been shivering.

"Lots of people rip out knitting projects." Charlotte managed to sound petulant despite her situation.

"You made the sweater as a gift for Pierre," Pamela said. "And the stitch was intended to cast a love spell. If I hadn't just been reading an article on the symbolism of traditional Celtic knitting patterns for *Fiber Craft*, I'd never have figured it out. You wanted Pierre to be free to love you after the magic had done its work, so you made sure to get Millicent out of the way before you presented your gift."

"It didn't work," Charlotte groaned, speaking as much to herself as to Pamela.

"No, it didn't," Pamela agreed. "I heard you declaring your love in the attic on the day I was there for the estate sale. I mistook your voice for someone else's, because of the sniffling and sneezing. But he resisted you—and thus resisted the charm—so he had to follow Millicent to the grave."

The siren meanwhile had been drawing closer. Soon its long rise and fall modulated into a resentful bleat, then the night was silent. Pamela stood up and hurried toward the street. When she reached the pool of light cast by the streetlamp she waved at the police, who had just climbed out of their car.

"Down here," she called, and turned the wave into a gesture that pointed toward where Richard and Charlotte still lay on the asphalt. "Down here along the side of the house."

One of the officers was Officer Sanchez, a young woman with dark hair and a sweet, heart-shaped face. Pamela had met her before. The other officer, a sturdy man, was someone she didn't recognize. As if on cue, both officers took flashlights from their belts.

Pamela let the officers lead the way, the two flashlight beams crisscrossing as they probed the gloom. The officers themselves were almost invisible in their dark uniforms. When the flashlight beams reached Charlotte and Richard, Officer Sanchez turned to Pamela.

"Do these individuals need medical attention?" she asked.

"Possibly," Pamela answered.

But Richard objected with a vigorous "No." With a ferocious grunt, he pushed himself up until he was kneeling again, and then lowered himself onto his haunches. "I'm fine," he said. "Just a little bruised."

Pamela took up where she left off. "That's not why we called 911," she said. "This woman"—she pointed at Charlotte—"wanted to shoot me with that rifle." She shifted the direction of her finger to where the rifle lay. The flashlight beams followed the gesture, and the rifle became visible, half buried in grimy snow. "And she ended up shooting at him," Pamela went on, waving toward Richard. "The rifle's been fired," she added. "You'll see that when it's tested."

Charlotte was in motion too. She struggled to a sitting position and tilted her head to look up at Officer Sanchez. The male officer edged closer to Charlotte. "She attacked me with a rolling pin," Charlotte said.

Despite her sweet face, Officer Sanchez could be stern. "Is that your rifle?" she demanded as her flashlight beam danced over what was visible of the rifle's barrel and stock.

"No!" Charlotte's tone of voice implied that the question was deeply offensive.

"It's true that it isn't hers," Pamela said. "But she brought it here and she fired it."

"Is *that* true?" Officer Sanchez asked.

Charlotte didn't respond. Suddenly she pushed herself up from the asphalt, whirled around, and began to sprint down the driveway. After a moment in which they seemed frozen, the two officers dashed after her.

Pamela followed them, but more slowly and at a distance. She watched as they easily overtook Charlotte and subdued her, each grabbing an arm. Pamela heard Officer Sanchez say, "I'll need an evidence bag for that rifle."

In a moment the male officer was escorting Charlotte across Pamela's snowy yard as Officer Sanchez hurried ahead to the police car. Carrying a large orange bag, she retraced her steps to where Pamela was standing. Richard, meanwhile, had managed to climb to his feet and was limping slowly toward Pamela.

As Pamela stared in the direction of the street, watching Charlotte being led away, headlights approached from the top of the block. The car whose arrival the headlights announced slowed and then turned into Bettina and Wilfred's driveway. The door of the police car had scarcely closed on Charlotte before Bettina was hurrying up Pamela's driveway. Her mouth was agape and her eyes were wide with alarm.

"What is happening?" she cried when she was within a few feet of Pamela. "The police car," she panted, "and"—she noticed Officer Sanchez—"the police!" She swung her head toward Richard. "Richard! And Pamela! Are you both all right?"

Wilfred had been thudding along behind Bettina and he joined the group now. "Dear wife!" he exclaimed. "Pamela! Rick! What is happening?"

"Sir, excuse me." Officer Sanchez stepped forward. "And ma'am." She nodded toward Bettina. "A police investigation is currently taking place. I'll have to ask you to return to your home."

"Police investigation!" Bettina gasped. "Pamela! What—?" Wilfred laid a protective hand on his wife's shoulder.

"It's okay," Pamela said. "Everything is okay."

"Ma'am! Sir!" Officer Sanchez advanced farther and Bettina and Wilfred retreated.

"I'll call you later," Pamela assured her friends. "Everything is really okay. Better than okay."

Half an hour later, Pamela was sitting on her sofa next to Richard Larkin. Officer Sanchez was perched on the rummage-sale chair with the carved wooden back and the needlepoint seat. Backup had arrived to transport Charlotte to the police station, and Pamela, Richard, and Officer Sanchez had repaired to Pamela's warm living room.

Officer Sanchez had nodded and taken notes as Pamela and Richard explained what had transpired before the police were summoned and what role the dress form had played. Now she tucked away her notepad and pen, and explained that Detective Clayborn would follow up the next day and that it might be necessary to search Pamela's driveway for the rifle bullet and shell casing. She also noted that Detective Clayborn would take a dim view of luring a murderer to incriminate herself by firing at a dress form set up as a decoy.

Pamela had no sooner seen Officer Sanchez out the door and turned off the porch light than the doorbell chimed.

"Was that Charlotte Sprague in the police car?" came an urgent voice out of the darkness. In a moment Bettina stepped over the threshold, followed by Wilfred. Bettina seized Pamela in an all-enveloping hug and then, still holding her arms, stepped back to study her. "What have you been up to?" she demanded.

"Catching a murderer," came Richard's comment from the next room. They all turned in his direction.

He tried to rise from the sofa, then winced and sank back down.

"Off with your coats," Pamela said. "Have a seat while I make coffee. You both deserve to hear the whole story."

Over coffee and poppy-seed cake, Pamela described the phone call she made to Charlotte hinting that she knew Charlotte was the murderer. "I suspected she'd show up here with the rifle," she explained, "and that would prove her guilt. But I didn't want her to actually shoot *me* so I set up a decoy in the driveway."

"The dress form made quite a convincing Pamela," Richard added, "until I tackled it and it tipped over with a clunk."

"That old dress form we hauled home from the estate sale?" Bettina laughed.

Pamela nodded. "It turned out to be quite useful— except my trap turned out a bit differently than I expected."

"But how did you figure out Charlotte was the murderer?" Bettina asked.

Pamela described what she'd learned about knitting designs as love charms from the *Fiber Craft* article. "But then," she added, "the charm didn't work, even though Millicent was out of the way," she added.

"I guess Charlotte didn't know about Jeannette," Bettina observed.

"No, she apparently didn't," Pamela said, "or Jeannette would have been the next to go."

"The charm didn't work, so Charlotte unraveled the sweater." Bettina reached for a second slice of poppy-seed cake. The four of them were grouped companionably around Pamela's coffee table.

Pamela nodded. "And then she killed Pierre. If she couldn't have him, then no one would. She probably shot both him and Millicent in those woods that surround the Wentworth mansion. No fear of neighbors hearing or seeing."

Wilfred spoke up. "With the same gun. The police confirmed that."

"The antique rifle came from the mansion's attic," Pamela said. "I'm sure of it—that puzzle piece fell right into place once I latched on to the idea that Charlotte was the killer."

"How?" Wilfred asked.

"A separate set of stairs led to the attic from the groom's quarters. I noticed it when we stopped in to tell Charlotte about the next Knit and Nibble meeting. Charlotte could have gone up there to rummage around anytime she felt like it, without anybody knowing. And that corner of the attic was where I heard the conversation I took to be Pierre and Jeannette, with a sneezy woman's voice telling Pierre how much she loved him. It was actually poor Charlotte—and Pierre was probably trying to escape the whole time. I could hear stuff falling over."

"You did a very reckless thing," Bettina said, folding her hands on her lap. She regarded Pamela with a stern expression quite at odds with the festive effect of her bright scarlet hair and her dangly earrings, which resembled miniature Christmas-tree balls. "Inviting a person to come to your house with a loaded rifle. And look what happened! She could have shot Richard."

"I *am* sorry," Pamela said meekly, "especially about that." She turned to Richard. "You were very brave to come to my rescue." He shifted his gaze from Bettina to her.

He *was* brave. And the fierce cast his strong features sometimes lent to his expression seemed appropriate now, appealing even. But as if catching himself looking more intense than he intended, he smiled and his face softened. Before he could say anything—or perhaps he hadn't planned to, Wilfred spoke up.

"All's well that ends well," he announced as his gaze traveled around the little group, his ruddy face the very picture of cheer.

Chapter Twenty-Four

"I hope you delivered that loaf of poppy-seed cake to Richard Larkin," Bettina said as soon as she opened her door. She was already bundled in her pumpkin-colored coat. "He saved your life last night."

"Not exactly." Pamela smiled. "But Charlotte could have done a lot of damage to the dress form if she'd managed to hit it."

"Well"—Bettina put her hands on her hips—"Richard *thought* he was saving your life. So . . . what about the poppy-seed cake?"

By this time Pamela had stepped into Bettina's living room, to which the lights on the Christmas tree gave a welcoming glow. Pamela's smile took on a teasing quality. "If I say I did, will you stop talking about him?"

"Did you?" Bettina's voice rose an octave. Woofus lifted his shaggy head at the sound but didn't stir from his comfortable sprawl on the sofa. Bettina clasped her hands in a praying gesture and stared at Pamela, her eyes bright with excitement.

Pamela lowered her gaze to the floor, controlling her desire to smile more broadly. "Yes," she whispered.

"What was it like?" Bettina whispered too, but urgently.

"He came to the door," Pamela said. "He's a little stiff from last night. I handed him the poppy-seed cake."

Bettina stared at Pamela as if watching a particularly mesmerizing drama unfold on a television screen. "And then . . . ?" she prompted.

"He said 'Thank you.' I said 'You're welcome.' And then I crossed the street to come here. We've got a Knit and Nibble meeting to get to."

"Ohhh!" Bettina twisted her lips into a disgusted knot. "It wouldn't have mattered if we were late." She lifted her handbag and gloves from a small table near the door. The gloves were the purple ones Penny had given her for Christmas. "I saw the reporters were around today," she commented.

Pamela nodded. "And I did speak with Clayborn," she said as they walked toward the driveway, where Bettina's faithful Toyota waited. "He reminded me that the residents of Arborville pay taxes so they don't have to solve crimes themselves. He didn't seem to want to get into the dress form issue."

The chilly air was scented with wood smoke from a nearby fireplace. There were no clouds, and the few stars were like bright pinpricks in an expanse of black. Bettina followed Pamela around the car and unlocked her door.

"Woofus seems calmer," Pamela said as she settled into the passenger seat.

"He is." Bettina nodded from behind the steering

wheel. "We're down to one kitten now, dear little Punkin."

"What happened to Midnight?" Pamela asked, startled. "I'd have taken him."

"He's back with Wilfred Jr.'s boys."

"I know the boys really missed him," Pamela said, "but Maxie can't be happy about keeping a pet that gives her boys a rash."

"It wasn't the kitten." Bettina laughed. "It was a new brand of laundry detergent. Maxie figured it out when she and Wilfred Jr. started itching too."

Pamela had no sooner settled onto Roland and Melanie's low-slung turquoise sofa than the questions began. Yes, she acknowledged, the *Register*'s description of the previous evening's events was accurate.

Holly looked up from rummaging in her knitting bag. "But what on earth made Charlotte decide she had to kill *you*?" she asked, a puzzled frown taking the place of her usual smile.

As Pamela hesitated, Bettina jumped in, breathlessly narrating—just as Pamela had described it to her—the prologue to the drama that had unfolded in the driveway: the sudden realization brought on by the article on the symbolism of knitting patterns, the phone call to Charlotte, the decision to set the dress form up as a decoy . . . But somehow, overnight, the disapproval Bettina had expressed so clearly the previous evening had turned to pride in her friend's clever ruse.

Disapproval, however, is always lurking, seeking a willing host. No sooner had Bettina finished than Nell spoke up from the comfortable armchair Melanie had offered her when she arrived. "That was a very, very foolish—and dangerous—thing to do," she said. Nell's faded blue eyes sought Pamela's and Pamela couldn't evade their gaze. Nell underlined the statement with a sorrowful headshake.

"I think it was amazing," Holly said, her dimply smile returning. Holly had come alone. Karen, still in the early stages of motherhood, was at home with her new baby. Holly looked across the room at Roland, who was sitting on the sleek turquoise chair that matched the sofa. "Don't you?" she inquired.

"That's one way to describe it." Roland looked up. He'd been knitting industriously as Bettina spoke. "Not quite the word I'd use," he added.

"Well, she saved the taxpayers some money." Bettina aimed a teasing smile his way. "You're always in favor of that."

Roland gave a grudging nod. "I suppose the Arborville police can wrap up the Farthingale case now."

"And Pierre's murder too," Bettina said. "All because of Pamela. Charlotte *did* confess, you know."

"Pamela was taking quite a risk." The expression on Roland's lean face sharpened. "Who do you suppose would have been liable if Richard Larkin had been shot? I would call that dress form a dangerous nuisance."

Nell had been glancing back and forth from Bettina to Roland. Now she put her knitting down and raised both of her wrinkled hands in a peacemaking gesture. "As Wilfred would say, all's well that ends well," she declared. "And I hope dear little Penny is at ease now. What a shocking start to her Christmas vacation." She let her kindly gaze travel around the room. "Now let's tend to our knitting."

Pamela smiled to herself. All's well that ends well indeed. And Penny had an Arborville boyfriend in the bargain.

Five people bent to their projects. Pamela fielded more questions, but this time about the lilac yarn and the lacy pattern taking shape under her needles. Holly was working on another orange square for her color-block afghan, Roland on an angora sweater for his mother, Bettina on the Nordic-style sweater for Wilfred.

"It might be his gift for *next* Christmas." She laughed in response to Holly's comment. "I'm not as speedy as all of you." She looked across the room to where Nell was nestled into the comfortable armchair. "That's not a stocking," she observed.

"No." Nell held up a needle from which a fuzzy pink object, slightly bowl-shaped, hung. "The Christmas stockings were a big hit with the children at the women's shelter. Now I'm making caps for newborns. The hospital loves to get them. Karen and Dave will be able to provide little Lily with everything she needs, but some new parents aren't so fortunate."

Pamela focused on her knitting, letting the rhythm of her needles and the soft buzz of conversation induce a welcome tranquility. Lined up next to her on the sofa, Bettina and Holly chatted about visits they'd made to Karen. Then they returned to the evening's earlier topic, but quietly, as across the room Nell and Roland knit on, undisturbed. Though Charlotte had been arrested, Bettina was explaining, not everything had been resolved—particularly Coot's claim on her mother's estate, which, with Pierre gone, might now be entirely hers if the DNA evidence held.

Pamela began to smell coffee brewing, and Roland began to stir, pushing back his shirt cuff to consult his impressive watch. His usual suit and tie had been set aside this evening in favor of slim wool slacks and an elegant V-neck sweater, though his shirt cuff was as aggressively starched as ever. But before he could announce that it was eight p.m. and time for refreshments, Melanie appeared in the living room doorway.

"It's so nice to see you all," she said with a smile. "All of you who are here, anyway—and I hope Karen is doing well." After her excursion into pink angora, Melanie had reverted to her customary look. Her well-toned legs were encased in black leggings, and an elegantly slouchy cardigan, knit from impossibly soft wool in tones of black, gray, and camel, topped a black turtleneck.

Roland set his knitting atop his closed briefcase and rose from the sleek turquoise chair. It was then that Pamela noticed he hadn't been the chair's only occupant. Lingering in the chair was a small ball of black fur. The ball of fur uncurled, leapt lightly to the floor, and scurried after him as he strode toward where Melanie stood. Pamela recognized the kitten Roland had adopted from Catrina's litter.

"That's Cuddles," Melanie explained. "They're inseparable."

"You started the coffee," Roland said, an edge of accusation in his voice. "I can take over from here."

"Of course, sweetheart." Melanie smiled serenely and Roland continued on to the kitchen, followed by the black kitten. "He's serving fruitcake," Melanie said with a shrug. "It's actually very good. His mother makes it and she sends it every year."

Roland was a busy host, popping back and forth between kitchen and living room countless times. The fruitcake arrived, carefully sliced and arranged on a platter, along with dessert plates, forks, and napkins. Cream and sugar were staged on the coffee table, the coffee-drinkers were provided with coffee, and a special pot of tea was delivered to the small table next to Nell's armchair.

The fruitcake *was* good. It was dark and fruity and nutty—and very moist, thanks to a noticeable infusion of brandy. Pamela savored the rich, bitter coffee and its contrast with the rich, sweet cake. Christmas wasn't really over yet, she reflected, gazing at Roland and Melanie's tree, with its sophisticated gold and silver ornaments set off by twinkling white lights. Now that Millicent's murder—and Pierre's—had been solved, she could enjoy what was left of the season. Penny would be home for another week, and as the carol reminded everyone, Christmas really lasted for twelve days.

Roland had settled back onto the turquoise chair with Cuddles perched on his thigh, contentedly kneading it with his tiny paws. Looking pleased with himself, Roland had fielded the compliments that came his way—his mother was to be congratulated on her fruitcake and his coffee was excellent (never mind that Melanie had made it). Now, in the lull that had fallen over the room, Nell spoke up.

"It's almost the New Year," she said. "Who has a resolution?"

"I do." Holly laughed gleefully. "I resolve to be part of this amazing knitting group forever. How about you, Roland?"

Roland looked puzzled. "I've never felt the need to make them," he said.

Bettina spoke up. "I can suggest a few things you might consider."

Nell leaned forward from the depths of her armchair. "If we're going to suggest resolutions other people might consider, I have one for Pamela." Pamela looked over the rim of her coffee cup to meet Nell's kindly gaze. "No more mysteries," Nell said firmly. "That's what the police are for. Will you promise me that?"

Pamela set her cup down. "Well . . . I . . ." she began, but before she could complete her thought, Bettina caught her eye. In a moment Bettina had leapt to her feet from the low-slung sofa, nearly defying gravity. "Let's all have more fruitcake," she cried, seizing up the platter. "Nell! You've only had one slice." She bounded across the room to offer the platter to Nell, then darted toward Roland.

The black kitten, interpreting Bettina's swooping approach as a threat to his master, reared up from Roland's thigh. Snarling, he leapt at Bettina with tiny claws extended. He landed on the fruitcake platter, which tipped, dumping the remaining slices of fruitcake onto Roland's lap. The kitten then regained his balance, scaled Bettina's arm, and clambered onto her shoulder. From there he launched himself toward the Christmas tree. He perched on a slender branch, setting ornaments to swaying. A gleaming golden ornament slipped off, bounced, and rolled across the carpet.

Roland stood up, shedding fruitcake slices, and Melanie dived for the fallen ornament. Bettina stood in the middle of the floor with the empty fruitcake platter, looking as if she was about to cry. The kitten burrowed into Holly's knitting bag.

In the general hubbub, no one noticed that Nell's question to Pamela had gone unanswered.

KNIT

Cozy Hands Fingerless Gloves

For this project you will need about 90 yards of medium-weight yarn. A typical skein of acrylic yarn from the hobby shop contains at least twice this amount. You will also need size 8 knitting needles, though 7 or 9 would work if that's what you have. The pattern is based on about 4 stitches to the inch and it makes fingerless gloves that fit a woman's rather large hands. You can recalibrate by measuring the hands you plan to fit and adjusting the number of stitches you cast on. These directions start with the glove for the left hand.

If you've never knitted anything at all, it's easier to learn the basics by watching than by reading. The Internet abounds in tutorials that show the process clearly, including casting on and off. Just search on "How to knit." These gloves use the stockinette stitch, the stitch you see, for example, in a typical sweater. To create the stockinette stitch, you knit one row, then purl going back the other direction, then knit, then purl, knit, purl, back and forth. Again, it's easier to understand "purl" by watching a video, but essentially when you purl you're creating the backside of "knit." To knit, you insert the right-hand needle front to back through the loop of yarn on the left-hand needle. To purl, you insert the needle back to front. The gloves also have ribbing, which will be described when we get to that point in the directions.

Cast on 28 stitches, using either the simple slip-knot cast-on process or the more complicated "long tail" process. If you are adjusting the size, try to cast on a number of stitches that is a multiple of 4. If you do this, the joint where one edge of your ribbing meets the other edge after you sew your gloves up will look nicer.

Ribbing is the effect often found at the cuffs of sweaters. It's the basic knit 2, purl 2 concept. For your first row, knit 2 stitches, then purl 2, then knit 2 more, purl 2 more and continue like that to the end of the row. On the way back, knit 2, purl 2 and so on again. But if you've cast on a multiple of 4, you'll see that now you're doing a knit where you did a purl, and vice versa. This is what creates the ribs. After you do a few rows you will see them starting to form and the concept will become clearer. One important note: after you knit the first two stitches, you must shift the yarn you're working with to the front of your work by passing it between the needles. After the two purls, you must shift it to the back, and so on back and forth. If you don't do this, extra loops of yarn will accumulate on your needles in a very confusing way.

Do the knitting and purling for about 9 rows or until you have about 1 to 2 inches of ribbing. You have now created the cuff of your first glove.

The body of the glove is worked in stockinette stitch. Knit, using the stockinette stitch, for about 18 rows or 3 or 4 inches. You are now ready to make the hole for the thumb, but you can hold the in-progress project up against the back of your hand to make sure you've knit far enough. At this point, with the ribbing

lying on your wrist in a natural position, the body of
the glove should reach the spot where your thumb
joins the rest of your hand.

It's best to do the thumb hole when you are on a
knit row rather than a purl row. Knit 4 stitches, then
cast off 4 stitches. Resume knitting and finish out
the row. On the way back you will be purling. Purl
20 stitches. (If you adjusted the size by casting on
fewer than 28 stitches, purl until you come to the spot
where you cast off the 4 stitches.) Cast on 4 stitches,
using the slip-knot process. Resume purling and finish
out the row. Keep on with the stockinette stitch for
about 8 rows, or 1½ inches. Again, you can hold the
in-progress work up against the back of your hand to
make sure you've knit far enough. At this point, the
body of the glove should reach the base of your fingers.
Cast off and clip your yarn, but leave a nice long tail.
You'll see why this is useful in a minute.

To make a glove for the right hand, follow these
directions again, except when you get to the row
where you cast off for the thumb hole, knit 20, cast off
4, then knit 4 to finish the row. As you work on the
second glove, you can hold it up against the completed
one to make sure your proportions are the same.

Now it's time to sew your gloves up. Start with either
one. Fold it so the right sides—the obvious stockinette
sides—are facing each other, in the same way that you
put right sides of fabric together when you sew a seam.
Use a yarn needle—a large needle with a large eye and
a blunt end. Thread the needle with the long tail you
left and stitch the two edges together. To make a neat
seam, use an overcast stitch and catch only the outer
loops along each side. When you get to the top of the
ribbing, pass your needle through a loop of yarn to

make a knot. Hide the smaller tail that remains by working the needle in and out of the knitted fabric for an inch or so. Pull the yarn through and cut off the bit of yarn that's left. Thread your yarn needle with the tail left from when you cast on and hide it too.

Turn your fingerless glove right side out and try it on. Sew up the other glove.

For a picture of the finished Cozy Hands,
visit the Knit & Nibble Mysteries page
at PeggyEhrhart.com.

NIBBLE

Christmas Poppy-Seed Cake

In *Silent Knit, Deadly Knit,* Pamela bakes a double recipe of poppy-seed cake. The directions below are for a single recipe. It makes two loaves about 4" by 8" or four loaves about 3" by 5".

Ingredients
- 1 cup poppy seeds
- 1 cup milk
- 2 cups flour—whole wheat or white or 1 cup of each
- 1½ tsp. salt
- 2½ tsp. baking powder
- 1 cup butter (two sticks)
- 2 cups sugar—brown or white or 1 cup of each
- 3 eggs
- 2 tsp. vanilla

In advance, cut the butter into small chunks, put it in a bowl large enough to eventually hold all the ingredients, and let it sit out unrefrigerated. You want the butter to be soft enough to cream easily when you begin your recipe. Also in advance, put the poppy seeds in a small saucepan and pour the milk over them. Bring the mixture almost to a boil and then turn the heat off and let the seeds and milk sit for at least an hour.

When you are ready to start, grease and flour your loaf pans. Sift the flour, salt, and baking powder into a small bowl and set it aside. Separate the eggs, catching the whites in a bowl large enough to accommodate beaters. Set the yolks aside in small bowl. Beat the whites until they are stiff but not dry and set the bowl aside.

With your mixer, cream the butter in the large bowl, adding the sugar slowly. When sugar and butter are blended well, add the yolks one by one and beat them in. Add the seeds, milk, and vanilla and continue to beat. Beat in the dry ingredients a little at a time. Using a rubber spatula, fold in the beaten egg whites.

Transfer the batter to the loaf pans. A large soup ladle works well for this step because you can apportion your batter evenly by counting the number of ladles for each loaf. Then use the spatula to collect every last dab of batter from the mixing bowl and add it to the loaf pans.

Bake the loaves at 350 degrees for 45 to 60 minutes. Check that your loaves are done by sticking a wooden toothpick into the middle of the tops. If the toothpick comes out clean, your loaves are baked. Cool them for half an hour or so before removing them from the pans.

For a picture of the finished
Christmas Poppy-Seed Cake,
visit the Knit & Nibble Mysteries page
at PeggyEhrhart.com.